A Place I've Never Been

ALSO BY DAVID LEAVITT

Family Dancing
The Lost Language of Cranes
Equal Affections

A Place I've Never Been

DAVID LEAVITT

VIKING

VIKING
Published by the Penguin Group
Viking Penguin, a division of Penguin Books USA Inc.,
375 Hudson Street, New York, New York 10014, U.S.A.
Penguin Books Ltd, 27 Wrights Lane, London W8 5TZ, England
Penguin Books Australia Ltd, Ringwood, Victoria, Australia
Penguin Books Canada Ltd, 2801 John Street, Markham, Ontario, Canada L3R 1B4
Penguin Books (N.Z.) Ltd, 182–190 Wairau Road, Auckland 10, New Zealand

Penguin Books Ltd, Registered Offices: Harmondsworth, Middlesex, England

First published in 1990 by Viking Penguin, a division of Penguin Books USA Inc.

3 5 7 9 10 8 6 4 2

Many of the stories in this collection originally appeared in the following magazines and anthologies, some in slightly different form: "A Place I've Never Been" in *Arete*; "Spouse Night" in *The Boston Globe Magazine* and *Winter's Tales* (England); "Chips Is Here" in *The Company of Dogs*; "Gravity" in *The East Hampton Star*; "Ayor" in *Men on Men 2: Best New Gay Fiction*; "My Marriage to Vengeance" in *Mother Jones* and, as "Braids," in *Soho Square* (England); "Houses" and "I See London, I See France" in *Savvy*.

LIBRARY OF CONGRESS CATALOGING IN PUBLICATION DATA
Leavitt, David, 1961–
A place I've never been : stories / by David Leavitt.
p. cm.
ISBN 0–670–82196–9
I. Title.
PS3562.E2618P57 1990
813'.54—dc20 90–50006

Printed in the United States of America
Set in Goudy Old Style
Designed by Fritz Metsch

For my father

ACKNOWLEDGMENTS

Many thanks to Jill Ciment, Gary Glickman, Amy Hempel, Fran Kiernan, and Sarah Schulman, for helpful readings; to my agent, Andrew Wylie, and his associates, Deborah Karl, Susan Schorr, and Sarah Chalfant; to the John Simon Guggenheim Foundation and its director, Joel Connaroe; and to the Institute of Catalan Letters of Barcelona, Spain, under whose auspices this book was finished.

In 1984, when I wrote the first of these stories, I was the part-time slush reader at Viking Press in New York; Dawn Seferian was an editorial assistant at Penguin Books. To be working again with her—this time as author and editor—is not only a great pleasure, but something of a homecoming.

ACKNOWLEDGMENTS

CONTENTS

A Place I've Never Been

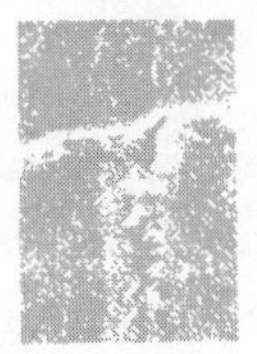

A PLACE I'VE NEVER BEEN

I *HAD* known Nathan for years—too many years, since we were in college—so when he went to Europe I wasn't sure how I'd survive it; he was my best friend, after all, my constant companion at Sunday afternoon double bills at the Thalia, my ever-present source of consolation and conversation. Still, such a turn can prove to be a blessing in disguise. It threw me off at first, his not being there—I had no one to watch *Jeopardy!* with, or talk to on the phone late at night—but then, gradually, I got over it, and I realized that maybe it was a good thing after all, that maybe now, with Nathan gone, I would be forced to go out into the world more, make new friends, maybe even find a boyfriend. And I had started: I lost weight, I went shopping. I was at Bloomingdale's one day on my lunch hour when a very skinny black woman with a French accent asked me if I'd like to have a makeover. I had always run away from such things, but this time, before I had a chance, this woman put her long hands on my cheeks and looked into my face—not my eyes, my face—and said, "You're really beautiful. You know that?" And I absolutely couldn't answer. After she was through with me I didn't even know what I looked like, but everyone at my office was amazed. "Celia," they said, "you look great. What happened?" I smiled, wondering if I'd be allowed to go back every day for a makeover, if I offered to pay.

There was even some interest from a man—a guy named Roy

who works downstairs, in contracts—and I was feeling pretty good about myself again, when the phone rang, and it was Nathan. At first I thought he must have been calling me from some European capital, but he said no, he was back in New York. "Celia," he said, "I have to see you. Something awful has happened."

Hearing those words, I pitched over—I assumed the worst. (And why not? He had been assuming the worst for over a year.) But he said, "No, no, I'm fine. I'm perfectly healthy. It's my apartment. Oh, Celia, it's awful. Could you come over?"

"Were you broken into?" I asked.

"I might as well have been!"

"Okay," I said. "I'll come over after work."

"I just got back last night. This is too much."

"I'll be there by six, Nathan."

"Thank you," he said, a little breathlessly, and hung up.

I drummed my nails—newly painted by another skinny woman at Bloomingdale's—against the black Formica of my desk, mostly to try out the sound. In truth I was a little happy he was back—I had missed him—and not at all surprised that he'd cut his trip short. Rich people are like that, I've observed; because they don't have to buy bargain-basement tickets on weird charter airlines, they feel free to change their minds. Probably he just got bored tooting around Europe, missed his old life, missed *Jeopardy!*, his friends. Oh, Nathan! How could I tell him the Thalia had closed?

I had to take several buses to get from my office to his neighborhood—a route I had once traversed almost daily, but which, since Nathan's departure, I hadn't had much occasion to take. Sitting on the Madison Avenue bus, I looked out the window at the rows of unaffordable shops, some still exactly what they'd been before, others boarded up, or reopened under new auspices—such a familiar panorama, unfolding, block by block, like a Chinese scroll I'd once been shown on a museum trip in junior high school. It was raining a little, and in the warm bus the long, unvarying progress of my love for Nathan seemed to unscroll as well—all the dinners and lunches and arguments, and all the trips back alone to my apartment, feeling ugly and fat, because Nathan had once again confirmed he could never love me the way he assured me he would someday love a man. How many hundreds of times I received that confirmation! And yet, somehow, it never occurred to me to give up that love I had nurtured for him since our earliest time together, that love which belonged to those days just past the brink of childhood, before I understood about Nathan, or rather, before Nathan understood about himself. So I persisted, and Nathan, in spite of his embarrassment at my occasional outbursts, continued to depend on me. I think he hoped that my feeling for him would one day transform itself into a more maternal kind of affection, that I would one day become the sort of woman who could tend to him without expecting anything in return. And that was, perhaps, a reasonable hope on his part, given my behavior. But: "If only," he said to me once, "you didn't have to act so crazy, Celia—" And that was how I realized I had to get out.

I got off the bus and walked the block and a half to his building—its façade, I noted, like almost every façade in the neighborhood, blemished by a bit of scaffolding—and, standing in that vestibule where I'd stood so often, waited for him to buzz me up. I read for diversion the now familiar list of tenants' names. The only difference today was that there were ragged ends of Scotch tape stuck around Nathan's name; probably his subletter had put his own name over Nathan's, and Nathan, returning, had torn the piece of paper off and left the ends of the tape. This didn't seem like him, and it made me suspicious. He was a scrupulous person about such things.

In due time—though slowly, for him—he let me in, and I walked the three flights of stairs to find him standing in the doorway, unshaven, looking as if he'd just gotten out of bed. He wasn't wearing any shoes, and he'd gained some weight. Almost immediately he fell into me—that is the only way to describe it, his big body limp in my arms. "Oh, God," he murmured into my hair, "am I glad to see you."

"Nathan," I said. "Nathan." And held him there. Usually he wriggled out of physical affection; kisses from him were little nips;

hugs were tight, jerky chokeholds. Now he lay absolutely still, his arms slung under mine, and I tried to keep from gasping from the weight of him. But finally—reluctantly—he let go, and putting his hand on his forehead, gestured toward the open door. "Prepare yourself," he said. "It's worse than you can imagine."

He led me into the apartment. I have to admit, I was shocked by what I saw. Nathan, unlike me, is a chronically neat person, everything in its place, all his perfect furniture glowing, polished, every state-of-the-art fountain pen and pencil tip-up in the blue glass jar on his desk. Today, however, the place was in havoc—newspapers and old Entenmann's cookie boxes spread over the floor, records piled on top of each other, inner sleeves crumpled behind the radiator, the blue glass jar overturned. The carpet was covered with dark mottlings, and a stench of old cigarette smoke and sweat and urine inhabited the place. "It gets worse," he said. "Look at the kitchen." A thick, yellowing layer of grease encrusted the stovetop. The bathroom was beyond the pale of my descriptive capacity for filth.

"Those bastards," Nathan was saying, shaking his head.

"Hold on to the security deposit," I suggested. "Make them pay for it."

He sat down on the sofa, the arms of which appeared to have been ground with cigarette butts, and shook his head. "There *is* no security deposit," he moaned. "I didn't take one because supposedly Denny was my friend, and this other guy—Hoop, or whatever his name was—he was Denny's friend. And look at this!" From the coffee table he handed me a thick stack of utility and phone bills, all unopened. "The phone's disconnected," he said. "Two of the rent checks have bounced. The landlord's about to evict me. I'm sure my credit rating has gone to hell. Jesus, why'd I do it?" He stood, marched into the corner, then turned again to face me. "You know what? I'm going to call my father. I'm going to have him sick every one of his bastard lawyers on those assholes until they pay."

"Nathan," I reminded, "they're unemployed actors. They're poor."

"Then let them rot in jail!" Nathan screamed. His voice was loud and sharp in my ears. It had been a long time since I'd had to witness another person's misery, a long time since anyone had asked of me what Nathan was now asking of me: to take care, to resolve, to smooth. Nonetheless I rallied my energies. I stood. "Look," I said. "I'm going to go out and buy sponges, Comet, Spic and Span, Fantastik, Windex. Everything. We're going to clean this place up. We're going to wash the sheets and shampoo the rug, we're going to scrub the toilet until it shines. I promise you, by the time you go to sleep tonight, it'll be what it was."

He stood silent in the corner.

"Okay?" I said.

"Okay."

"So you wait here," I said. "I'll be right back."

"Thank you."

I picked up my purse and closed the door, thus, once again, saving him from disaster.

But there were certain things I could not save Nathan from. A year ago, his ex-lover Martin had called him up and told him he had tested positive. This was the secret fact he had to live with every day of his life, the secret fact that had brought him to Xanax and Halcion, Darvon and Valium—all crude efforts to cut the fear firing through his blood, exploding like the tiny viral time bombs he believed were lying in wait, expertly planted. It was the day after he found out that he started talking about clearing out. He had no obligations—he had quit his job a few months before and was just doing free-lance work anyway—and so, he reasoned, what was keeping him in New York? "I need to get away from all this," he said, gesturing frantically at the air. I believe he really thought back then that by running away to somewhere where it was less well known, he might be able to escape the disease. This is something I've noticed: The men act as if they think the power of infection exists in direct proportion to its publicity, that in places far from New York City it can, in effect, be outrun. And who's to say they are wrong, with all this talk about stress and the immune system? In Italy, in the countryside, Nathan seemed to feel he'd feel safer. And probably he was right; he would feel safer. Over there, away from the American cityscape with its streets full of gaunt sufferers, you're able to forget the last ten years, you can remember how old the world is and how there was a time when sex wasn't something likely to kill you.

It should be pointed out that Nathan had no symptoms; he hadn't even had the test for the virus itself. He refused to have it, saying he could think of no reason to give up at least the hope of freedom. Not that this made any difference, of course. The fear itself is a brutal enough enemy.

But he gave up sex. No sex, he said, was safe enough for him. He bought a VCR and began to hoard pornographic videotapes. And I think he was having phone sex too, because once I picked up the phone in his apartment and before I could say hello, a husky-voiced man said, "You stud," and then, when I said "Excuse me?" got flustered-sounding and hung up. Some people would probably count that as sex, but I'm not sure I would.

All the time, meanwhile, he was frenzied. I could never guess what time he'd call—six in the morning, sometimes, he'd drag me from sleep. "I figured you'd still be up," he'd say, which gave me a clue to how he was living. It got so bad that by the time he actually left I felt as if a great burden had been lifted from my shoulders. Not that I didn't miss him, but from that day on my time was, miraculously, my own. Nathan is a terrible correspondent—I don't think he's sent me one postcard or letter in all the time we've known each other—and so for months my only news of him came through the phone. Strangers would call me, Germans, Italians, nervous-sounding young men who spoke bad English, who were staying at the YMCA, who were in New York for the first time and to whom he had given my number. I don't think any of them actually wanted to see me; I think they just wanted me to tell them which bars were good and which subway lines were safe—information I happily dispensed. Of course, there was a time when I would have taken them on the subways, shown them around the bars, but I have thankfully passed out of that phase.

And of course, as sex became more and more a possibility, then a likelihood once again in my life, I began to worry myself about the very things that were torturing Nathan. What should I say, say, to Roy in contracts, when he asked me to sleep with him, which I was fairly sure he was going to do within a lunch or two? Certainly I wanted to sleep with him. But did I dare ask him to use a condom? Did I dare even broach the subject? I was frightened that he might get furious, that he might overreact, and I considered saying nothing, taking my chances. Then again, for me in particular, it was a very big chance to take; I have a pattern of falling in love with men who at some point or other have fallen in love with other men. All trivial, selfish, this line of worry, I recognize now, but at that point Nathan was gone, and I had no one around to remind me of how high the stakes were for other people. I slipped back into a kind of women's-magazine attitude toward the whole thing: for the moment, at least, *I* was safe, and I cherished that safety without even knowing it, I gloried in it. All my speculations were merely matters of prevention; that place where Nathan had been exiled was a place I'd never been. I am ashamed to admit it, but there was even a moment when I took a kind of vengeful pleasure in the whole matter—the years I had hardly slept with anyone, for which I had been taught to feel ashamed and freakish, I now wanted to rub in someone's face: I was right and you were wrong! I wanted to say. I'm not proud of having had such thoughts, and I can only say, in my defense, that they passed quickly—but a strict accounting of all feelings, at this point, seems to me necessary. We have to be rigorous with ourselves these days.

In any case, Nathan was back, and I didn't dare think about myself. I went to the grocery store, I bought every cleaner I could find. And when I got back to the apartment he was still standing where he'd been standing, in the corner. "Nate," I said, "here's everything. Let's get to work."

"Okay," he said glumly, even though he is an ace cleaner, and we began.

As we cleaned, the truth came out. This Denny to whom he'd sublet the apartment, Nathan had had a crush on. "To the extent that a crush is a relevant thing in my life anymore," he said, "since God knows, there's nothing to be done about it. But there you are. The libido doesn't stop, the heart doesn't stop, no matter how hard you try to make them."

None of this—especially that last part—was news to me, though Nathan had managed to overlook that aspect of our relationship for years. I had understood from the beginning about the skipping-over of the security payment, the laxness of the setup, because these were the sorts of things I would have willingly done for Nathan at a different time. I think he was privately so excited at the prospect of this virile young man, Denny, sleeping, and perhaps having sex, between his sheets, that he would have taken any number of risks to assure it. Crush: what an oddly appropriate word, considering what it makes you do to yourself. His apartment was, in a sense, the most Nathan could offer, and probably the most Denny would accept. I understood: You want to get as close as you can, even if it's only at arm's length. And when you come back, maybe, you want to breathe in the smell of the person you love loving someone else.

Europe, he said, had been a failure. He had wandered, having dinner with old friends of his parents, visiting college acquaintances who were busy with exotic lives. He'd gone to bars, which was merely frustrating; there was nothing to be done. "What about safe sex?" I asked, and he said, "Celia, please. There is no such thing, as far as I'm concerned." Once again this started a panicked thumping in my chest as I thought about Roy, and Nathan said, "It's really true. Suppose something lands on you—you know what I'm saying—and there's a microscopic cut in your skin. Bingo."

"Nathan, come on," I said. "That sounds crazy to me."

"Yeah?" he said. "Just wait till some ex-lover of yours calls you up with a little piece of news. Then see how you feel."

He returned to his furious scrubbing of the bathroom sink. I returned to my furious scrubbing of the tub. Somehow, even now, I'm always stuck with the worst of it.

Finally we were done. The place looked okay—it didn't smell anymore—though it was hardly what it had been. Some long-preserved pristineness was gone from the apartment, and both of us knew without saying a word that it would never be restored. We breathed in exhausted—no, not exhausted triumph. It was more like relief. We had beaten something back, yet again.

My hands were red from detergents, my stomach and forehead sweaty. I went into the now-bearable bathroom and washed up, and then Nathan said he would take me out to dinner—my choice. And so we ended up, as we had a thousand other nights, sitting by the window at the Empire Szechuan down the block from his apartment, eating cold noodles with sesame sauce, which, when we had finished them, Nathan ordered more of. "God, how I've missed these," he said, as he scooped the brown slimy noodles into his mouth. "You don't know."

In between slurps he looked at me and said, "You look good, Celia. Have you lost weight?"

"Yes, as a matter of fact," I said.

"I thought so."

I looked back at him, trying to recreate the expression on the French woman's face, and didn't say anything, but as it turned out I didn't need to. "I know what you're thinking," he said, "and you're right. Twelve pounds since you last saw me. But I don't care. I mean, you lose weight when you're sick. At least this way, gaining weight, I know I don't have it."

He continued eating. I looked outside. Past the plate-glass window that separated us from the sidewalk, crowds of people walked, young and old, good-looking and bad-looking, healthy and sick, some of them staring in at our food and our eating. Suddenly—urgently—I wanted to be out among them, I wanted to be walking in that crowd, pushed along in it, and not sitting here, locked into this tiny two-person table with Nathan. And yet I knew that escape was probably impossible. I looked once again at Nathan, eating happily, resigned, perhaps, to the fate of his apartment, and the knowledge that everything would work out, that this had, in fact, been merely a run-of-the-mill crisis. For the moment he was appeased, his hungry anxiety sated; for the moment. But who could guess what would set him off next? I steadied my chin on my palm, drank some water, watched Nathan eat like a happy child.

The next few weeks were thorny with events. Nathan bought a new sofa, had his place recarpeted, threw several small dinners. Then it was time for Lizzie Fischman's birthday party—one of the few annual events in our lives. We had known Lizzie since college—she was a tragic, trying sort of person, the sort who carries with her a constant aura of fatedness, of doom. So many bad things happen to Lizzie you can't help but wonder, after a while, if she doesn't hold out a beacon for disaster. This year alone, she was in a taxi that got hit by a bus; then she was mugged in the subway by a man who called her an "ugly dyke bitch"; then she started feeling sick all the time, and no one could figure out what was wrong, until it was revealed that her building's heating system was leaking small quantities of carbon monoxide into her awful little apartment. The tenants sued, and in the course of the suit, Lizzie, exposed as an illegal subletter, was evicted. She now lived with her father in one half of a two-family house in Plainfield, New Jersey, because she couldn't find another apartment she could afford. (Her job, incidentally, in addition to being wretchedly low-paying, is one of the dreariest I know of: proofreading accounting textbooks in an office on Forty-second Street.)

Anyway, each year Lizzie threw a big birthday party for herself in her father's house in Plainfield, and we all went, her friends, because of course we couldn't bear to disappoint her and add ourselves to her roster of worldwide enemies. It was invariably a miserable party—everyone drunk on bourbon, and Lizzie, eager to recreate the slumber parties of her childhood, dancing around in pink pajamas with feet. We were making s'mores over the gas stove—shoving the chocolate bars and the graham crackers onto fondue forks rather than old sticks—and *Beach Blanket Bingo* was playing on the VCR and no one was having a good time, particularly Nathan, who was overdressed in a beige Giorgio Armani linen suit he'd bought in Italy, and was standing in the corner idly pressing his neck, feeling for swollen lymph nodes. Lizzie's circle dwindled each year, as her friends moved on, or found ways to get out of it. This year eight of us had made it to the party, plus a newcomer from Lizzie's office, a very fat girl with very red nails named Dorrie Friedman, who, in spite of her heaviness, was what my mother would have called dainty. She ate a lot, but unless you were observant, you'd never have noticed it. The image of the fat person stuffing food into her face is mythic: I know from experience, when fat you eat slowly, chew methodically, in order not to draw attention to your mouth. Over the course of an hour I watched Dorrie Friedman put away six of those s'mores with a tidiness worthy of Emily Post, I watched her dab her cheek with her napkin after each bite, and I understood: This was shame, but also, in some peculiar way, this was innocence. A state to envy.

There is a point in Lizzie's parties when she invariably suggests we play Deprivation, a game that had been terribly popular among our crowd in college. The way you play it is you sit in a big circle, and everyone is given ten pennies. (In this case the pennies were unceremoniously taken from a huge bowl that sat on top of Lizzie's mother's refrigerator, and that she had upended on the linoleum floor—no doubt a long-contemplated act of desecration.) You go around the circle, and each person announces something he or she has never done, or a place they've never been—"I've never been to Borneo" is a good example—and then everyone who has been to Borneo is obliged to throw you a penny. Needless to say, especially in college, the game degenerates rather quickly to matters of sex and drugs.

I remembered the first time I ever played Deprivation, my sophomore year, I had been reading Blake's *Songs of Innocence* and *Songs of Experience.* Everything in our lives seemed a question of innocence and experience back then, so this seemed appropriate. There was a tacit assumption among my friends that "experience"—by that term we meant, I think, almost exclusively sex and drugs—was something you strove to get as much of as you could, that innocence, for all the praise it received in literature, was a state so essentially tedious that those of us still stuck in it deserved the childish recompense of shiny new pennies. (None of us, of course, imagining that five years from now the "experiences" we urged on one another might spread a murderous germ, that five years from now some of our friends, still in their youth, would be lost. Youth! You were supposed to sow your wild oats, weren't you? Those of us who didn't—we were the ones who failed, weren't we?)

One problem with Deprivation is that the older you get, the less interesting it becomes; every year, it seemed, my friends had fewer gaps in their lives to confess, and as our embarrassments began to stack up on the positive side, it was what we *had* done that was titillating. Indeed, Nick Walsh, who was to Lizzie what Nathan was to me, complained as the game began, "I can't play this. There's nothing I haven't done." But Lizzie, who has a naive faith in ritual, merely smiled and said, "Oh come on, Nick. No one's done *everything.* For instance, you could say, 'I've never been to Togo,' or 'I've never been made love to simultaneously by twelve Arab boys in a back alley on Mott Street.' "

"Well, Lizzie," Nick said, "it *is* true that I've never been to Togo." His leering smile surveyed the circle, and of course, there *was* someone there—Gracie Wong, I think—who had, in fact, been to Togo.

The next person in the circle was Nathan. He's never liked this game, but he also plays it more cleverly than anyone. "Hmm," he said, stroking his chin as if there were a beard there, "let's see . . . Ah, I've got it. I've never had sex with anyone in this group." He smiled boldly, and everyone laughed—everyone, that is, except for me and Bill Darlington, and Lizzie herself—all three of us now, for the wretched experiments of our early youth, obliged to throw Nathan a penny.

Next was Dorrie Friedman's turn, which I had been dreading. She sat on the floor, her legs crossed under her, her very fat fingers intertwined, and said, "Hmm . . . Something I've never done. Well—I've never ridden a bicycle."

An awful silence greeted this confession, and then a tinkling sound, like wind chimes, as the pennies flew. "Gee," Dorrie Friedman said, "I won big that time." I couldn't tell if she was genuinely pleased.

And as the game went on, we settled, all of us, into more or less parallel states of innocence and experience, except for Lizzie and Nick, whose piles had rapidly dwindled, and Dorrie Friedman, who, it seemed, by virtue of lifelong fatness, had done nearly nothing. She had never been to Europe; she had never swum; she had never played tennis; she had never skied; she had never been on a boat. Even someone else's turn could be an awful moment for Dorrie, as when Nick said, "I've never had a vaginal orgasm." But fortunately, there, she did throw in her penny. I was relieved; I don't think I could have stood it if she hadn't.

After a while, in an effort not to look at Dorrie and her immense pile of pennies, we all started trying to trip up Lizzie and Nick, whose respective caches of sexual experience seemed limitless. "I've never had sex in my parents' bed," I offered. The pennies flew. "I've never had sex under a dry-docked boat." "I've never had sex with more than one other person." "Two other people." "Three other people." By then Lizzie was out of pennies, and declared the game over.

"I guess I won," Dorrie said rather softly. She had her pennies neatly piled in identically sized stacks.

I wondered if Lizzie was worried. I wondered if she was thinking about the disease, if she was frightened, the way Nathan was, or if she just assumed death was coming anyway, the final blow in her life of unendurable misfortunes. She started to gather the pennies back into their bowl, and I glanced across the room at Nathan, to see if he was ready to go. All through the game, of course, he had been looking pretty miserable—he always looks miserable at parties.

Worse, he has a way of turning his misery around, making me responsible for it. Across the circle of our nearest and dearest friends he glared at me angrily, and I knew that by the time we were back in his car and on our way home to Manhattan he would have contrived a way for the evening to be my fault. And yet tonight, his occasional knowing sneers, inviting my complicity in looking down on the party, only enraged me. I was angry at him, in advance, for what I was sure he was going to do in the car, and I was also angry at him for being such a snob, for having no sympathy toward this evening, which, in spite of all its displeasures, was nevertheless an event of some interest, perhaps the very last hurrah of our youth, our own little big chill. And that was something: Up until now I had always assumed Nathan's version of things to be the correct one, and cast my own into the background. Now his perception seemed meager, insufficient: Here was an historic night, after all, and all he seemed to want to think about was his own boredom, his own unhappiness.

Finally, reluctantly, Lizzie let us go, and relinquished from her grip, we got into Nathan's car and headed onto the Garden State Parkway. "Never again," Nathan was saying, "will I allow you to convince me to attend one of Lizzie Fischman's awful parties. This is the last." I didn't even bother answering, it all seemed so predictable. Instead I just settled back into the comfortable velour of the car seat and switched on the radio. Dionne Warwick and Elton John were singing "That's What Friends Are For," and Nathan said, "You know, of course, that that's the song they wrote to raise money for AIDS."

"I'd heard," I said.

"Have you seen the video? It makes me furious. All these famous singers up there, grinning these huge grins, rocking back and forth. Why the hell are they smiling, I'd like to ask?"

For a second, I considered answering that question, then decided I'd better not. We were slipping into the Holland Tunnel, and by the time we got through to Manhattan I was ready to call it a night. I wanted to get back to my apartment and see if Roy had left a message on my answering machine. But Nathan said, "It's Saturday night, Celia, it's still early. Won't you have a drink with me or something?"

"I don't want to go to any more gay bars, Nathan, I told you that."

"So we'll go to a straight bar. I don't care. I just can't bear to go back to my apartment at eleven o'clock." We stopped for a red light, and he leaned closer to me. "The truth is, I don't think I can bear to be alone. Please."

"All right," I said. What else could I say?

"Goody," Nathan said.

We parked the car in a garage and walked to a darkish café on Greenwich Avenue, just a few doors down from the huge gay bar Nathan used to frequent, and which he jokingly referred to as "the airport." No mention was made of that bar in the café, however, where he ordered latte machiato for both of us. "Aren't you going to have some dessert?" he said. "I know I am. Baba au rhum, perhaps. Or tiramisu. You know '*tirami su*' means 'pick me up,' but if you want to offend an Italian waiter, you say 'I'll have the *tiramilo su*,' which means 'pick up my dick.' "

"I'm trying to lose weight, Nathan," I said. "Please don't encourage me to eat desserts."

"Sorry." He coughed. Our latte machiatos came, and Nathan raised his cup and said, "Here's to us. Here's to Lizzie Fischman. Here's to never playing that dumb game again as long as we live." These days, I noticed, Nathan used the phrase "as long as we live" a bit too frequently for comfort.

Reluctantly I touched my glass to his. "You know," he said, "I think I've always hated that game. Even in college, when I won, it made me jealous. Everyone else had done so much more than me. Back then I figured I'd have time to explore the sexual world. Guess the joke's on me, huh?"

I shrugged. I wasn't sure.

"What's with you tonight, anyway?" he said. "You're so distant."

"I just have things on my mind, Nathan, that's all."

"You've been acting weird ever since I got back from Europe, Celia. Sometimes I think you don't even want to see me."

Clearly he was expecting reassurances to the contrary. I didn't say anything.

"Well," he said, "is that it? You don't want to see me?"

I twisted my shoulders in confusion. "Nathan—"

"Great," he said, and laughed so that I couldn't tell if he was kidding. "Your best friend for nearly ten years. Jesus."

"Look, Nathan, don't melodramatize," I said. "It's not that simple. It's just that I have to think a little about myself. My own life, my own needs. I mean, I'm going to be thirty soon. You know how long it's been since I've had a boyfriend?"

"I'm not against your having a boyfriend," Nathan said. "Have I ever tried to stop you from having a boyfriend?"

"But, Nathan," I said, "I never get to meet anyone when I'm with you all the time. I love you and I want to be your friend, but you can't expect me to just keep giving and giving and giving my time to you without anything in return. It's not fair."

I was looking away from him as I said this. From the corner of my vision I could see him glancing to the side, his mouth a small, tight line.

"You're all I have," he said quietly.

"That's not true, Nathan," I said.

"Yes it is true, Celia."

"Nathan, you have lots of other friends."

"But none of them count. No one but you counts."

The waitress arrived with his goblet of tiramisu, put it down in front of him. "Go on with your life, you say," he was muttering. "Find a boyfriend. Don't you think I'd do the same thing if I could? But all those options are closed to me, Celia. There's nowhere for me to go, no route that isn't dangerous. I mean, getting on with my life—I just can't talk about that simply anymore, the way you can." He leaned closer, over the table. "Do you want to know something?" he said. "Every time I see someone I'm attracted to I go into a cold sweat. And I imagine that they're dead, that if I touch them, the part of them I touch will die. Don't you see? It's bad enough to be afraid you might get it. But to be afraid you might give it—and to someone you loved—" He shook his head, put his hand to his forehead.

What could I say to that? What possibly was there to say? I took his hand, suddenly, I squeezed his hand until the edges of his fingers were white. I was remembering how Nathan looked the first time I saw him, in line at a college dining hall, his hands on his hips, his head erect, staring worriedly at the old lady dishing out food, as if he feared she might run out, or not give him enough. I have always loved the boyish hungers—for food, for sex—because they are so perpetual, so faithful in their daily revival, and even though I hadn't met Nathan yet, I think, in my mind, I already understood: I wanted to feed him, to fill him up; I wanted to give him everything.

Across from us, now, two girls were smoking cigarettes and talking about what art was. A man and a woman, in love, intertwined their fingers. Nathan's hand was getting warm and damp in mine, so I let it go, and eventually he blew his nose and lit a cigarette.

"You know," he said after a while, "it's not the sex, really. That's not what I regret missing. It's just that— Do you realize, Celia, I've never been in love? Never once in my life have I actually been in love?" And he looked at me very earnestly, not knowing, not having the slightest idea, that once again he was counting me for nothing.

"Nathan," I said. "Oh, my Nathan." Still, he didn't seem satisfied, and I knew he had been hoping for something better than my limp consolation. He looked away from me, across the café, listening, I suppose, for that wind-chime peal as all the world's pennies flew his way.

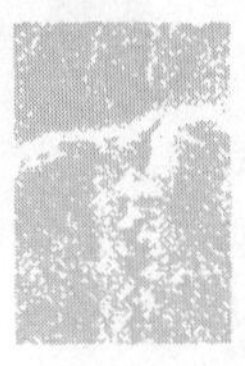

SPOUSE NIGHT

DURING the day, when Arthur is at work, the puppy listens to the radio—"Anything with voices," Mrs. Theodorus advised when Arthur went to pick up the puppy; "it calms them." And so, sitting in her pen in Arthur's decaying kitchen, while she chews on the newspaper that is meant to be her toilet, or urinates on the towel that is meant to be her bed, the puppy is surrounded by a comforting haze of half-human noise. For a while Arthur tried KQRT, the leftist station, and the puppy heard interviews with experts on Central American insurgency and radical women of color. Then he tuned in to a station that broadcast exclusively for the Polish community. "Mrs. Byziewicz, who has requested this polka, is eighty-five, the mother of three and the grandmother of eleven," the puppy heard as she pounced on her rubber newspaper, or tried to scale the chicken-wire walls of her pen. Now Arthur's settled on KSXT, a peculiar station which claims to feature "lite" programming, and which Arthur thinks is ideally suited to the listening needs of a dog, so the puppy is hearing a ten-minute-long radio play about Edgar Allan Poe when Arthur rushes in the door with Mrs. Theodorus, both breathing hard.

"Edgar, why are your poems so strange and weird?" Mrs. Poe is asking her husband on the radio, and the puppy looks at the woman who midwifed her birth ten weeks earlier. Mrs. Theodorus's blouse is partially undone, and the drawstring on her purple sweatpants is loosened, but all the puppy notices is the faint, half-familiar smell of her mother, and smelling it, she cries, barks and, for the first time in her short life, leaps over the edge of her pen. No one is there to congratulate her. Sniffing, the puppy makes her way into the bedroom, where Arthur and Mrs. Theodorus are in the midst of a sweaty half-naked tumble. The puppy jumps into the fray, barking, and Mrs. Theodorus screams.

"Arthur, you have got to teach her who's boss," she says, and climbs off him. "Remember—you must be in control at all times." She looks down at the puppy, who sits on the floor now, humbled before the sight of Mrs. Theodorus, naked except for her black bra, disapproval shining in her eyes. A small trickle of moisture snakes through the thick-pile carpet, darkening its yellow whorls, and quickly, quicker than Arthur can believe, Mrs. Theodorus has the puppy in hand and is carrying her back into the kitchen, shouting "No! No!" She returns with a sponge and a bottle of urine-stain remover. "I'm a whiz at this," she says.

"Eva," Arthur says, rolling over and unbuttoning his pants, "you never fail to amaze me."

Across the house the puppy wails for her mother.

In Arthur's bathroom one medicine cabinet is full, one empty, but still, for some reason, on the soap dish, one of Claire's earrings hangs haphazardly, as if she'd just pulled it out of the tiny hole in her earlobe. Next to it lies a fake gold tooth, from the days when crowns were removable, which Claire wore most of her life and only took out during her last stay in the hospital. Arthur saved the earring because he couldn't find its partner; for hours he searched the bedroom and the bathroom, desperate to complete his inventory of Claire's jewelry so that he could finally get rid of it all, but the second earring failed to materialize. Finally he gave up. After the rest of the jewelry was distributed among the children and Claire's sisters he could not bring himself to throw the one earring away—

it would have killed him, he said in group. It is a gold earring, shaped like a dolphin; its tiny jade eye glints up at him from the syrupy moat of the soap dish.

"Have you been brushing her regularly?" Mrs. Theodorus asks, examining the puppy on the kitchen table. "Her furnishings look a little matted. Remember, Arthur, this is a high-maintenance dog you've got here, and you'd better get in the habit of taking care of her now if you don't want her to scream when she goes to the groomer later on."

"I'm sorry, Eva," Arthur says.

Mrs. Theodorus smiles. "Well, I'll be happy to help you," she says, as, yelping loudly, the puppy tries to bite the comb that is pulling the fur from her skin. "But you've got to remember," Mrs. Theodorus adds, looking at Arthur sternly, "she's your puppy, and finally it's your responsibility to take care of her. You can't count on me being around all the time to do it."

"We're going to be late, Eva," Arthur says.

"I know. I'll be done in a minute."

She finishes, and the puppy is returned to the dark, private world in which she spends most of her time. "What I'm interested in, Kathy," a voice on the radio says, "is how *you* feel when your husband makes these suggestions. You have to think about your own desires, too."

"That puppy is going to be ruined, listening to Dr. Pleasure," Mrs. Theodorus says as she gets into her car. They still go in separate cars.

It is the third Thursday of the month—spouse night—and even though Arthur and Mrs. Theodorus are no longer technically spouses—both have recently lost their loved ones—they still attend with needful regularity. Claire, Arthur's wife, died two months ago of a sudden, searing chemical burn, a drug reaction, which over five days crisped and opened her skin until she lay in the burn unit, her face tomato-red, her body wrapped in mummylike bandages, and wrote to Arthur, her hand shaking, "I'm scared."

"Scared of what?" Arthur asked, and she pointed a bloody finger, as best she could, to the tubes thrust down her throat to keep her breathing; she had pneumonia. In the terrible humidity of the burn unit, surrounded by the screams of injured children, Arthur tried to reassure her. He had on three gowns, two masks, a flowered surgical cap, rubber gloves. His spectacled eyes stared out from all that fabric. A children's tape deck he had bought at Walgreen's played Hoagy Carmichael songs in the corner. Above it the nurse had written: "Hello, my name is Claire. Please turn over the tape in my tape deck. Thanx."

Meanwhile, Mr. Theodorus—jolly, warm, wonderful Mr. Theodorus, with his black suits, his little mustache, his slicked-back hair; Spiro Theodorus, brother of the maitre d' at the Greek Tycoon's, mixer of the best daiquiris and joy of group night—was in a coma a few floors below. Arthur and Mrs. Theodorus met to drink coffee in the cafeteria with the tired-out residents. They shook their heads, and sometimes they wept, before returning to the ordeal, the vigil. Mrs. Theodorus told Arthur that her champion bitch Alicia was dying as well, of canine degenerative myelopathy; when she wasn't with Spiro she was at the animal hospital, stroking Alicia and feeding her small pieces of boiled chicken through the slats in her cage. She talked often, while she drank her coffee, about Alicia's coat. It was the best coat in the country, she said. Walking out of the cafeteria, Mrs. Theodorus said she honestly did not know which was going to hurt more: the death of her husband or that of her dog. They parted at the third floor. Riding back to the burn unit, Arthur rallied to face his own terrible dilemma of which-was-worse: the possibility that Claire had died without him versus the probability that she was still alive.

Arthur and Mrs. Theodorus now return to the hospital only once a month, for spouse night. Olivia, the social worker, insists that they are welcome to continue coming to group as long as they want.

And Arthur does want to come. He depends on the group not only for continuity but because toward the end it constituted the very center of Claire's life; in some ways the members were more important to her than he was, or the children. Still, he is afraid of becoming like Mrs. Jaroslavsky, who attends spouse night faithfully even now, a year after Mr. Jaroslavsky's passing. Because of Mrs. Jaroslavsky, the big conference table is covered each spouse night with a pink tablecloth and platters of poppy-seed cake, chocolate cake, pudding cake, blueberry pie. Each month there is an excuse, because each month brings dark news, death and sudden spasms of hope in equal quantity. This week, Mrs. Jaroslavsky explains, the cakes are because Christa is having her six-month interim X rays, and she wants to help. "Everyone does what they can," she says to Christa.

Across the room, Christa—freckled arms, a long sandy braid and a spigot in her arm for the chemotherapy to be poured into—looks away from the food, biting the thumbnail of one of her hands, while Chuck, her husband, holds the other. They are both professional ski instructors but have been living in this snowless climate since the illness, hand-to-mouth. Kitty Mitsui got Chuck a job busing dishes at Beefsteak Hirosha's, but that hardly scratches the surface of the bills.

"Thank you, Mrs. Jaroslavsky," Chuck says now, smiling faintly, then turning again to make sure Christa isn't going to cry.

"Well, you're welcome," Mrs. Jaroslavsky says. "You know I do what I can. And if you need anything else—anything cooked, anything cleaned—don't hesitate to ask."

She sits back, satisfied, in her chair, and takes out her knitting. She is a large, amiable-looking woman with red cheeks and hair, and oddly, the odor that dominates the room tonight is not that of the food, but the faint, sickly-sweet, waxy perfume of her lips. Arthur and Mrs. Theodorus, taking off their coats, know, as some do not, that underneath the pink cloth is a table stained with cigarette burns, and pale, slightly swollen lesions where coffee cups have leaked, and chicken-scratched nicks in the wood where hands have idly ground pencils or scissor points or the ends of ballpoint pens. The carpet is pale yellow and worn in places, and above the table is a poster, its corners worn through with pinprickings, of a cat clinging to a chinning bar. "We all have days like this," the poster says.

It is a hard room for the healthy; it looks like death. But the members of the group don't seem to notice, much less mind it. When she came home from group those first few Thursday nights, in fact, her tires skidding on the gravel, Arthur sometimes asked Claire what the room was like, and she said, "Oh, you know. Just a room." This was before Arthur stopped repressing and started going to spouse night. After taking off her coat, Claire went straight out onto the porch and smoked a cigarette, and Arthur stood by the kitchen window, watching her as she blew rings into the night. She stared at the sky, at the stars, and that was how Arthur knew the group was changing her life. She looked exhilarated, like a girl dropped off from a date during which a boy she could not care less about has told her that he loves her.

Arthur still cannot quite believe, looking at her this spouse night, that he and Mrs. Theodorus have become lovers. It seems a most unlikely thing for them to be doing, not three months after their loved ones' deaths. Still, even now, staring at her across the room, he is filled with the panicked desire for Eva that has characterized this affair since it began. For the first time in his life Arthur feels lust, insatiable lust, and apparently Eva feels it too. They make love wildly, whispering obscene phrases in each other's ears, howling with pleasure. He has scratch marks on his back from Eva's long nails. Sometimes, in the middle of the night, they get up and sit in her kitchen and eat giant pieces of the chocolate cream pie and Black Forest cake that Mr. Theodorus's brother sends over from his restaurant. The whipped cream dots their noses and chins. Once they spread it on each other and licked it off, which Arthur had read about people doing in *Penthouse;* it was Eva's idea, however.

She is not the sort of woman Arthur ever imagined when he

imagined lust. Tall, with big breasts, high hips, a heavy behind, she has steel-gray hair which she wears piled on her head, stuck randomly with bobby pins. Her face is rubbery and slightly squashed-looking. Her clothes are uniformly stretchy; they smell of dog. And still, Arthur feels for her an attraction stronger than any he has felt for any woman in his life, even Claire. He wonders if this is grief, insatiable grief, masquerading as lust to trick him, or spare him something. Sundays he lies all day in Eva's bed, reading the copies of *Dog World* and *Dog Fancy* that cover the floor. He can identify any breed now, from Chinese crested to owczarek nizinny, from Jack Russell terrier to bichon frise. She has infected him with her expertise.

And now Mrs. Theodorus gently nudges him, points to Mrs. Jaroslavsky, who sits across the table. She knits. He sees stitches being counted and measured in the raising of eyebrows, the slight parting of lips. He once read that all human gestures, if filmed in slow motion, can be shown to be coordinated with sounds, and he is trying to see if Mrs. Jaroslavsky's eyes and lips are indeed pursing and opening to the calm voice of Olivia, the social worker. Olivia's voice is like water, and so is her bluish hair, which falls down her back in an effortless ponytail.

Christa, tears in her eyes, tells the group, "If he makes me wait three hours again tomorrow, I don't know—I'll just give up." She shakes her head. "I'm ready to give up," she says. "I stare at the stupid fish tank. I read *Highlights for Children.* Sometimes I just want to say to hell with it."

Collectively, the members of the group have spent close to three of the past ten years in doctors' waiting rooms. Cheerily, Bud Israeloff reminds everyone of this statistic, and the group responds with a low murmur of laughter. Only the spouses are silent. They sit next to their sick beloved, clutching hands, looking worriedly across the table to see whose husbands and wives are worse off than theirs.

"We all understand, Christa," Kitty Mitsui says. "You know what happened to me once? I had to wait two hours in the waiting room, and then I had to wait an hour and a half in the examining room for the doctor, and then I had to wait another hour for them to take my blood. So when I heard the B.R. finally coming I pulled the sheet up over my face and pretended I was dead. It gave him a shock, I'll tell you."

"What's a B.R.?" a new wife asks sheepishly.

"That's just group talk, honey," responds a more experienced spouse. "It means 'bastard resident.' "

Olivia does not like to encourage this particular subject. "Let's talk about what to do, practically, to allay waiting anxiety," she says. "How can we help Christa get through tomorrow?"

"One of us could go with her," Kitty Mitsui says. "Christa, do you play Scrabble?"

"I don't know," Christa says.

"I could do it," Kitty says. "I've got the day off. I'll sit with you. I'll bring my portable Scrabble set. We'll play Scrabble, and when we get bored with that, we'll make origami animals. I know it's not much, but it's better than the fish tank."

"Waiting to hear if I'm going to live or not, if I can have a baby," Christa says, "and they keep me in the waiting room. Christ, my life is on the line here and they make me wait."

Under the table, Eva's hand takes Arthur's. He folds the note she has given him into quarters, then furtively reads it.

"Have you been putting the oil in her dinner?" Eva has written. "You need to for her coat."

It is decided. Kitty will go with Christa and Chuck to Christa's doctor's office tomorrow. She'll bring her portable Scrabble set. And now, that matter concluded, Iris Pearlstein takes the floor and says, "If no one minds, I have something I'd like to address, and it's this food. It's hard enough for me to come here without it looking like I'm at a bar mitzvah."

For once Mrs. Jaroslavsky stares up from her knitting. "What?" she says.

"This food, this food," Iris says, and waves at it. "It makes me sick, having to stare at it all night."

"I just wanted to make things a little more cheerful," Mrs. Jaroslavsky says, her mouth trembling. She puts down her knitting.

"Oh, who're you kidding, Doris? You want to make it more pleasant, but I'm sorry, there's nothing nice about any of this." She looks at her husband, Joe, broken by recent radiation, dozing next to her, and puts her hand on her forehead. "Christ," she says, lighting a cigarette, "we don't want to stare at fucking cake."

Arthur wonders if Mrs. Jaroslavsky is going to cry. But she holds her own. "Now just one minute, Iris," she says. "Don't think any of this is easy for me. When Morry was in the hospital, I was up every night, I was half crazy. What was I supposed to do? So I baked. That food was the fruit of suffering for my dying husband. You know how it was. I kept thinking that maybe if I just keep baking it'll keep the clock ticking, thinking, God, for one more cake, give him six months." She frowns. "Well, God defaulted. Now Morry's gone, and my freezers are stuffed. The truth is I bake for all of you the way I baked for him. There's nothing nice about it."

She resumes her knitting. Iris Pearlstein takes out a Kleenex to blow her nose. Once again Mrs. Theodorus takes Arthur's hand under the table. Mrs. Jaroslavsky looks vibrant.

"Ask if you can take home the poppy-seed," Arthur reads when he unfolds Eva's note.

Arthur got the puppy when Mrs. Theodorus offered the group a discount on her new litter. "A pet can really cheer you up," she explained at spouse night. "The human-animal bond is so important in this stressful world."

After that, Arthur approached Mrs. Theodorus and said, "I might be interested in a puppy. Since Claire passed on—"

"I know, I know," she said. "Come tomorrow, in the afternoon."

He drove through a rainstorm. Mrs. Theodorus lived in a small, sleek, cobalt-blue house in a neighborhood where the streets flounced into cul-de-sacs and children played capture the flag with unusual viciousness. The puppies stared up at him from their kitchen enclosure, mewing and rubbing against one another, vying for his attention. "This little girl is the one for you," Mrs. Theodorus said, and he was amazed that she could tell them apart. "Look at this." She pried the puppy's mouth open, revealing young fangs.

"Looks okay," Arthur said.

"Can't you tell?" said Mrs. Theodorus. "Her bite's off. She'll never show. A pity, because her coat's really good, almost as good as Alicia's was, and she's got the best bone structure of any of them."

"We had a dog once, a Yorkie," Arthur said. "She died when my oldest daughter was twelve. Just went to sleep and never woke up."

"Oh, I can't talk about the death of dogs right now," Mrs. Theodorus said.

He took the puppy home with him that day. Claire had been gone a week, and still he was finding things he could not bear—today it was a half-finished *New York Times* acrostic puzzle. It was three weeks old. Already her handwriting was shaky. Did she have any idea then, he wondered, that the rash creeping over her skin, that unbearable itchy rash, was going to kill her? He certainly didn't. You don't die from a rash. A rash would have been embarrassing to bring up in group, where hematomas and bone loss were the norm. Claire's bane, her great guilt, in the group was that she was one of the healthier ones, but she hoped that meant she could help. "What the group does—what we mostly do—is figure out how to help each other," Arthur remembered Claire saying, as the two of them sat at the kitchen table, drinking coffee. She had just come back from her second night at group. The third night she didn't come back until four in the morning, and he went half mad with panic. "We went to the Greek Tycoon's," she explained blithely. "Mr. Theodorus bought us all drinks."

The fourth night was spouse night, and he went.

He sat down at the kitchen table with the acrostic and tried to finish it; one of the clues Claire hadn't been able to get was a river that ran through the Dolomites, and he became obsessed with figuring it out, but as soon as he saw how thick and strong his own handwriting looked in comparison with the jagged, frail letters of Claire's decline, he laid his head down on the newsprint and wept. The puppy watched him from the corner. When he got up, he used Claire's last puzzle to line her pen.

Just before spouse night ends, Kitty Mitsui announces that she and Mike Watkins and Ronni Holtzman will be going to Poncho's for margaritas and nachos. "It'll be a good time," she says halfheartedly. But everyone knows she is fighting a losing battle. Since Mr. Theodorus died the after-group outings have lost their momentum.

Then, in the group's golden age, its giddy second childhood, in the reign of Mr. Theodorus, there was wild revelry, screaming laughter in the hospital parking lot, until finally Mrs. Leon, a Mormon, brought up her moral objections at group.

The next week Mr. Theodorus arrived with a rubber dog's snout tied over his nose. That was the end of Mrs. Leon, Claire reported afterwards to Arthur, her eyes gleaming. He smiled. It seemed that Claire's greatest ambition was to be fully accepted into that subgroup of the group which played charades until four in the morning, drank, and drove all night, one Thursday, to watch the sun rise over Echo Lake, where Kitty Mitsui had a cabin. Claire reported it all—the wind on her cheeks, the crispness of the air, the glory of the mountain sunrise. They built a fire and lay bundled together in sleeping bags, five of them, like campfire girls, she said.

Claire believed until the end that she was peripheral, barely accepted. She believed that Spiro and Kitty and the others were going out together without her, excluding her from the best, the most intimate gatherings. This was ironic, for as Arthur learned after her death, Claire was, if anything, the group's spiritual center; without her it fragmented. Mournful couples went home alone on spouse night, the healthy clinging testily to the sick. Then Mr. Theodorus died, and the group entered a period of adolescent turmoil. Furious explosions occurred; well-buried animosities were laid bare. For the first time the group included enemies, who sat as far across the table from each other as possible, avoiding each other's glances.

Arthur can't help but wonder sometimes if any of it was sexual; if Claire might have slept with one of the men. It's hard for him to imagine. Usually, when he tries to envision those post-group revels, or when he dreams about them, he sees only five bodies huddled in sleeping bags by a lake as dawn breaks. Sometimes he wakes up with itchy hands, and bursts into tears because he wasn't there.

When spouse night ends, Mrs. Theodorus says to Mrs. Jaroslavsky, "Doris, if you don't need it—well, I could sure use that spice cake. I have this important show judge coming over tomorrow."

"Don't do me any favors," Mrs. Jaroslavsky says. She is grim-faced, puffy. Then, cautiously: "You really want it?"

"If you don't mind. This judge is very powerful, and God knows, I could never bake anything like that. All I have around are these horrible Black Forest things Spiro's brother sends over, with ten pounds of synthetic whipped cream."

"Terrible, the things they call a cake," Mrs. Jaroslavsky says, as, smiling, she hands Mrs. Theodorus an aluminum-wrapped package.

They walk out to the parking lot together. "I know when I've outstayed my welcome," Mrs. Jaroslavsky explains to Mrs. Theodorus and Arthur. "I know it's been too long. I feel I can talk about that with you two, since we're all in the same position. The rest of them, they're fickle. When Morry died, they couldn't have been nicer, they kept saying, 'Doris, anything you want, anything you want.' Now they'd like to slap my face. And that Olivia. She gets my goat. Every day it's, 'Stay as long as you need, Doris, anything you need, Doris,' but I know the score. She'd like to get rid of me too." She blows out breath, resigned. "So this is it, Mrs. Jaroslavsky," she says. "No more spouse night. The rest of the way you have to go it alone."

"I know how you feel, Doris," Arthur says. "The group's my last link to Claire. How can I leave them? Toward the end, sometimes I think, they knew her better than I did."

"Oh, but they don't, don't you see?" Mrs. Jaroslavsky says. "That's just their illusion. They have each other for a year, maybe a little more. But what I have to remember, what I must remember, is I had Morry a lifetime." She smiles, breathes deeply. "The wind feels wonderful, doesn't it?" she says, and turning from Arthur, opens her face to the sky, as if to absorb the starlight.

Across the parking lot Kitty Mitsui calls, "Hey, you guys want to come for a nightcap? Come on! It'll be fun!" She smiles too widely at them, as if she imagines that by sheer force of will she can muster the energy to bring the dead back to life.

Arthur smiles back. "No thanks," he says. "You go ahead."

"Suit yourself," Kitty Mitsui says, "but you're missing a big blow-out." She has four with her, including Christa and Chuck. Clearly she is destined to become the group's perpetual cheerleader, unflagging in her determination to bring back the glory of the past with a few loudly-called-out cries. Poor Kitty Mitsui. The rest of them had lives, but she's thirty-two and unmarried. The group is her life, and it will be her doomed nostalgia.

Mrs. Jaroslavsky winces as Kitty's car roars off. "That smell," she says. "That particular smell of burnt rubber. I remember it from Morry's room when he was dying. It must have been something in one of the machines. Now I smell it—and I can hardly keep myself standing up." She looks at the ground, clearly cried out for an entire lifetime, and Arthur is suddenly grateful to have Mrs. Theodorus, grateful for the nights they may spend together in her dog-hair-covered bed. He will lie awake, listening for occasional yelps from the kennel.

"What you need," Mrs. Theodorus says, "is a puppy," and Mrs. Jaroslavsky's mouth opens into a wide smile. "My dear girl," she says, "I'm allergic." Her face, against the dark sky, expands into a comic vision of the moon, eager-eyed and white-faced.

* * *

When Claire died, Arthur arranged for her ashes to be scattered at sea. It was what she had wanted. Everyone in the group had decided what they wanted, "B vs. C," or burial versus cremation, being one of the most popular discussion topics at the post-group gatherings. He and the children took the plastic vial of ashes out on a boat, which they had to share with another family—a staunch couple named MacGiver who had lost their son, and who resembled the protagonists of *American Gothic.* Arthur felt faintly embarrassed as the two families engaged in nervous small talk. The wind was too strong to go out to sea that day, the young captain informed them; the scattering would have to take place in the bay. Arthur, as he figures it now, went crazy. "She said the ocean," he kept repeating to the captain, who in turn kept explaining, calmly and compassionately, that the wind situation simply made it impossible for them to go to the ocean. "It's okay, Dad," Arthur's daughters told him. "The bay's almost the ocean anyway." But he was adamant. "I told her the ocean," he kept saying. "I told her she'd be scattered over the ocean." He clutched the vial to his chest, while the MacGivers discreetly did their own dumping, shaking the little plastic bag over the water as if it were a sand-filled towel. "Mister," the captain said, "we're going to have to turn back soon." It was getting to be dusk. Finally, miserably, Arthur said, "Oh, the hell with it," and without even warning his children (Jane was in the bathroom at the time) dumped the vial over the side of the boat in a rage. The ashes swirled into the water like foam; the big chunks plopped and sank instantly. Nothing was left but a fine powder of ash, coating the inside of the bag, and in a moment of turmoil and indecision Arthur bent over and touched his tongue to the white crust, lapped it up. He was crying wildly. Dismayed, the MacGivers pretended to look the other way, pointing out to one another the Golden Gate Bridge, Angel Island, Alcatraz.

At Mrs. Theodorus's house, the puppy writhes on the floor, urinates, rolls onto her back. Her mother ignores her. "It's the hormonal change," Mrs. Theodorus explains blithely. "After a few months, the mothers don't recognize their offspring anymore."

"I think that's sad," Arthur says, even though he doesn't quite believe it, and Mrs. Theodorus shrugs and pours out coffee. "In a sense, it's better," she says. "They're spared the sensation of loss."

She looks out at the grooming table, empty now, but still festooned with Alicia's ribbons and silver cups and photographs of Mrs. Theodorus posed with her prize bitch. Across the room the remaining puppies lie with their mother in various states of repose. Only Arthur's puppy wags her tail, and stretches her legs behind herself, barely holding herself back from her uninterested mother.

"I think they slept together," Mrs. Theodorus says.

For a moment Arthur thinks she is talking about the dogs. "All of them," Eva goes on, and her voice is low. "That night they went to Echo Lake."

"Eva," he says, "why are you saying this?"

"Oh, I think it's pretty obvious," she says. "You see, there were things I overheard—on the phone."

Arthur is surprised at how panicked he feels, and tries to hide it. "What did you hear?" he asks finally—not wanting to sound too curious, though he is.

"I heard Spiro talking to a woman. A woman he was clearly . . . intimate with. I think it was Kitty. But then again, now that I think about it, it might just as well have been Claire." She is quiet a moment. "It wasn't just the two of them, if you know what I mean. So I thought I would ask you if you knew anything—"

"I don't know anything," Arthur says. He stares up at the ceiling. "And I don't want to know anything. I don't want to know another bloody thing about that group."

"Don't sound so holier-than-thou, Arthur. The two of us aren't exactly being saintly in our loyalty to the memory of our lost loved ones. So what if Claire was sleeping with Spiro? So what if they were all sleeping together? Look at us."

"Claire is in the water," Arthur says. "Spiro is buried."

"He wouldn't have had it any other way," Mrs. Theodorus says.

They are again quiet. In the bright light of the kennel Arthur can see the portrait of Alicia that hangs over the table. Mouth open, red tongue hanging, the dog stares. Does anyone know how long it takes? Did Claire guess, that morning she woke up and said, "My hands are itching, Arthur. Were we near any poison oak last night?" All it took was three short weeks, and she was fighting to live. What did the group matter then? He was an egotist, a child, to think that his losing Claire to the group was anything even close to tragedy, to think his suffering came anywhere close to hers.

"Oh, Arthur," Mrs. Theodorus says. "I shouldn't impose my weird ideas on you. Since Spiro died, I just don't know what I'm saying or thinking, or where I'm going. I could have read a lot into that conversation, I realize now. It was hard to make it all out. I just think that if I knew . . . maybe I wouldn't feel so lost."

"Neither of us exactly feels found," Arthur says. "Remember how that first night at group after Claire died, I almost hit Ronni Holtzman when she said she was sorry? What was I supposed to say to that? It's okay? Claire's not really dead? It wasn't your fault?"

"Oh, Arthur," Mrs. Theodorus says. "I know how you feel." But Arthur doesn't answer. To know how *Claire* felt—that is the knowledge he longs for: lying in that bed, skin cracked and bleeding, tubes in his kidneys, his lungs, his arms. That is what he wants, craves, lusts to know—that harsh condition by which Claire was taken from him. Isn't it the great lie of the living, after all, that grieving is worse, is anything near death?

Distantly he feels hands, lips on him. It is Eva, wanting, he supposes, to make love, and he obeys, allowing her to walk him into her bedroom. But in his mind he is still on that boat, clinging to the vial of Claire's ashes. "All right, already," is what he thinks he shouted, when the captain said they would have to leave, and in fury he threw to the water those ashes he had cradled in his arms, those ashes he had loved and lived with. His daughters, he is sure, still murmur together about "Dad's awful moment," "Dad's terrible behavior," but in truth he is still angry at how grief carped around on that boat, pretending to dignity. "Why did you have to embarrass us like that?" his daughter Jane said to him in the car—it was she who had been in the bathroom—and yet he knows he would do it again; he would throw those ashes over in graceless fury, again and again.

"Kiss me," Eva says nervously. He takes her in his arms. Through the window, the moon illuminates Mr. Theodorus's supply of after-shave lotion, hair tonic, shoe polish—a row of dark bottles lined up carefully, like sentries, guarding the way in.

MY MARRIAGE TO VENGEANCE

WHEN I got the invitation to Diana's wedding—elegantly embossed, archaically formal (the ceremony, it stated, would take place at "twelve-thirty o'clock")—the first thing I did was the *TV Guide* crossword puzzle. I was not so much surprised by Diana getting married as I was by her inviting me. What, I wondered, would motivate a person like Diana to ask her former lover, a woman she had lived with for a year and a month and whose heart she had suddenly and callously broken, to a celebration of her union with a man? It seems to me that that is asking for trouble.

I decided to call Leonore, who had been a close friend of Diana's and mine during the days when we were together, and who always seemed to have answers. "Leonore, Diana's getting married," I said when she picked up the phone.

"If you ask me," Leonore said, "she's wanted a man since day one. Remember that gay guy she tried to make it with? He said he wanted to change, have kids and all?" She paused ominously. "It's not him, is it?"

I looked at the invitation. "Mark Charles Cadwallader," I said.

"Well, for his sake," Leonore said, "I only hope he knows what he's getting into. As for Miss Diana, her doings are of no interest to me."

"But, Leonore," I said, "the question is: Should I go to the wedding?" imagining myself, suddenly, in my red T-shirt that said

BABY BUTCH (a present from Diana), reintroducing myself to her thin, severe, long-necked mother, Marjorie Winters.

"I think that would depend on the food," Leonore said.

After I hung up, I poured myself some coffee and propped the invitation in front of me to look at. For the first few seconds it hadn't even clicked who was getting married. I had read: "Mr. and Mrs. Humphrey Winters cordially invite you to celebrate the wedding of their daughter, Diana Helaine," and thought: Who is Diana Helaine? Then it hit me, because for the whole year and a month, Diana had refused to tell me what her middle initial stood for—positively refused, she said, out of embarrassment, while I tried to imagine what horrors could lie behind that "H"—Hildegarde? Hester? Hulga? She was coyly, irritatingly insistent about not letting the secret out, like certain girls who would have nothing to do with me in eighth grade. Now she was making public to the world what she insisted on hiding from me, and it made perfect sense. Diana Helaine, not a different person, is getting married, I thought, and it was true, the fact in and of itself didn't surprise me. During the year and a month, combing the ghost of her once knee-length hair, I couldn't count how many times she'd said, very off-the-cuff, "You know, Ellen, sometimes I think this lesbian life is for the birds. Maybe I should just give it up, get married and have two point four babies." I'd smile and say, "If you do that, Diana, you can count on my coming to the wedding with a shotgun and shooting myself there in front of everybody." To which, still strumming her hair like a guitar and staring into the mirror, she would respond only with a faint smile, as if she could think of nothing in the world she would enjoy more.

First things first: We were lovers, and I don't mean schoolgirls touching each other in exploratory ways in dormitories after dark. I mean, we lived together, shared tampons and toothpaste, had one bed to sleep in, and for all the world (and ourselves) to see. Diana was in law school in San Francisco, and I had a job at Milpitas State Hospital (I still do). Each day I'd drive an hour and a half there and an hour and a half back, and when I got home Diana would be waiting for me in bed, a fat textbook propped on her lap. We had couple friends, Leonore and Callie, for instance, and were always invited to things together, and when she left me, we were even thinking about getting power of attorney over each other. I was Diana's first woman lover, though she had had plenty of boyfriends. I had never slept with a boy, but had been making love with girls since early in high school. Which meant that for me, being a lesbian was just how things were. But for Diana—well, from day one it was adventure, event and episode. For a while we just had long blushing talks over pizza, during which she confessed she was "curious." It's ridiculous how many supposedly straight girls come on to you that way—plopping themselves down on your lap and fully expecting you to go through all the hard work of initiating them into Sapphic love out of sheer lust for recruitment. No way, I said. The last thing I need is to play guinea pig, testing ground, only to be left when the fun's over and a new boyfriend shows up on the horizon. But no, Diana said. I mean, yes. I think I *do.* I mean, I think I *am.* At which point she would always have just missed the last bus home and have to spend the night in my bed, where it was only a matter of time before I had no more defenses.

After we became lovers, Diana cut her hair off, and bought me the BABY BUTCH T-shirt. She joined all sorts of groups and organizations, dragged me to unsavory bars, insisted, fiercely, on telling her parents everything. (They did not respond well.) Only in private did she muse over her other options. I think she thought she was rich enough not to have to take any vow or promise all that seriously. Rich people are like that, I have noticed. They think a love affair is like a shared real estate venture they can just buy out of when they get tired of it.

Diana had always said the one reason she definitely wanted to get married was for the presents, so the day before the wedding I took my credit card and went to Nordstrom's, where I found her name in the bridal registry and was handed a computer printout with her china pattern, silver, stainless and other assorted requirements. I was already over my spending limit, so I bought her the ultimate—a Cuisinart—which I had wrapped to carry in white crêpe paper with a huge yellow bow. Next came the equally important matter of buying myself a dress for the wedding. It had been maybe five, six years since I'd owned a dress. But buying clothes is like riding a bicycle—it comes back—and soon, remembering age-old advice from my mother on hems and necklines, I had picked out a pretty yellow sundress with a spattering of daisies, and a big, wide-brimmed hat.

The invitation had been addressed to Miss Ellen Britchkey and guest, and afterwards, in the parking lot, that made me think about my life—how there was no one in it. And then, as I was driving home from Nordstrom's, for the first time in years I had a seizure of accident panic. I couldn't believe I was traveling sixty miles an hour, part of a herd of speeding cars which passed and raced each other, coming within five or six inches of collision and death every ten seconds. It astonished me to realize that I drove every day of my life, that every day of my life I risked ending my life, that all I had to do was swerve the wrong way, or look only in the front and not the side mirror, and I might hit another car, or hit a child on the way to a wedding, and have to live for the rest of my life with the guilt, or die. Horrified, I headed right, into the slow lane. The slow lane was full of scared women, crawling home alone. It was no surprise to me. I was one with the scared women crawling home alone. After Diana left me, I moved down the peninsula to a miniature house—that is the only way to describe it—two rooms with a roof, and shingles, and big pretty windows. It was my solitude house, my self-indulgence house, my remorse-and-secret-pleasure house. There I ate take-out Chinese food, read and reread *Little House on the Prairie,* stayed up late watching reruns of *Star Trek* and *The Honeymooners.* I lived by my wits, by survival measures. The television was one of those tiny ones, the screen smaller than a human face.

* * *

Diana—I only have one picture of her, and it is not a good likeness. In it she wears glasses and has long, long hair, sweeping below the white fringe of the picture, to her behind. She cut all her hair off as an offering to me the day after the first night we made love, and presented it that evening in a box—two neat braids, clipped easily as toenail parings, offered like a dozen roses. I stared at them, the hair still braided, still fresh with the smell of shampoo, and joked that I had bought her a comb, like in "The Gift of the Magi." "Don't you see?" she said. "I did it for you—I changed myself for you, as an act of love." I looked at her, her new boyish bangs, her face suddenly so thin-seeming without its frame of yellow hair. She was used to big gestures, to gifts that made an impact.

"Diana," I lied (for I had loved her long hair), "it's the most generous thing anyone's ever done for me." To say she'd done it for me—well, it was a little bit like a mean trick my sister pulled on me one Christmas when we were kids. She had this thing about getting a little tiny tree to put on top of the piano. And I, of course, wanted a great big one, like the Wagner family down the block. And then, about ten days before Christmas, she said, "Ellen, I have an early Christmas present for you," and she handed me a box, inside which were about a hundred miniature Christmas-tree ornaments.

I can recognize a present with its own motive.

If I've learned one thing from Diana, it's that there's more to a gift than just giving.

The next day was the day of the wedding, and somehow, without hitting any children, I drove to the hotel in Hillsborough where the ceremony and reception were taking place. A doorman escorted me to a private drawing room where, nervous about being recognized, I kept the Cuisinart in front of my face as long as I could, until finally an older woman with a carnation over her breast, apparently an aunt or something, said, "May I take that, dear?" and I had to surrender the Cuisinart to a table full of presents, some of which were hugely and awkwardly wrapped and looked like human heads. I thanked her, suddenly naked in my shame, and sturdied myself to brave the drawing room, where the guests milled. I recognized two or three faces from college, all part of Diana's set—rich, straight, preppy, not the sort I had hung around with at all. And in the distance I saw her very prepared parents, her mother thin and severe-looking as ever in a sleeveless black dress, her streaked hair cut short, like Diana's, her neck and throat nakedly displaying a brilliant jade necklace, while her father, in his tuxedo, talked with some other men and puffed at a cigar. Turning to avoid them, I almost walked right into Walter Bevins, who was Diana's gay best friend, or "hag fag," in college, and we were so relieved to see each other we grabbed a couple of whiskey sours and headed to as secluded a corner as we could find. "Boy, am I glad to see a familiar face," Walter said. "Can you believe this? Though I must say, I never doubted Diana would get married in anything less than splendor."

"Me neither," I admitted. "I was just a little surprised that Diana was getting married at all."

"Weren't we all!" Walter said. "But he seems like a nice guy. A lawyer, of course. *Very* cute, a real shame that he's heterosexual, if you ask me. But apparently she loves him and he loves her, and that's just fine. Look, there he is."

Walter pointed to a tall, dark man with a mustache and beard who stood in the middle of a circle of elderly women. To my horror, his eye caught ours, and he disentangled himself from the old women and walked over to where we were sitting. "Walter," he said. Then he looked at me and said, "Ellen?"

I nodded and smiled.

"Ellen, Ellen," he said, and reached out a hand which, when I took it, lifted me from the safety of my sofa onto my feet. "It is such a pleasure to meet you," he said. "Come with me for a second. I've wanted a chance to talk with you for so long, and once the wedding takes place—who knows?"

I smiled nervously at Walter, who raised a hand in comradeship, and was led by the groom through a door to an antechamber, empty except for a card table piled high with bridesmaids' bouquets. "I just want you to know," he said, "how happy Diana and I are that you could make it. She speaks so warmly of you. And I also want you to know, just so there's no tension, Diana's told me everything, and I'm fully accepting of her past."

"Thank you, Mark," I said, horrified that at my age I could already be part of someone's "past." It sounded fake to me, as if lesbianism was just a stage Diana had passed through, and I was some sort of perpetual adolescent, never seeing the adult light of heterosexuality.

"Charlie," Mark said. "I'm called Charlie."

He opened the door, and as we were heading back out into the drawing room, he said, "Oh, by the way, we've seated you next to the schizophrenic girl. Your being a social worker and all, we figured you wouldn't mind."

"Me?" I said. "Mind? Not at all."

"Thanks. Boy, is Diana going to be thrilled to see you."

Then he was gone into the crowd.

Once back in the drawing room I searched for Walter, but couldn't seem to find him. I was surrounded on all sides by elderly women with elaborate, peroxided hairdos. Their purses fascinated me. Some were hard as shell and shaped like kidneys, others made out of punctured leather that reminded me of birth control pill dispensers. Suddenly I found myself face to nose with Marjorie Winters, whose eyes visibly bulged upon recognizing me. We had met once, when Diana had brought me home for a weekend, but that was before she had told her mother the nature of our relationship. After Diana came out—well, I believe the exact words were, "I never want that woman in my house again."

"Ellen," Marjorie said now, just as I had imagined she might. "What a surprise." She smiled, whether with contempt or triumph I couldn't tell.

"Well, you know I wouldn't miss Diana's wedding, Mrs. Winters," I said, smiling. "And this certainly is a lovely hotel."

She smiled. "Yes, isn't it? Red, look who's here," she said, and motioned over her husband, who for no particular reason except that his name was Humphrey was called Red. He was an amiable, absent-minded man, and he stared at me in earnest, trying to figure out who I was.

"You remember Diana's friend Ellen, from college, don't you?"

"Oh yes," he said. "Of course." Clearly he knew nothing. I believe his wife liked to keep him in a perpetual dark like that, so that he wouldn't be distracted from earning money.

"Ellen's a social worker," Marjorie said, "at the state hospital at Milpitas. So Diana and I thought it would be a good idea to seat her next to the schizophrenic girl, don't you think?"

"Oh yes," Red said. "Definitely. I imagine they'll have a lot of things to talk about."

A little tinkling bell rang, and Marjorie said, "Oh goodness, that's my cue. Be a dear, and do take care of Natalie." Squeezing my hand, she was gone. She had won, and she was glorying in her victory. And not for the first time that day, I wondered: Why is it that the people who always win always win?

The guests were beginning to move outdoors, to the garden, where the ceremony was taking place. Lost in the crowd, I spied Walter and maneuvered my way next to him. "How's it going, little one?" he said.

"I feel like a piece of shit," I said. I wasn't in the mood to make small talk.

"That's what weddings are for," he said cheerfully. We headed through a pair of french doors into a small, beautiful garden, full of blooming roses and wreaths and huge baskets of wisteria and lilies. Handsome, uniformed men—mostly brothers of the groom, I presumed—were helping everyone to their seats. Thinking we were a couple, one of them escorted Walter and me to one of the back rows, along with several other young couples, who had brought their babies and might have to run out to change a diaper or something in the middle of the ceremony.

As soon as everyone was seated the string quartet in the corner began to play something sweet and Chopin-like, and then the procession started—first Diana's sister, who was matron of honor;

then the bridesmaids, each arm in arm with an usher, each dressed in a different pastel dress which was coordinated perfectly with her bouquet; and then, finally, Diana herself, looking resplendent in her white dress. Everyone gave out little oohs and aahs as she entered, locked tight between her parents. It had been two years since we'd seen each other, and looking at her, I thought I'd cry. I felt like such a piece of nothing, such a worthless piece of garbage without her—she was really that beautiful. Her hair was growing back, which was the worst thing. She had it braided and piled on her head and woven with wildflowers. Her skin was flawless, smooth—skin I'd touched hundreds, thousands of times—and there was an astonishing brightness about her eyes, as if she could see right through everything to its very heart. From the altar, the groom looked on, grinning like an idiot, a proud possessor who seemed to be saying, with his teary grin, see, look what I've got, look what chose me. And Diana too, approaching him at the altar, was all bright smiles, no doubt, no regret or hesitation registering in her face, and I wondered what she was thinking now: if she was thinking about her other life, her long committed days and nights as a lesbian.

The music stopped. They stood, backs to us, the audience, before the reverent reverend. He began to lecture them solemnly. And then I saw it. I saw myself stand up, run to the front of the garden, and before anyone could say anything, do anything, pull out the gun and consummate, all over the grass, my own splendid marriage to vengeance.

But of course I didn't do anything like that. Instead I just sat there with Walter and listened as Diana, love of my life, my lover, my life, repeated the marriage vows, her voice a little trembly, as if to suggest she was just barely holding in her tears. They said their "I do"s. They exchanged rings. They kissed, and everyone cheered.

At my table in the dining room were seated Walter; the Winterses' maid, Juanita; her son; the schizophrenic girl; and the schizophrenic girl's mother. It was in the darkest, most invisible corner of the room, and I could see it was no accident that Marjorie Winters had gathered us all here—all the misfits and minorities, the kooks and oddities of the wedding. For a minute, sitting down and gazing out at the other tables, which were full of beautiful women and men in tuxedos, I was so mad at Diana I wanted to run back to the presents table and reclaim my Cuisinart, which I really couldn't afford to be giving her anyway, and which she certainly didn't deserve. But then I realized that people would probably think I was a thief and call the hotel detective or the police, and I decided not to.

The food, Leonore would have been pleased to know, was mediocre. Next to me, the schizophrenic girl stabbed with her knife at a pathetic-looking little bowl of melon balls and greenish strawberries, while her mother looked out exhaustedly, impatiently, at the expanse of the hotel dining room. Seeing that the schizophrenic girl had started, Juanita's son, who must have been seven feet tall, began eating as well, but she slapped his hand. Not wanting to embarrass him by staring, I looked at the schizophrenic girl. I knew she was the schizophrenic girl by her glasses—big, ugly, red ones from the seventies, the kind where the temples start at the bottom of the frames—and the way she slumped over her fruit salad, as if she was afraid someone might steal it.

"Hello," I said to her.

She didn't say anything. Her mother, dragged back into focus, looked down at her and said, "Oh now, Natalie."

"Hello," Natalie said.

The mother smiled. "Are you with the bride or the groom?" she asked.

"The bride."

"Relation?"

"Friend from college."

"How nice," the mother said. "We're with the groom. Old neighbors. Natalie and Charlie were born the same day in the same hospital, isn't that right, Nat?"

"Yes," Natalie said.

"She's very shy," the mother said to me, and winked.

Across the table Walter was asking Juanita's son if he played basketball. Shyly, in a Jamaican accent, he admitted that he did. His face was as arch and stern as that of his mother, a fat brown woman with the eyes of a prison guard. She smelled very clean, almost antiseptic.

"Natalie, are you in school?" I asked.

She continued to stab at her fruit salad, not really eating it as much as trying to decimate the pieces of melon.

"Tell the lady, Natalie," said her mother.

"Yes."

"Natalie's in a very special school," the mother said.

"I'm a social worker," I said. "I understand about Natalie."

"Oh really, you are?" the mother said, and relief flushed her face. "I'm so glad. It's so painful, having to explain—you know—"

Walter was trying to get Juanita to reveal the secret location of the honeymoon. "I'm not saying," Juanita said. "Not one word."

"Come on," said Walter. "I won't tell a soul, I swear."

"I'm on TV," Natalie said.

"Oh now," said her mother.

"I am. I'm on *The Facts of Life.* I'm Tuti."

"Now, Natalie, you know you're not."

"And I'm also on *All My Children* during the day. It's a tough life, but I manage."

"Natalie, you know you're not to tell these stories."

"Did someone mention *All My Children?*" asked Juanita's son. Walter, too, looked interested.

"My lips are forever sealed," Juanita said to no one in particular. "There's no chance no way no one's going to get me to say one word."

Diana and Ellen. Ellen and Diana. When we were together, everything about us seethed. We lived from seizure to seizure. Our fights were glorious, manic, our need to fight like an allergy, something that reddens and irritates the edges of everything and demands release. Once Diana broke the air conditioner and I wouldn't forgive her. "Leave me alone," I screamed.

"No," she said. "I want to talk about it. Now."

"Well, I don't."

"Why are you punishing me?" Diana said. "It's not my fault."

"I'm not punishing you."

"You are. You're shutting me up when I have something I want to say."

"Damn it, won't you just leave me alone? Can't you leave anything alone?"

"Let me say what I have to say, damn it!"

"What?"

"I didn't break it on purpose! I broke it by accident!"

"Damn it, Diana, leave me the fuck alone! Why don't you just go away?"

"You are so hard!" Diana said, tears in her eyes, and slammed out the door into the bedroom.

After we fought, consumed, crazed, we made love like animals, then crawled about the house for days, cats in a cage, lost in a torpor of lazy carnality. It helped that the air conditioner was broken. It kept us slick. There was always, between us, heat and itch.

Once, in those most desperate, most remorse-filled days after Diana left, before I moved down the peninsula to my escape-hatch dream house, I made a list which was titled "Reasons I love her."

1. Her hair.
2. Her eyes.
3. Her skin. (Actually, most of her body except maybe her elbows.)
4. The way she does voices for the plants when she waters them, saying things like "Boy was I thirsty, thanks for the drink." [This one was a lie. That habit actually infuriated me.]

5. Her advantages: smart and nice.
6. Her devotion to me, to us as a couple.
7. How much she loved me.
8. Her love for me.
9. How she loves me.

There was less to that list than met the eye. When Diana left me—and it must be stated, here and now, she did so cruelly, callously, and suddenly—she said that the one thing she wanted me to know was that she still considered herself a lesbian. It was only me she was leaving. "Don't think I'm just another straight girl who used you," she insisted, as she gathered all her things into monogrammed suitcases. "I just don't feel we're right for each other. You're a social worker. I'm not good enough for you. Our lives, our ideas about the world—they're just never going to mesh."

Outside, I knew, her mother's station wagon waited in ambush. Still I pleaded. "Diana," I said, "you got me into this thing. You lured me in, pulled me in against my will. You can't leave just like that."

But she was already at the door. "I want you to know," she said, "because of you, I'll be able to say, loud and clear, for the rest of my life, I am a lesbian," and kissed me on the cheek.

In tears I stared at her, astonished that this late in the game she still thought my misery at her departure might be quelled by abstract gestures to sisterhood. Also that she could think me that stupid. I saw through her quaking, frightened face, her little-boy locks.

"You're a liar," I said, and, grateful for the anger, she crumpled up her face, screamed, "Damn you, Ellen," and ran out the door.

As I said, our fights were glorious.

All she left behind were her braids.

Across the dining room, Diana stood with Charlie, holding a big knife over the wedding cake. Everyone was cheering. The knife sank into the soft white flesh of the cake, came out again clung with silken frosting and crumbs. Diana cut two pieces. Their arms intertwined, she and Charlie fed each other.

Then they danced. A high-hipped young woman in sequins got up on the bandstand and sang, "Graduation's almost here, my love, teach me tonight."

After the bride and groom had been given their five minutes of single glory on the dance floor, and the parents and grandparents had joined them, I felt a tap on my shoulder. "Care to tango *avec moi*, my dear?" Walter said.

"Walter," I said, "I'd be delighted."

We got up from the table and moved out onto the floor. I was extremely nervous, sweating through my dress. I hadn't actually spoken to Diana yet, doubted she'd even seen me. Now, not three feet away, she stood, dancing and laughing, Mrs. Mark Charles Cadwallader.

I kept my eyes on Walter's lapel. The song ended. The couples broke up. And then, there she was, approaching me, all smiles, all bright eyes. "Ellen," she said, embracing me, and her mother shot us a wrathful glance. "Ellen. Let me look at you."

She looked at me. I looked at her. Close up, she looked slightly unraveled, her makeup smeared, her eyes red and a little tense. "Come with me to the ladies' room," she said. "My contacts are killing me."

She took my hand and swept me out of the ballroom into the main hotel lobby. Everyone in the lobby stared at us frankly, presuming, I suppose, that she was a runaway bride, and I her maid. But we were only running away to the ladies' room.

"These contacts!" she said once we got there, and opening one eye wide peeled off a small sheath of plastic. "I'm glad you came," she said, placing the lens on the end of her tongue and licking it. "I was worried that you wouldn't. I've felt so bad about you, Ellen, worried about you so much, since—well, since things ended between us. I was hoping this wedding could be a reconciliation for us. That now we could start again. As friends."

She turned away from the lamplit mirror and flashed me a big smile. I just looked up at her.

"Yes," I said. "I'd like that."

Diana removed the other lens and licked it. It seemed to me a highly unorthodox method of cleaning. Then, nervously, she replaced the lens and looked at herself in the mirror. She had let down her guard. Her face looked haggard, and red blush was streaming off her cheeks.

"I didn't invite Leonore for a reason," she said. "I knew she'd do something to embarrass me, come all dyked out or something. I'm not trying to deny my past, you know. Charlie knows everything. Have you met him?"

"Yes," I said.

"And isn't he a wonderful guy?"

"Yes."

"I have nothing against Leonore. I just believe in subtlety these days. You, I knew I could count on you for some subtlety, some class. Leonore definitely lacks class."

It astonished me, all that wasn't being said. I wanted to mention it all—her promise on the doorstep, the gun, the schizophrenic girl. But there was so much. Too much. Nowhere to begin.

When she'd finished with her ablutions, we sat down in parallel toilets. "It is nearly impossible to pee in this damned dress," she said to me through the divider. "I can't wait to get out of it."

"I can imagine," I said.

Then there was a loud spilling noise, and Diana gave out a little sigh of relief. "I've got a terrible bladder infection," she said. "Remember in college how it was such a big status symbol to have a bladder infection because it meant you were having sex? Girls used to come into the dining hall clutching big jars of cranberry juice and moaning, and the rest of us would look at them a little jealously." She faltered. "Or some of us did," she added. "I guess not you, huh, Ellen?"

"No, I was a lesbian," I said, "and still am, and will be until the day I die." I don't know why I said that, but it shut her up.

For about thirty seconds there was not a sound from the other side of the divider, and then I heard Diana sniffling. I didn't know what to say.

"Christ," Diana said, after a few seconds, and blew her nose. "Christ. Why'd I get married?"

I hesitated. "I'm not sure I'm the person to ask," I said. "Did your mother have anything to do with it?"

"Oh, Ellen," Diana said, "please!" I heard her spinning the toilet paper roll. "Look," she said, "you probably resent me incredibly. You probably think I'm a sellout and a fool and that I was a royal bitch to you. You probably think when Charlie does it to me I lie there and pretend I'm feeling something when I'm not. Well, it's not true. Not in the least." She paused. "I was just not prepared to go through my life as a social freak, Ellen. I want a normal life, just like everybody. I want to go to parties and not have to die inside trying to explain who it is I'm with. Charlie's very good for me in that way, he's very understanding and generous." She blew her nose again. "I'm not denying you were part of my life, that our relationship was a big thing for me. I'm just saying it's finished. That part's finished."

Defiantly she flushed.

We stood up, pulled up our underpants and stepped out of the toilet booths to face each other. I looked Diana right in the eye, and I noticed her weaken. I saw it. I could have kissed her or something, I knew, and made her even more unhappy. But I didn't really see the point.

Afterwards, we walked together out of the ladies' room, back into the ballroom, where we were accosted by huge crowds of elderly women with purses that looked to me like the shellacked sushi in certain Japanese restaurant windows.

"Was it okay?" Walter asked me, taking my arm and leading me back to our table for cake.

"Yes," I said. "Okay." But he could see from my face how utterly miserable I was.

"Don't even try," Juanita said, giggling hysterically to herself as we got back to the table. "You're not getting a word out of me, so don't even begin to ask me questions."

Once I knew a schizophrenic girl. Her name was Holly Reardon and she was my best friend from age five to eight. We played house a lot, and sometimes we played spaceship, crawling together into a cubbyhole behind my parents' sofa bed, then turning off the lights and pretending the living room was some fantastic planet. We did well with our limited resources. But then money started disappearing, and my mother sat me down one day and asked me if I had noticed the money always disappeared when Holly came to visit. I shook my head vigorously no, refusing to believe her. And then one day my favorite stuffed animal, a dog called Rufus, disappeared, and I didn't tell my mother, and didn't tell my mother, until one day she said to me, "Ellen, what happened to Rufus?" and I started to cry. We never found Rufus. Holly had done something with him. And it wasn't because of me that she went away, my parents assured me, it wasn't because of me that her parents closed up the house and had to move into an apartment. Holly was not well. Years later, when I went to work at the state hospital, I think somewhere, secretly, I hoped Holly might be there, a patient there, that we might play house and spaceship in the linen closets. But of course she wasn't. Who knows where she is now?

After the wedding I felt so depressed I had ice cream for dinner. I did several acrostic puzzles. I watched *The Honeymooners* and I watched *Star Trek.* I watched Sally Jessy Raphael. I watched *The Twilight Zone.* Fortunately, it was not one of the boring Western ones, but an episode I like particularly, about a little girl with a doll that says things like, "My name is Talking Tina and I'm going to kill you." I wished I'd had a doll like that when I was growing up. Next was *Night Gallery.* I almost never watch *Night Gallery,* but when I do, it seems I always see the same episode, the one about two people who meet on a road and are filled with a mysterious sense of déjà vu, of having met before. It turns out they live in the mind of a writer who has been rewriting the same scene a thousand times. Near the end they rail at their creator to stop tormenting them by summoning them into existence over and over, to suffer over and over. At the risk of mysticism, it seems to me significant that every time I have tuned into *Night Gallery* in my life it is this episode I have seen.

Then there was nothing more good to watch.

I got up, paced around the house, tried not to think about any of it: Holly Reardon, or Natalie, or Diana, or those poor people living in the mind of a writer and getting rewritten over and over again. I tried not to think about all the Chinese dinners I wasn't going to be able to have because I'd spent so much money on that Cuisinart for Diana, who probably could afford to buy herself a hundred Cuisinarts if she wanted. I tried not to think about their honeymoon, about what secret, glorious place they were bound for. It was too late for it to still make me mad that the whole world, fired up to stop me and Diana, was in a conspiracy to protect the privacy of the angelic married couple she had leapt into to save herself, to make sure their perfect honeymoon wasn't invaded by crazy lesbian ex-lovers with shotguns and a whole lot of unfinished business on their minds. Unfortunately, any anger I felt, which might have saved me, was counteracted by how incredibly sorry I felt for Diana, how sad she had seemed, weeping in the ladies' room on her wedding day.

I went to the closet and took out Diana's braids. God knows I hadn't opened the box for ages. There they were, the braids, only a little faded, a little tangled, and of course, no longer smelling of shampoo. I lifted one up. I was surprised at how silky the hair felt, even this old. Carefully, to protect myself, I rubbed just a little of it against my face. I shuddered. It could have been her.

I went to the bed, carrying the braids with me. I laid them along my chest. I have never had long hair. Now I tried to imagine what it felt like, tried to imagine I was Diana imagining me, a woman she had loved, a woman she had given her hair, a woman who now lay on a bed somewhere, crying, using all the strength she could muster just to not force the braids down her throat. But I knew

Diana was on a plane somewhere in the sky, or in a car, or more likely than that, lying in a heart-shaped bed while a man hovered over her, his hands running through her new hair, and that probably all she was thinking was how much better off she was than me, how much richer, and how lucky to have escaped before she was sucked so far in, like me, that it would be too late to ever get out. Was I so pathetic? Possibly. And possibly Diana was going to be happier for the choice she had made. But I think, more likely, lying on that mysterious bed, she was contemplating a whole life of mistakes spinning out from one act of compromise, and realizing she preferred a life of easy mistakes to one that was harder but better. Who was I to criticize? Diana had her tricks, and so did Juanita, and so, for that matter, did that schizophrenic girl stabbing at her melon balls. We all had our little tricks.

I took the braids off myself. I stood up. A few hairs broke loose from the gathered ropes, fell lightly to the floor. They didn't even look like anything; they might have been pieces of straw.

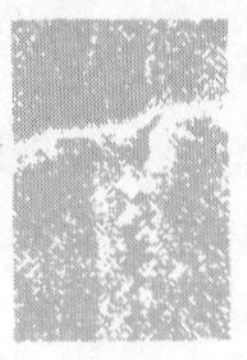

AYOR

THE summer I turned nineteen I took a short, sad, circular trip to the Great Smoky Mountains National Park, in Tennessee, with a friend I was in love with, or would have been in love with, had I known more about him or about myself. His name was Craig Rosen, and he lived down the hall from me freshman year in college. When he suggested taking the trip as a way of passing the interval between the end of school and the beginning of our summer jobs, I said yes in a second. Craig was good-looking, dark-haired and dark-eyed, and I desperately wanted to see him naked. I didn't know much about him except that he was an economics major, and sang in the glee club, and spent most of his time with a fellow glee-clubber, a thin-mouthed Japanese girl named Barbara Love. Nevertheless I had certain suspicions, not to mention a rabid eagerness to be seduced, which, in the end, was never satisfied. For five nights Craig and I shared a bed in that curry-smelling motel in Gatlinburg, and for five nights we never touched each other—a fact which, in all the years since, we have not talked about once. There is a code which applies here, I think, having to do with friendship and sex and their exclusivity, a code at least as mysterious and hermetic as the code of the *Spartacus Guide* which led us through Europe a few summers later. But that is jumping ahead of things.

We were, then, nineteen, East Coast college boys, Jews, homosexuals (though this we hadn't admitted). Gatlinburg, Tennessee, on the fringe of the park, with its sticky candy shops, its born-again bookstores and hillbilly hayrides, may seem an unlikely place for us to have confronted (as we never did, it turned out) our shared secret sexuality. But I had grown up in amusement parks, glorying in the smell of diesel fuel and cotton candy, in roller coasters, in the wildness of rides that whirled at high speeds, round and round. I had had my first inkling of erotic feeling on those rides, when I was eleven, when the heavy artificial wind of a machine called a Lobster pushed my best friend Eric's body into mine, so that I couldn't breathe. Gatlinburg, with Craig, was full of that same erotic heat, that camaraderie of boys which seems always on the verge of dissolving into lust. Like children released from the better advice of our parents, we ate only the junk food that was on sale everywhere in the town—candied apples, wheels of fried dough swirling in vats of grease, gargantuan hamburgers and cheeseburgers. Craig shaved in his underwear, like a man in a television commercial, something I imagined to be a gesture of sexual display. Soon, I hoped, his eyes would meet mine; he would turn away from the mirror in the bathroom, his face still half covered with shaving cream, and begin walking toward me. But it never happened. Why? I wondered each night, curled into my half of the bedsheets, far away from Craig. It would have been so easy for him to have done me that favor, I thought, and liberated me from my crabbed, frightened little body. And though I have come up, over the years, with many elaborate psychological explanations for why Craig and I didn't sleep together in Gatlinburg, only recently have I been able to admit the simple truth: we didn't sleep together because Craig didn't want to; to put it flatly, he wasn't in the least attracted to my body. I did not know it yet, but even at nineteen he had already had hundreds of men, including a famous porn star. Sex—for me a quaking, romantic, nearly unimaginable dream—was for him an athletic exercise in alleviating boredom. It was—and this, I think, is the key—a way of determining self-worth; he wanted only the most beautiful, most perfect men, not in order to possess them, but because their interest in him, their lust for him, confirmed that he was part of their elite. It was a matter of class, pure and simple; like his father before him, he wanted into a country club. And though it probably gratified him, on some mean level, to see his preening self reflected in my burning eyes in the bathroom mirror, sleeping with me not only wouldn't have gained him any points, it probably would have lost him some.

So why did Craig want me to come to Tennessee in the first place? It occurs to me now that my very lack of sexual appeal might have made me appealing to Craig in other ways, that week we spent together. I think I offered him a kind of escape, a safety hatch through which he could flee a life that, as I would later learn, was beginning to consist of little other than showers at the gym, circle jerks in Central Park, afternoons at the glory holes near Times Square. Perhaps he craved my innocence; perhaps he envisioned a wholesome, rejuvenating week in the wilderness; perhaps he was recovering from some casually transmitted disease. I don't know because, as I said, Craig and I have never discussed that week in Gatlinburg, and I doubt we ever will.

When we arrived at the Great Smoky Mountains National Park, the first thing we did was go to the ranger station to plan our trip. We were going to do a six-day circle of the park, long planned by Craig, hiking seventy-five miles of forested mountain, much of it along the famous Appalachian Trail. The ranger girl chewed gum as she drew us a map. When she explained that we would probably be four days without human contact, four days in the depths of the park, more than a day's hike away from civilization, we looked at each other. Perhaps, in all this organizing, we simply hadn't thought enough about the realities of camping out for so long. What if something went wrong? What if a bear attacked us? Six days, alone, sleeping outdoors, the weather unpredictable—the prospect was terrifying to us.

So instead of risking the dangers of the forest, we "camped out" in a motel in Gatlinburg that was operated by a family of Sikhs. The proprietress painted a dot on her forehead each morning which by nighttime, when we saw her drift by in her mass of sari, was beginning to stream out like a black-rayed sun. She and her family lived in a group of rooms behind the desk from which a strong odor of cumin emanated, wafting down the linoleum hallways, inhabiting our room like an incense. There was only one bed. We lay far apart, on either side of it, Craig in his skimpy underpants, me in pajamas. I tried to engage him in the closest thing I could muster to sexy talk: I asked him why he preferred jockeys to boxers. He said he liked the "tighter feel," whatever that means. Then he fell asleep.

For lunch, out of guilt, we sat at a picnic site and ate the dehydrated spaghetti and meatballs and chicken à la king I had been so eager to taste ever since we had bought them in that camping store on Park Row. Afterwards—having made our perfunctory stab at the park—we headed back into town, to wander the shopping malls of Gatlinburg, ride the funicular, play at the hillbilly miniature-golf courses. Craig had never said anything explicit to me about his sexual life, though he was always mentioning his ex-girlfriend in Connecticut. Eager for signs, evidence, some sort of recognition, I tried to give off feeble signals of my own—that is, I glanced at him needfully, and sat with him, smiling like an indulgent mother, while he ate the fried dough he so loved. None of these techniques worked. As I have witnessed a hundred times over the years we've known each other, Craig is not in the least impressed by romantic mooning; in fact, it rather disgusts him. If he spared me his contempt, that week in Gatlinburg, it was probably only because he didn't recognize how far gone I was into fantasy.

The fourth day, having done everything else, we went to the Ripley's Believe-It-or-Not Museum. It didn't seem like much of a place at first. In the window a mock witch's den was set up, with a wax witch, a little cauldron, many elaborate rugs, a crystal ball. I was looking in the window rather uninterestedly when I heard a voice say, "Hey, you!" I looked around, behind me, but there was no one. "You," the voice said, "in the green shirt. I'm in here." I looked in the window, and saw the face of a pale girl reflected in the crystal ball. "I'm the Genie of the Crystal," she said, with a strong Southern accent, "and I want to tell you what a great time you'll have here in the Gatlinburg Ripley's Believe-It-or-Not Museum."

"What the hell is that?" Craig said.

"And you too, in the red shirt, with the dark hair and pretty eyes," said the Genie of the Crystal. "Y'all can have a wonderful time here in the Gatlinburg Ripley's Believe-It-or-Not Museum, so why not come on in?"

Craig and I looked at each other. "Can she see us?" I asked.

"Sure I can," said the Genie of the Crystal, "just like you can see me. So why don't you come on in? A couple of cute guys like you could have lots of fun."

She was flirting with us—or rather, flirting with Craig. I imagined her in her little room in the back, looking at us on a television screen like the ones in the corners in drugstores, noticing Craig. Even through two layers of glass and several TVs, it was obvious where her eyes were focused.

"What happens inside?" I asked.

The Genie of the Crystal laughed. "You get to see all the attractions," she said and, smiling some more at Craig, added, "like me."

Craig smiled thinly.

"Do you want to go in?" I said. "I think it might be fun."

He tried for anger. "Look," he said, "I didn't come camping for a week to spend all my time in stupid museums like this." But I persisted. "Come on, Craig," I said. "When are we ever going to have the chance again?" The Genie's flirtation titillated me, as if she and I were conspirators in Craig's seduction.

"Listen to your friend, Craig," she said. "Don't you want to see the inside of my lamp?"

Craig looked for a moment through the window, at the crystal ball. He sighed loudly. "All right," he said finally, making it clear he was doing me a big favor.

"Good," I said.

We paid our three seventy-five each and slipped through the turnstile, where a comforting sign which could only have existed in Tennessee assured us, "This is not a scary museum." For an hour we wandered among stuffed six-toed cats and immense toothpick mansions. We looked at pictures of a family of giants, listened to a tape recording of twins who had invented their own language. But the Genie of the Crystal really had been only doing her job; she was nowhere to be found.

"Did y'all have a good time?" she asked us afterwards, all mock-innocence, and we glared at her. Then a family—grandparents, parents, a blur of children—was crowding around the window, pushing us out of the Genie's view and mind. "What's that?" a little girl asked.

"I'm the Genie of the Crystal, honey," said the Genie of the Crystal.

The little girl started to cry.

"Don't be scared," the Genie said. "I'm your friend. And y'all can have a wonderful time here at the Gatlinburg Ripley's Believe-It-or-Not Museum."

Now—as Craig would say—"time warp." Five years passed. I was still a sexual innocent, compared to Craig, but I believed genuinely that I was making up for lack of experience with density of experience. Not Craig. Fear of AIDS had not compelled him to limit his activities, only to reduce their scope. He had as much sex as ever, but it was "safe sex," the rules outlined clearly from the beginning: no kissing, no fluid exchange, no collision of mucous-membrane areas. I don't think it was really much of a sacrifice for him; he claimed to have always liked it best that way anyway, watching someone watch him make love to himself.

We were both living in New York that summer just out of college. I had a stupid job at a bookstore, and Craig had an impressive job at a law firm which allowed him to make his own hours. Since I didn't have that many other friends in the city, I found myself becoming quite dependent on Craig—as a teacher, a tour guide, a mentor. We would go out to coffee shops together, in the afternoons, and he would tell me about having sex with soap in the West Side Y showers, and then about how he had developed bad sores between his legs from having sex with soap in the West Side Y showers. He described to me in detail the bizarre sexual practice of "felching," and what Kwell was. I memorized these words, imagining they would be as important in my life as they appeared to be in his. At night, when we went to bars together, vain Craig refused to wear his glasses, and insisted I act as his Seeing Eye dog. "That guy over there," he'd say. "Is he cute? Is he looking at me?" I'd tell him faithfully, though often our opinions differed. Always the tourist, I went home from these nocturnal expeditions alone, and woke up to Craig's phone call the next morning, describing the night's experience, usually bad. He was living with his parents, and had an immense collection of pornography stashed right under their noses, which he liked to trade from and bargain with, like a child with baseball cards. He claimed he could always tell how much hair a man had on his ass by looking at his wrists. And once, when we were in the park, he led me on a circuitous route through bushes where men stood leaning against trees, caressing the prominent erections outlined in their pockets, and I burst out laughing. "Shut up," he whispered, grabbing my arm and dragging me away, back onto one of the park's main avenues. "How could you do that? How could you embarrass me like that?"—as if I'd told a dirty joke to his grandmother. I kept laughing. I don't know why I was laughing—what I'd seen in the bushes hadn't struck me as particularly funny—but somehow I couldn't get hold of myself. The laughter controlled me, like hiccups, and would not abate, the same way a sly smile sometimes crept across my face just after I'd heard a piece of terrible news. It was as if a demon were shifting circuits inside my brain to turn Craig against me.

In the end, when I finally stopped laughing, I apologized to Craig. I did not, after all, want to offend him. I needed Craig a lot that summer because I felt safe doing things with him that I would never dare do by myself. When I entered the bars and pornographic bookstores alone, they were full of threats, and the biggest threat was that I might become, like Craig, their denizen. I could feel that urge in myself—it would be so easy to slip through the turnstile into the Adonis Theatre, as Craig often did, and once there, do what was beckoned of you, in the dark. With Craig I was protected. I could live vicariously. I was never tempted, because no man, seeing me and Craig together, would even notice me. He was dazzling in his dark, Semitic handsomeness, the perfect Jewish lawyer every mother wants her girl to marry. Neat tufts of hair poked out of his shirt collar. He was everyone's freshman-year roommate, the president of the debate society, your sister's sexy boyfriend. I used his attractiveness as a shield; in its shadow I was invisible, and could watch, fascinated, as men approached him, as he absorbed all the damage that might be inflicted in those late-night places. It was Craig who got crabs, amoebas, warts. I always ended up at home—alone, but unscathed. Safe.

Craig's appeal, in truth, is limited. What boyfriends he has managed to keep more than a week have emerged from extended relationships with him itchy and unsatisfied, for no matter how irresistible the prospect of a night with Craig, there is not much to warm up to in the thought of a life with him. This is, perhaps, his greatest tragedy, for when he does fall in love, it is with an intensity and fervor unlike any I've ever seen. So used is he to sexual control that, robbed of it, he becomes a madman, furious in his jealousy, pathetic in his adoration. If Craig loves a man, the man must be a god. It is a condition of his ego. I remember Sam, the blond architect he saw for a month, and finally scared out of New York with his loud worship; and Willie, the downtown artist, whose ripe body odor Craig found ambrosial, and spoke about with everyone, until Willie found out and got so embarrassed he refused even to speak to Craig. After his lovers broke up with him, Craig was bitter, churlish, stingy. His contempt was loud and cruel, and usually directed toward those men who made the mistake of trying to court him in conventional ways—that is, with phone calls, letters, (God forbid) love poems. I remember one poor man who approached him on a Friday night at Boy Bar, an elementary-school teacher who wanted to make him dinner. "I'm a competent cook," he kept saying, pleadingly. I think he only really meant that—that he wanted to cook him dinner. He just kept talking, telling everything to Craig, who never said a word, never even looked at him. And I thought, as I often thought when I was with him, how glad I was to be Craig's friend, because it meant I was spared the indignity of being his suitor.

At the end of the summer I quit my job at the bookstore and started business school—a mistake, I realize now, calculated primarily to please my father. It did not go well, but I passed most of my courses, and my parents, for my birthday, gave me what I'd been begging them for—a round-trip ticket to Paris, where I'd spent the spring semester of my junior year in college, and where I'd felt happier, I believed, than anywhere else I'd ever lived. When the ticket arrived, it was sealed in a red gift envelope bearing the airline's name, and there was wrapped around it a wildflower-patterned note from my mother on which she'd written a poem to me: "You've worked hard all year / To make your career / But now the term's done / So go have some fun! XXX, Mom." She fully believed, of course, that I was going to be coming back from Paris, that I was going to return to business school, and I wasn't about to tell her otherwise. Not that I had alternative plans. I had simply decided, in my own mind, that I wasn't going to come back. My life in New York was starting to repulse me, and I had to get away from it, from the endless repetition of my nights with Craig, or rather, the endless repetition of Craig's nights, the ragged edges of which I clung to. Perhaps I was also beginning to want things Craig would never have been able to get for himself, much less for me: a lover, nights watching television in bed instead of in bars. And I knew I wouldn't be able to free myself from my dependency on Craig unless I got far, far away from him.

In Paris, I lived in a beautiful apartment that belonged to an Italian woman, a friend of my parents'—a sleek, modern studio in a crumbling fifteenth-century building near the Pompidou Center, in the Marais. *Marais* means swamp, and riding to the airport on the JFK Express, I looked out the window at the bayoulike hinterlands of Queens: a muddy delta of broken-down houses, their little jetties thrust out into the sludge. It was a depressing view, and it didn't bode well for the summer. But the Marais turned out to be no swamp; it was an ancient neighborhood of tiny cobblestoned streets, too narrow for most cars, in which art galleries and fancy bookstores, like newly planted exotic flowers, were just beginning to bloom. There were chickens and urinating children in the courtyard, sawdust on the uneven steps. Most of my neighbors were stooped old women who eyed me suspiciously, muttering *"L'Italienne"* to one another under their breath. Their rooms were as squalid as the courtyard; they shared squat toilets in the hall. I suspect they resented *L'Italienne* not because she was young and chic and was part of a growing movement to gentrify their neighborhood, but because she had her own fancy bathroom and water heater. I myself had never met *L'Italienne,* my patroness, so kindly allowing me to live rent-free in her pied-à-terre, though she made her presence and personality known to me in the form of little notes stuck all over the apartment, instructing me how to turn on the water, which drawers to use, how to light the stove, not to mention the many notes which said "Privé," or "Personal Drawer—Do Not Touch." I never did.

June afternoons in Paris are melancholic. Craig, who was himself going to be spending the summer Eurailing his way through Spain and Italy and Greece, had encouraged me to buy the *Spartacus Guide for Gay Men* before I left, and according to its instructions, I walked up and down the Tuileries each night at dusk, astonished at how many men there were there, some shirtless, others dressed head to toe in leather, lounging on benches, or leaning against the Orangerie, or staring dissolutely at the Seine. The *Spartacus Guide* really was, as it claimed, a world unto itself. Its entire middle was composed of advertisements from various pedophiliac presses for novels, short-story collections, diatribes and defenses of the "boy-loving man" and "man-loving boy." When you looked up a bar, or a bathhouse, or an "outdoor cruising area" in the *Spartacus Guide,* you would get an entry something like this: B D LX M OG AYOR. You would then look in the key at the front of the book for a translation. B meant bar, D dancing, LX lesbians excluded, all the way down to AYOR—"At Your Own Risk." This last abbreviation appealed to me especially because I read it as a word—"ayor." "Ayor," I'd say to myself, walking up and down the length of the dusky Tuileries. I loved the sound of it, the way it rolled off my tongue into definitiveness. It was like a signal, a code of unwelcome, the opposite of "ahoy." "Ayor." Stay away. There are dangers here.

Because I was a good boy, I avoided the places that were labeled AYOR. I only went to Le Broad, the big disco that the guide gave four stars and described as "certainly the classiest and best-run gay establishment in Paris." It was a giant, cavernous place, with elaborate catacombs, dark links of rooms where who knows what happened, where I might have ventured with Craig, but never alone. Instead, I stayed on the dance floor, where, as it was perfectly acceptable to do so in Paris, I often danced by myself, for hours, caught up in the frenzy of music and movement, swept to my feet by the moment. The biggest song that summer was a ridiculous, campy concoction by Eartha Kitt, called "I Love Men," though she sang it "I Love-ah Men-ah."

In the end, they always resist-ah
And pretend you didn't exist-ah
But, my friend, somehow they persist-ah
And remain at the top of my list-ah . . .

I remember how the French men—so exotic-looking to me, with their thick syrupy smell of *parfum* and cigarettes, their shirts open to the waist, their dark skin, thin lips, huge black eyes—tried so hard to sing along with Eartha Kitt, though they didn't understand anything she was saying. Drunk and in love with themselves, they howled animalistically some rough approximation of the song. They made out in pairs and trios on the fringes of the dance floor.

They were joyous in their collectivity. And why not? "*Le SIDA*" hadn't caught up with them yet. It was the first time in my life and the only place in the world where I have ever been able to imagine sex with a man without feeling fear or guilt. Instead, I imagined the prospect of adventure, celebration. I could taste it on my lips.

I met Laurent the second night I went to that disco. A fight had broken out somewhere across the dance floor, and the ripples of movement threw us literally into each other's arms. Laughing, we just stayed there. It was a glorious, easy meeting. Laurent was twenty, a literature student at Nanterre, son of an Italian mother and a French father, and the birthdate carved on the gold chain around his neck was a lie. "Why?" I asked him that night, while we lay naked and sweating in my big bed, in the heat of the night, and I, at least, in the heat of love. He explained that his mother was already two months pregnant when she married his father, and that they had had to lie to the Italian relatives about the birthday to avoid a *scandale.* He didn't mind because it meant he had two birthdays a year—one in France and another, two months later, in Italy. Except that he rarely saw the Italian relatives. His father, whom he hated, who drove a silver "Bay-Em-Double-vay," had left his mother for her cousin. His mother had not been the same since; he had had to move home with her, to take care of her. He also had to babysit his own *petite cousine,* Marianne, every morning at nine, and therefore couldn't spend the night. (This seemed to be the ultimate, consequential point of the saga.) I said that was fine. I was ready to agree to just about anything.

From the moment I let Laurent out the door, in the early hours of the morning, I was jubilant with love for him—for his long, dark eyelashes, his slightly contemptuous mouth, his odd insistence on wearing only white socks. ("*Non, ce n'est pas les Français,*" he explained when I asked him, "*c'est seulement moi.*") Like most Europeans, he was uncircumcised—the only uncircumcised lover I have ever had. That small flap of skin, long removed from me in some deeply historical *bris,* was the embodiment of our difference. It fascinated me, and my fascination chafed poor Laurent, who couldn't understand what the big deal was—I, the American, was the one who was altered, *pas normal,* after all. I pulled at it, played with it, curious and delighted, until he made me stop. "*Tu me fais mal,*" he protested. Craig's eyes would have lit up.

But Craig was nowhere near, and I was in a limited way happy. My love affair with Laurent was simple and regular, a series of afternoons, one blending into the other. Around eleven-thirty in the morning, after finishing with *la petite Marianne*, he would arrive at my apartment, and I would feed him lunch. Then we would make love, perfunctorily, for an hour or so. Then we would take a walk to his car, and he would drive me for a while through the suburbs of Paris—Choisy-le-Roi, Vincennes, Clamart, Pantin. He classified these suburbs as either *pas beau, beau* or *joli,* adjectives which seemed to have more to do with class than aesthetics. I was inept at understanding the distinctions. "*Neuilly est joli, n'est-ce pas?*" I'd ask him, as we drove down tree-lined avenues, past big, imposing houses. "*Non, c'est beau.*" "*Clamart, c'est aussi beau, n'est-ce pas?*" "*Non, c'est joli.*" Eventually I'd give up, and Laurent, frustrated by my intransigence, would drop me off at my apartment before going off to his job. All night he sold Walkmans in a Parisian "drugstore," a giant, futuristic shopping mall of red Formica and chrome that featured at its heart a seventy-foot wall on which sixty-four televisions played rock videos simultaneously. This huge and garish place is the sentimental center of my memories of that summer, for I used to go there often in the evenings to visit Laurent, unable to resist his company, though I feared he might grow tired of me. Then I'd stand under the light of the videos, pretending not to know him, while he explained to someone the advantages of Aiwa over Sony. When he wasn't with a customer, we'd talk, or (more aptly) he'd play with one of the little credit-card-sized calculators he had in his display case, and I'd stare at him. But I couldn't stay at the drugstore forever. After twenty minutes or so, fearful of rousing the suspicions of the ash-blond woman who was in charge of Laurent, I'd bid him adieu, and he'd wink at me before returning to his work. That wink meant everything to me. It meant my life. Powered by it, I might walk for miles afterwards down the Rue de Rivoli, along the Seine, across the brilliant bridges to the Latin Quarter, filled in summer with joyous young Americans singing in the streets, eating take-out couscous, smiling and laughing just to be there. Often friends from college were among their number. We'd wave across the street as casually as if we were seeing each other in New York. It astonishes me to think how many miles I must have charted that summer, zigzagging aimlessly across the Parisian night for love of Laurent. It was almost enough, walking like that, wanting him. That wink was almost enough.

Laurent had been to America only once, when he was fourteen. His parents had sent him to New York, where he was to meet an aunt who lived in Washington, but the aunt's son was in a car accident and she couldn't come. For a week he had stayed alone at the Waldorf-Astoria, a little French boy who didn't speak English, instructed by his mother to avoid at all costs the subways, the streets, the world. These days, when the meanderings of my life take me to the giant, glittering lobby of the Waldorf-Astoria, I sometimes think I see him, in his French schoolboy's suit, hiding behind a giant ficus, or cautiously fingering magazines in the gift shop. I imagine him running down the halls, or pacing the confines of his four-walled room, or sitting on the big bed, entranced by the babbling cartoon creatures inhabiting his television.

Craig is by nature a suburbanite. He grew up in Westport, Connecticut, where his father is a prominent dermatologist and the first Jew ever admitted to the country club. One evening in college he embarrassed me by getting into a long argument with a girl from Mount Kisco on the ridiculous subject of which was a better suburb—Mount Kisco or Westport. On the way back to our dorm, I berated him. "Jesus, Craig," I said, "I can't believe you'd stoop so low as to argue about a subject as ridiculous as who grew up in a better suburb." But he didn't care. "She's crazy," he insisted. "Mount Kisco doesn't compare to Westport. I'm not arguing about it because I have a stake in it, only because it's true. Westport is much nicer—the houses are much farther apart, and the people, they're just classier, better-looking and with higher-up positions. Mount Kisco's where you go on the way to Westport."

Suburbs mattered to Craig. He apparently saw no implicit contradiction in their mattering to him at the same moment that he was, say, being given a blowjob by a law student in one of the infamous library men's rooms, or offering me a list of call numbers that would point to the library's hidden stashes of pornography. But Craig has never been given much to introspection. He is blessed by a remarkable clarity of vision, which allows him to see through the levels, the aboves and belows, that plague the rest of us. There are no contradictions in his world; nothing is profane, but then again, nothing is sacred.

He was in Europe, that same summer as me, on his parents' money, on a last big bash before law school. In Paris I'd get postcards from Ibiza, from Barcelona, where he'd had his passport stolen, from Florence (this one showing a close-up of the *David*'s genitalia), and he would talk about Nils, Rutger and especially Nino, whom he'd met in the men's room at the train station. I enjoyed his postcards. They provided a much-needed connection with my old life, my pre-Paris self. Things were not going well with Laurent, who, it had taken me only a few days to learn, lived in a state of continuous and deep depression. He would arrive afternoons in my apartment, silent, and land in the armchair, where for hours, his eyes lowered, he would read the Tintin books I kept around to improve my French, and sometimes watch *Les Quatres Fantastiques* on television. The candy-colored cartoon adventures of Tintin, androgynous boy reporter, kept him busy until it was nearly time for him to go to work, at which point I would nudge my way into his lap and say, "*Qu'est-ce que c'est?* I want to help you." But all he would tell me was that he was depressed because he was losing his car. His aunt, who owned it, was taking it back, and now he would have to ride the train in to work every day, and take a cab back late at night. I suggested he might stay with me, and he shook his head. "*La petite Marianne*," he reminded me. Of course. *La petite Marianne*.

I think now that in continually begging Laurent to tell me what was worrying him, it was I who pushed him away. My assumption that "talking about it" or "opening up" was the only way for him to feel better was very American, and probably misguided. And of course, my motives were not, as I imagined, entirely unselfish, for at the heart of all that badgering was a deep fear that he did not love me, and that that was why he held back from me, refused to tell me what was wrong. Now I look back on Laurent's life in those days, and I see he probably wasn't hiding things from me. He probably really was depressed because he was losing his car, though that was only the tip of the iceberg. His fragile mother depended on him totally, his father was nowhere to be seen, his future, as a literature student at a second-rate university, was not rosy. It is quite possible, I see now, that in his sadness it was comforting for him simply to be in my presence, my warm apartment on a late afternoon, reading Tintin books, drinking tea. But I wasn't content to offer him just that. I wanted him to notice me. I wanted to be his cure. I wish I'd known that then; I might not have driven him off.

In any case, I was very happy when Craig finally came to visit, that summer, because it meant I would have something to occupy my time other than my worrisome thoughts about Laurent. It was late July by then, and the prospect of August, when Paris empties itself of its native population and becomes a desiccated land of closed shops, wandered by aimless foreigners, was almost sufficiently unappealing to send me back to business school. In ten days Laurent would quit his job and take off to the seaside with his mother. There was no mention of my possibly going with him, though I would have gladly done so, and could imagine with relish staying by myself in a little pension near the big, elegant hotel where Laurent and his mother went every year, going for tea and sitting near them on the outdoor promenade, watching them, waiting for

Laurent's wink. There would be secret rendezvous, long walks on beaches—but it was all a dream. Laurent would have been furious if I'd shown up.

And so I was happily looking forward to Craig, to the stories I knew he'd tell, the sexual exploits he'd so willingly narrate, and in such great detail. I met his train at the Gare de Lyon. There he was, on schedule, in alpine shorts and Harvard T-shirt, the big ubiquitous backpack stooping him over. We embraced, and took the métro back to my apartment. He looked tired, thin. He had lost his traveler's checks in Milan, he explained, had had his wallet stolen in Venice. He had also wasted a lot of money renting double rooms at exorbitant prices just for himself, and was worried that his parents wouldn't agree to wire him more. I tried to sympathize, but it seemed somehow fitting that he should now be suffering the consequences of his irresponsibility. Stingy with anyone else, he was rapacious in spending his parents' money on himself—a trait I have observed often in firstborn sons of Jewish families. (I myself was the second-born son, and live frugally to this day.)

We went out, that night, for dinner, to a Vietnamese restaurant I liked and ate in often, and Craig started to tell me about his trip—the beaches at Ibiza, the bars in Amsterdam. "It's been fun," he concluded. "Everything's been pretty good, except this one bad thing happened."

"What was that?" I asked.

"Well, I was raped in Madrid."

Delicately he wrapped a spring roll in a sprig of mint and popped it in his mouth.

"What?" I said.

"Just what I told you. I was raped in Madrid."

I put down my fork. "Craig," I said. "Come on. What do you mean, 'raped'?"

"Forcibly taken. Fucked against my will. What better definition do you want?"

He took a swig of water.

I sat back in my chair. As often happens to me when I'm struck speechless, a lewd, involuntary smile pulled apart my lips. I tried to suppress it.

"How did it happen?" I asked, as casually as I could.

"The usual way," he said, and laughed. "I was walking down the street, cruising a little bit, and this guy said '*Hola*' to me. He was cute, young. I said '*Hola*' back. Well, to make a long story short, we ended up back at his apartment. He spoke a little English, and he explained to me that he was in a big hurry. Then there was a knock on the door and this other guy walked in. They talked very quickly in Spanish, and he told me to get undressed. I didn't much want to do it anymore, but I took off my clothes—"

"Why?" I interrupted.

He shrugged. "Once you've gone that far it's hard not to," he said. "Anyway, as far as I could gather, he and his friend were arguing over whether the friend would have sex with us or just watch. After a while I stopped trying to understand and just sat down on the bed. It didn't take me too long to figure out the guy was married and that was why he was in such a hurry. I could tell from all the woman's things around the apartment.

"Anyway, they finally decided the friend would just watch. The first guy—the one who said '*Hola*'—saw I was naked and he took off his clothes and then— Well, I tried to explain I only did certain things, 'safe sex' and all, but he didn't listen to me. He just jumped me. He was very strong, and the worst thing was, he really smelled. He hadn't washed for a long time, he was really disgusting." Craig leaned closer to me. "You know," he said, "that I don't get fucked. I don't like it and I won't do it. And I kept trying to tell him this, but he just wouldn't listen to me. I don't think he meant to force me. I think he just thought I was playing games and that I was really enjoying it. I mean, he didn't hit me or anything, though he held my wrists behind my back for a while. But then he stopped."

He ate another spring roll, and called the waiter over to ask for chopsticks. There were no tears in his eyes; no change was visible in his face. A deep horror welled in me, stronger than anything I'd ever felt with Craig, so strong I just wanted to laugh, the same way I'd laughed that afternoon in Central Park when he showed me the secret places where men meet other men.

"Are you okay?" I asked instead, mustering a sudden, surprising self-control. "Do you need to see a doctor?"

He shrugged. "I'm just mad because he came in my ass even though I asked him not to. Who knows what he might have been carrying? Also, it hurt. But I didn't bleed or anything. I didn't come, of course, and he couldn't have cared less, which really pissed me off. He finished, told me to get dressed fast. I guess he was worried his wife would come home."

I looked at the table, and Craig served himself more food.

"I think if that happened to me I'd have to kill myself," I said quietly.

"I don't see why you're making such a big deal out of it," Craig said. "I mean, it didn't hurt *that* much or anything. Anyway, it was just once."

I pushed back my chair, stretched out my legs. I had no idea what to say next. "Aren't you going to eat any more?" Craig asked, and I nodded no, I had lost my appetite.

"Well, I'm going to finish these noodles," he said, and scooped some onto his plate. I watched him eat. I wanted to know if he was really feeling nothing, as he claimed. But his face was impassive, unreadable. Clearly he was not going to let me know.

Afterwards, we walked along the mossy sidewalks of the Seine—"good cruising," the *Spartacus Guide* had advised us, but "very AYOR"—and Craig told me about Nils, Rutger, Nino, etc. I, in turn, told him about Laurent. He was mostly interested in the matter of his foreskin. When I started discussing our problems—Laurent's depression, my fear that he was pulling away from me—Craig grew distant, hardly seemed to be listening to me. "Uh-huh," he'd say, in response to every phrase I'd offer, and look away, or over his shoulder, until finally I gave up.

We crossed the Île de la Cité, and Craig asked about going to a bar, but I told him I was too tired, and he admitted he probably was as well. He hadn't gotten a *couchette* on the train up here, and the passport-control people had woken him up six or seven times during the night.

Back at my apartment, we undressed together. (Since Laurent, I had lost my modesty.) I watched as Craig, like any good first son, carefully folded his shirt and balled his socks before climbing into the makeshift bed I had created for him on my floor. These old habits, taught long ago by his mother, were second nature to him, which I found touching. I looked at him in the bed. He had lost weight, and a spray of fine red pimples covered his back.

Raped. I can hardly say that word. Besides Craig, the only person I know who was raped was a friend in my dorm in college named Sandra. After it happened, I avoided her for weeks. I imagined, stupidly, that simply because I was male, I'd remind her of what she'd gone through, make her break down, melt, weep. But finally she cornered me one afternoon in the library. "Stop avoiding me," she said. "Just because I was raped doesn't mean I'm made out of glass." And it was true. It was always Sandra who brought up the fact of the rape—often in front of strangers. "I was raped," she'd say, as if to get the facts out of the way, as if saying it like that—casually, without preparation—helped to alleviate the terror, gave her strength. Craig had told me with a similar studied casualness. And yet I suspect his motive was not so much to console himself as to do some sort of penance; I suspect he genuinely believed that he had been asking for it, and that he deserved it, deserved whatever he got.

Perhaps I am wrong to use the word "underside" when I describe the world Craig led me through that first summer in New York, perhaps wrong in assuming that for Craig, it has been a matter of surfaces and depths, hells and heavens. For me, yes. But for him, I think, there really wasn't much of a distance to travel between the Westport of his childhood and the dark places he seemed to end up in, guide or no guide, in whatever city he visited. Wallets, traveler's checks, your life: these were just the risks you took. I lived in two worlds; I went in and out of the underside as I pleased, with Craig to protect me. I could not say it was my fault that he was raped. But I realized, that night, that on some level I had been encouraging him to live in the world's danger zones, its ayor zones, for years now, to satisfy my own curiosity, my own lust. And I wondered: How much had I contributed to Craig's apparent downfall? To what extent had I, in living through him, made him, molded him into some person I secretly, fearfully longed to be?

He lay on my floor, gently snoring. He always slept gently. But I had no desire to embrace him or to try to save him. He seemed, somehow, ruined to me, beyond hope. He had lost all allure. It is cruel to record now, but the truth was, I hoped he'd be gone by morning.

The next afternoon, we had lunch with Laurent. Because Craig spoke no French and Laurent spoke no English, there was not much conversation. I translated, remedially, between them. Craig did not seem very impressed by Laurent, which disappointed me, and Laurent did not seem very impressed by Craig, which pleased me.

Afterwards, Laurent and I drove Craig to the Gare du Nord, where he was catching a train to Munich. He had relatives there who he hoped would give him money to spend at least a few weeks in Germany. For a couple of minutes, through me, he and Laurent discussed whether or not he should go to see Dachau. Laurent had found it very moving, he said. But Craig's only response was, "Uh-huh."

Then we were saying good-bye, and then he was gone, lost in the depths of the *gare.*

On the way back to my apartment I told Laurent about Craig's rape. His eyes bulged in surprise. "*Ton ami,*" he said, when I had finished the story, "*sa vie est tragique.*" I was glad, somehow, that the rape meant something to Laurent, and for a moment, in spite of all our problems, I wanted to embrace him, to celebrate the fact of all we had escaped, all we hadn't suffered. But my French wasn't good enough to convey what I wanted to convey. And Laurent was depressed.

He dropped me off at my apartment, continued on to work. I

couldn't bear the thought of sitting alone indoors, so I took a walk over to the Rue St. Denis and Les Halles. The shops had just reopened for the afternoon, and the streets were full of people—giggly Americans and Germans, trios of teenaged boys.

I sat down in a café and tried to stare at the men in the streets. I wondered what it must have been like, that "*Hola,*" whispered on a busy Madrid sidewalk, that face turning toward him. Was the face clear, vivid in its intent? I think not. I think it was probably as vague and convex as the face of the Genie of the Crystal in Gatlinburg. Then, too, it was the surprise of recognition, the surprise of being noticed; it will do it every time. The Genie of the Crystal, she, too, had wanted Craig, and even then I had urged him on, thinking myself safe in his shadow.

I drank a cup of coffee, then another. I stared unceasingly at men in the street, men in the café, sometimes getting cracked smiles in response. But in truth, as Craig has endlessly told me, I simply do not have the patience for cruising. Finally I paid my bill, and then I heard the church bells of Notre Dame strike seven. Only five days left in July. Soon it would be time to head up to Montmartre, to the drugstore, where Laurent, like it or not, was going to get my company.

GRAVITY

THEO had a choice between a drug that would save his sight and a drug that would keep him alive, so he chose not to go blind. He stopped the pills and started the injections—these required the implantation of an unpleasant and painful catheter just above his heart—and within a few days the clouds in his eyes started to clear up; he could see again. He remembered going into New York City to a show with his mother, when he was twelve and didn't want to admit he needed glasses. "Can you read that?" she'd shouted, pointing to a Broadway marquee, and when he'd squinted, making out only one or two letters, she'd taken off her own glasses—harlequins with tiny rhinestones in the corners—and shoved them onto his face. The world came into focus, and he gasped, astonished at the precision around the edges of things, the legibility, the hard, sharp, colorful landscape. Sylvia had to squint through *Fiddler on the Roof* that day, but for Theo, his face masked by his mother's huge glasses, everything was as bright and vivid as a comic book. Even though people stared at him, and muttered things, Sylvia didn't care; he could *see.*

Because he was dying again, Theo moved back to his mother's house in New Jersey. The DHPG injections she took in stride—she'd seen her own mother through *her* dying, after all. Four times a day, with the equanimity of a nurse, she cleaned out the plastic tube implanted in his chest, inserted a sterilized hypodermic and slowly dripped the bag of sight-giving liquid into his veins. They endured this procedure silently, Sylvia sitting on the side of the hospital bed she'd rented for the duration of Theo's stay—his life, he sometimes thought—watching reruns of *I Love Lucy* or the news, while he tried not to think about the hard piece of pipe stuck into him, even though it was a constant reminder of how wide and unswimmable the gulf was becoming between him and the ever-receding shoreline of the well. And Sylvia was intricately cheerful. Each day she urged him to go out with her somewhere—to the library, or the little museum with the dinosaur replicas he'd been fond of as a child—and when his thinness and the cane drew stares, she'd maneuver him around the people who were staring, determined to shield him from whatever they might say or do. It had been the same that afternoon so many years ago, when she'd pushed him through a lobbyful of curious and laughing faces, determined that nothing should interfere with the spectacle of his seeing. What a pair they must have made, a boy in ugly glasses and a mother daring the world to say a word about it!

This warm, breezy afternoon in May they were shopping for revenge. "Your cousin Howard's engagement party is next month," Sylvia explained in the car. "A very nice girl from Livingston. I met her a few weeks ago, and really, she's a superior person."

"I'm glad," Theo said. "Congratulate Howie for me."

"Do you think you'll be up to going to the party?"

"I'm not sure. Would it be okay for me just to give him a gift?"

"You already have. A lovely silver tray, if I say so myself. The thank-you note's in the living room."

"Mom," Theo said, "why do you always have to—"

Sylvia honked her horn at a truck making an illegal left turn. "Better they should get something than no present at all, is what I say," she said. "But now, the problem is, *I* have to give Howie something, to be from me, and it better be good. It better be very, very good."

"Why?"

"Don't you remember that cheap little nothing Bibi gave you for your graduation? It was disgusting."

"I can't remember what she gave me."

"Of course you can't. It was a tacky pen-and-pencil set. Not even a real leather box. So naturally, it stands to reason that I have to get something truly spectacular for Howard's engagement. Something that will make Bibi blanch. Anyway, I think I've found just the thing, but I need your advice."

"Advice? Well, when my old roommate Nick got married, I gave him a garlic press. It cost five dollars and reflected exactly how much I felt, at that moment, our friendship was worth."

Sylvia laughed. "Clever. But my idea is much more brilliant, because it makes it possible for me to get back at Bibi *and* give Howard the nice gift he and his girl deserve." She smiled, clearly pleased with herself. "Ah, you live and learn."

"You live," Theo said.

Sylvia blinked. "Well, look, here we are." She pulled the car into a handicapped-parking place on Morris Avenue and got out to help Theo, but he was already hoisting himself up out of his seat, using the door handle for leverage. "I can manage myself," he said with some irritation. Sylvia stepped back.

"Clearly one advantage to all this for you," Theo said, balancing on his cane, "is that it's suddenly so much easier to get a parking place."

"Oh Theo, please," Sylvia said. "Look, here's where we're going."

She leaned him into a gift shop filled with porcelain statuettes of Snow White and all seven of the dwarves, music boxes which, when you opened them, played "The Shadow of Your Smile," complicated-smelling potpourris in purple wallpapered boxes, and stuffed snakes you were supposed to push up against drafty windows and doors.

"Mrs. Greenman," said an expansive, gray-haired man in a cream-colored cardigan sweater. "Look who's here, Archie, it's Mrs. Greenman."

Another man, this one thinner and balding, but dressed in an identical cardigan, peered out from the back of the shop. "Hello there!" he said, smiling. He looked at Theo, and his expression changed.

"Mr. Sherman, Mr. Baker. This is my son, Theo."

"Hello," Mr. Sherman and Mr. Baker said. They didn't offer to shake hands.

"Are you here for that item we discussed last week?" Mr. Sherman asked.

"Yes," Sylvia said. "I want advice from my son here." She walked over to a large ridged crystal bowl, a very fifties sort of bowl, stalwart and square-jawed. "What do you think? Beautiful, isn't it?"

"Mom, to tell the truth, I think it's kind of ugly."

"Four hundred and twenty-five dollars," Sylvia said admiringly. "You have to feel it."

Then she picked up the big bowl and tossed it to Theo, like a football.

The gentlemen in the cardigan sweaters gasped and did not exhale. When Theo caught it, it sank his hands. His cane rattled as it hit the floor.

"That's heavy," Sylvia said, observing with satisfaction how the bowl had weighted Theo's arms down. "And where crystal is concerned, heavy is impressive."

She took the bowl back from him and carried it to the counter. Mr. Sherman was mopping his brow. Theo looked at the floor, still surprised not to see shards of glass around his feet.

Since no one else seemed to be volunteering, he bent over and picked up the cane.

"Four hundred and fifty-nine, with tax," Mr. Sherman said, his voice still a bit shaky, and a look of relish came over Sylvia's face as she pulled out her checkbook to pay. Behind the counter, Theo could see Mr. Baker put his hand on his forehead and cast his eyes to the ceiling.

It seemed Sylvia had been looking a long time for something like this, something heavy enough to leave an impression, yet so fragile it could make you sorry.

* * *

They headed back out to the car.

"Where can we go now?" Sylvia asked, as she got in. "There must be someplace else to go."

"Home," Theo said. "It's almost time for my medicine."

"Really? Oh. All right." She pulled on her seat belt, inserted the car key in the ignition and sat there.

For just a moment, but perceptibly, her face broke. She squeezed her eyes shut so tight the blue shadow on the lids cracked.

Almost as quickly she was back to normal again, and they were driving. "It's getting hotter," Sylvia said. "Shall I put on the air?"

"Sure," Theo said. He was thinking about the bowl, or more specifically, about how surprising its weight had been, pulling his hands down. For a while now he'd been worried about his mother, worried about what damage his illness might secretly be doing to her that of course she would never admit. On the surface things seemed all right. She still broiled herself a skinned chicken breast for dinner every night, still swam a mile and a half a day, still kept used teabags wrapped in foil in the refrigerator. Yet she had also, at about three o'clock one morning, woken him up to tell him she was going to the twenty-four-hour supermarket, and was there anything he wanted. Then there was the gift shop: She had literally pitched that bowl toward him, pitched it like a ball, and as that great gleam of flight and potential regret came sailing his direction, it had occurred to him that she was trusting his two feeble hands, out of the whole world, to keep it from shattering. What was she trying to test? Was it his newly regained vision? Was it the assurance that he was there, alive, that he hadn't yet slipped past all her caring, a little lost boy in rhinestone-studded glasses? There are certain things you've already done before you even think how to do them—a child pulled from in front of a car, for instance, or the bowl, which Theo was holding before he could even begin to calculate its brief trajectory. It had pulled his arms down, and from that apish posture he'd looked at his mother, who smiled broadly, as if, in the war between heaviness and shattering, he'd just helped her win some small but sustaining victory.

HOUSES

WHEN I arrived at my office that morning—the morning after Susan took me back—an old man and woman wearing wide-brimmed hats and sweatpants were peering at the little snapshots of houses pinned up in the window, discussing their prices in loud voices. There was nothing surprising in this, except that it was still spring, and the costume and demeanor of the couple emphatically suggested summer vacations. It was very early in the day as well as the season—not yet eight and not yet April. They had the look of people who never slept, people who propelled themselves through life on sheer adrenaline, and they also had the look of kindness and good intention gone awry which so often seems to motivate people like that.

I lingered for a few moments outside the office door before going in, so that I could hear their conversation. I had taken a lot of the snapshots myself, and written the descriptive tags underneath them, and I was curious which houses would pique their interest. At first, of course, they looked at the mansions—one of them, oceanfront with ten bathrooms and two pools, was listed for $10.5 million. "Can you imagine?" the wife said. "Mostly it's corporations that buy those," the husband answered. Then their attentions shifted to some more moderately priced, but still expensive, contemporaries. "I don't know, it's like living on the starship *Enterprise*, if you ask me," the wife said. "Personally, I never would get used to a house like that." The husband chuckled. Then the wife's mouth opened and she said, "Will you look at this, Ed? Just look!" and pointed to a snapshot of a small, cedar-shingled house which I happened to know stood not five hundred feet from the office—$165,000, price negotiable. "It's adorable!" the wife said. "It's just like the house in my dream!"

I wanted to tell her it was my dream house too, my dream house first, to beg her not to buy it. But I held back. I reminded myself I already had a house. I reminded myself I had a wife, a dog.

Ed took off his glasses and peered skeptically at the picture. "It doesn't look too bad," he said. "Still, something must be wrong with it. The price is just too low."

"It's the house in my dream, Ed! The one I dreamed about! I swear it is!"

"I told you, Grace-Anne, the last thing I need is a handyman's special. These are my retirement years."

"But how can you know it needs work? We haven't even seen it! Can't we just look at it? Please?"

"Let's have breakfast and talk it over."

"Okay, okay. No point in getting overeager, right?" They headed toward the coffee shop across the street, and I leaned back against the window.

It was just an ordinary house, the plainest of houses. And yet, as I unlocked the office door to let myself in, I found myself swearing I'd burn it down before I'd let that couple take possession of it. Love can push you to all sorts of unlikely threats.

What had happened was this: The night before, I had gone back to my wife after three months of living with a man. I was thirty-two years old, and more than anything in the world, I wanted things to slow, slow down.

It was a quiet morning. We live year-round in a resort town, and except for the summer months, not a whole lot goes on here. Next week things would start gearing up for the Memorial Day closings—my wife Susan's law firm was already frantic with work—but for the moment I was in a lull. It was still early—not even the receptionist had come in yet—so I sat at my desk, and looked at the one picture I kept there, of Susan running on the beach with our golden retriever, Charlotte. Susan held out a tennis ball in the picture, toward which Charlotte, barely out of puppyhood, was inclining her head. And of course I remembered that even now Susan didn't know the extent to which Charlotte was wound up in all of it.

Around nine forty-five I called Ted at the Elegant Canine. I was halfway through dialing before I realized that it was probably improper for me to be doing this, now that I'd officially gone back to Susan, that Susan, if she knew I was calling him, would more than likely have sent me packing—our reconciliation was that fragile. One of her conditions for taking me back was that I not see, not even speak to Ted, and in my shame I'd agreed. Nonetheless, here I was, listening as the phone rang. His boss, Patricia, answered. In the background was the usual cacophony of yelps and barks.

"I don't have much time," Ted said, when he picked up a few seconds later. "I have Mrs. Morrison's poodle to blow-dry."

"I didn't mean to bother you," I said. "I just wondered how you were doing."

"Fine," Ted said. "How are you doing?"

"Oh, okay."

"How did things go with Susan last night?"

"Okay."

"Just okay?"

"Well—it felt so good to be home again—in my own bed, with Susan and Charlotte—" I closed my eyes and pressed the bridge of my nose with my fingers. "Anyway," I said, "it's not fair of me to impose all of this on you. Not fair at all. I mean, here I am, back with Susan, leaving you—"

"Don't worry about it."

"I do worry about it. I do."

There was a barely muffled canine scream in the background, and then I could hear Patricia calling for Ted.

"I have to go, Paul—"

"I guess I just wanted to say I miss you. There, I've said it. There's nothing to do about it, but I wanted to say it, because it's what I feel."

"I miss you too, Paul, but listen, I have to go—"

"Wait, wait. There's something I have to tell you."

"What?"

"There was a couple today. Outside the office. They were looking at our house."

"Paul—"

"I don't know what I'd do if they bought it."

"Paul," Ted said, "it's not our house. It never was."

"No, I guess it wasn't." Again I squeezed the bridge of my nose. I could hear the barking in the background grow louder, but this time Ted didn't tell me he had to go.

"Ted?"

"What?"

"Would you mind if I called you tomorrow?"

"You can call me whenever you want."

"Thanks," I said, and then he said a quick good-bye, and all the dogs were gone.

Three months before, things had been simpler. There was Susan, and me, and Charlotte. Charlotte was starting to smell, and the monthly ordeal of bathing her was getting to be too much for both of us, and anyway, Susan reasoned, now that she'd finally paid off the last of her law school loans, we really did have the right to hire someone to bathe our dog. (We were both raised in penny-pinching families; even in relative affluence, we had no cleaning woman, no gardener. I mowed our lawn.) And so, on a drab Wednesday morning before work, I bundled Charlotte into the car and drove her over to the Elegant Canine. There, among the fake emerald collars, the squeaky toys in the shape of mice and hamburgers, the rawhide bones and shoes and pizzas, was Ted. He had wheat-colored hair and green eyes, and he smiled at me in a frank and unwavering way I found difficult to turn away from. I smiled back, left Charlotte in his capable-seeming hands and headed off to work. The morning proceeded lazily. At noon I drove back to fetch Charlotte, and found her looking golden and glorious, leashed to a small post in a waiting area just to the side of the main desk. Through the door behind the desk I saw a very wet Pekingese being shampooed in a tub and a West Highland white terrier sitting alertly on a metal table, a chain around its neck. I rang a bell, and Ted emerged, waving to me with an arm around which a large bloody bandage had been carefully wrapped.

"My God," I said. "Was it—"

"I'm afraid so," Ted said. "You say she's never been to a groomer's?"

"I assure you, never in her entire life—we've left her alone with small children—our friends joke that she could be a babysitter—" I turned to Charlotte, who looked up at me, panting in that retriever way. "What got into you?" I said, rather hesitantly. And even more hesitantly: "Bad, bad dog—"

"Don't worry about it," Ted said, laughing. "It's happened before and it'll happen again."

"I am so sorry. I am just so—sorry. I had no idea, really."

"Look, it's an occupational hazard. Anyway we're great at first aid around here." He smiled again, and, calmed for the moment, I smiled back. "I just can't imagine what got into her. She's supposed to go to the vet next week, so I'll ask him what he thinks."

"Well, Charlotte's a sweetheart," Ted said. "After our initial hostilities, we got to be great friends, right, Charlotte?" He ruffled the top of her head, and she looked up at him adoringly. We were both looking at Charlotte. Then we were looking at each other. Ted raised his eyebrows. I flushed. The look went on just a beat too long, before I turned away, and he was totaling the bill.

Afterwards, at home, I told Susan about it, and she got into a state. "What if he sues?" she said, running her left hand nervously through her hair. She had taken her shoes off; the heels of her panty hose were black with the dye from her shoes.

"Susan, he's not going to sue. He's a very nice kid, very friendly."

I put my arms around her, but she pushed me away. "Was he the boss?" she said. "You said someone else was the boss."

"Yes, a woman."

"Oh, great. Women are much more vicious than men, Paul, believe me. Especially professional women. He's perfectly friendly and wants to forget it, but for all we know she's been dreaming about going on *People's Court* her whole life." She hit the palm of her hand against her forehead.

"Susan," I said, "I really don't think—"

"Did you give him anything?"

"Give him anything?"

"You know, a tip. Something."

"No."

"Jesus, hasn't being married to a lawyer all these years taught you anything?" She sat down and stood up again. "All right, all right, here's what we're going to do. I want you to have a bottle of champagne sent over to the guy. With an apology, a note. Marcia Grossman did that after she hit that tree, and it worked wonders." She blew out breath. "I don't see what else we *can* do at this point, except wait, and hope—"

"Susan, I really think you're making too much of all this. This isn't New York City, after all, and really, he didn't seem to mind at all—"

"Paul, honey, please trust me. You've always been very naive about these things. Just send the champagne, all right?"

Her voice had reached an unendurable pitch of annoyance. I stood up. She looked at me guardedly. It was the beginning of a familiar fight between us—in her anxiety, she'd say something to imply, not so subtly, how much more she understood about the world than I did, and in response I would stalk off, insulted and pouty. But this time I did not stalk off—I just stood there—and Susan, closing her eyes in a manner which suggested profound regret at having acted rashly, said in a very soft voice, "I don't mean to yell. It's just that you know how insecure I get about things like this, and really, it'll make me feel so much better to know we've done something. So send the champagne for my sake, okay?" Suddenly she was small and vulnerable, a little girl victimized by her own anxieties. It was a transformation she made easily, and often used to explain her entire life.

"Okay," I said, as I always said, and that was the end of it.

The next day I sent the champagne. The note read (according to Susan's instructions): "Dear Ted: Please accept this little gift as a token of thanks for your professionalism and good humor. Sincerely, Paul Hoover and Charlotte." I should add that at this point I believed I was leaving Susan's name off only because she hadn't been there.

The phone at my office rang the next morning at nine-thirty. "Listen," Ted said, "thanks for the champagne! That was so thoughtful of you."

"Oh, it was nothing."

"No, but it means a lot that you cared enough to send it." He was quiet for a moment. "So few clients do, you know. Care."

"Oh, well," I said. "My pleasure."

Then Ted asked me if I wanted to have dinner with him sometime during the week.

"Dinner? Um—well—"

"I know, you're probably thinking this is sudden and rash of me, but— Well, you seemed like such a nice guy, and—I don't know—I don't meet many people I can really even stand to be around—men, that is—so what's the point of pussyfooting around?"

"No, no, I understand," I said. "That sounds great. Dinner, that is—sounds great."

Ted made noises of relief. "Terrific, terrific. What night would be good for you?"

"Oh, I don't know. Thursday?" Thursday Susan was going to New York to sell her mother's apartment.

"Thursday's terrific," Ted said. "Do you like Dunes?"

"Sure." Dunes was a gay bar and restaurant I'd never been to.

"So I'll make a reservation. Eight o'clock? We'll meet there?"

"That's fine."

"I'm so glad," Ted said. "I'm really looking forward to it."

It may be hard to believe, but even then I still told myself I was doing it to make sure he didn't sue us.

Now, I should point out that not *all* of this was a new experience for me. It's true I'd never been to Dunes, but in my town, late at night, there is a beach, and not too far down the highway, a parking area. Those nights Susan and I fought, it was usually at one of these places that I ended up.

Still, nothing I'd done in the dark prepared me for Dunes, when I got there Thursday night. Not that it was so different from any other restaurant I'd gone to—it was your basic scrubbed-oak, piano-bar sort of place. Only everyone was a man. The maitre d', white-bearded and red-cheeked, a displaced Santa Claus, smiled at me and said, "Meeting someone?"

"Yes, in fact." I scanned the row of young and youngish men sitting at the bar, looking for Ted. "He doesn't seem to be here yet."

"Ted Potter, right?"

I didn't know Ted's last name. "Yes, I think so."

"The dog groomer?"

"Right."

The maitre d', I thought, smirked. "Well, I can seat you now, or you can wait at the bar."

"Oh, I think I'll just wait here, thanks, if that's okay."

"Whatever you want," the maitre d' said. He drifted off toward a large, familial-looking group of young men who'd just walked in the door. Guardedly I surveyed the restaurant for a familiar face which, thankfully, never materialized. I had two or three co-workers who I suspected ate here regularly.

I had to go to the bathroom, which was across the room. As far as I could tell there was no ladies' room at all. As for the men's room, it was small and cramped, with a long trough reminiscent of junior high school summer camp instead of urinals. Above the trough a mirror had been strategically tilted at a downward angle.

By the time I'd finished, and emerged once again into the restaurant, Ted had arrived. He looked breathless and a little worried and was consulting busily with the maitre d'. I waved; he waved back with his bandaged hand, said a few more words to the maitre d' and strode up briskly to greet me. "Hello," he said, clasping my hand with his unbandaged one. It was a large hand, cool and powdery. "Gosh, I'm sorry I'm late. I have to say, when I got here, and didn't see you, I was worried you might have left. Joey—that's the owner—said you'd been standing there one minute and the next you were gone."

"I was just in the bathroom."

"I'm glad you didn't leave." He exhaled what seemed an enormous quantity of breath. "Wow, it's great to see you! You look great!"

"Thanks," I said. "So do you." He did. He was wearing a white oxford shirt with the first couple of buttons unbuttoned, and a blazer the color of the beach.

"There you are," said Joey—the maitre d'. "We were wondering where you'd run off to. Well, your table's ready." He escorted us to the middle of the hubbub. "Let's order some wine," Ted said as we sat down. "What kind do you like?"

I wasn't a big wine expert—Susan had always done the ordering for us—so I deferred to Ted, who, after conferring for a few moments with Joey, mentioned something that sounded Italian. Then he leaned back and cracked his knuckles, bewildered, apparently, to be suddenly without tasks.

"So," he said.

"So," I said.

"I'm glad to see you."

"I'm glad to see you too."

We both blushed. "You're a real estate broker, right? At least, that's what I figured from your business card."

"That's right."

"How long have you been doing that?"

I dug back. "Oh, eight years or so."

"That's great. Have you been out here the whole time?"

"No, no, we moved out here six years ago."

"We?"

"Uh—Charlotte and I."

"Oh." Again Ted smiled. "So do you like it, living year-round in a resort town?"

"Sure. How about you?"

"I ended up out here by accident and just sort of stayed. A lot of people I've met have the same story. They'd like to leave, but you know—the climate is nice, life's not too difficult. It's hard to pull yourself away."

I nodded nervously.

"Is that your story too?"

"Oh—well, sort of," I said. "I was born in Queens, and then—I was living in Manhattan for a while—and then we decided to move out here—Charlotte and I—because I'd always loved the beach, and wanted to have a house, and here you could sell real estate and live all year round." I looked at Ted: Had I caught myself up in a lie or a contradiction? What I was telling him, essentially, was my history, but without Susan—and that was ridiculous, since my history was bound up with Susan's every step of the way. We'd started dating in high school, gone to the same college. The truth was I'd lived in Manhattan only while she was in law school, and had started selling real estate to help pay her tuition. No wonder the story sounded so strangely motiveless as I told it. I'd left out the reasons for everything. Susan was the reason for everything.

A waiter—a youngish blond man with a mustache so pale you could barely see it—gave us menus. He was wearing a white T-shirt and had a corkscrew outlined in the pocket of his jeans.

"Hello, Teddy," he said to Ted. Then he looked at me and said very fast, as if it were one sentence, "I'm Bobby and I'll be your waiter for the evening would you like something from the bar?"

"We've already ordered some wine," Ted said. "You want anything else, Paul?"

"I'm fine."

"Okay, would you like to hear the specials now?"

We both nodded, and Bobby rattled off a list of complex-sounding dishes. It was hard for me to separate one from the other. I had no appetite. He handed us our menus and moved on to another table.

I opened the menu. Everything I read sounded like it would make me sick.

"So do you like selling houses?" Ted asked.

"Oh yes, I love it—I love houses." I looked up, suddenly nervous that I was talking too much about myself. Shouldn't I ask him something about himself? I hadn't been on a date for fifteen years, after all, and even then the only girl I dated was Susan, whom I'd known forever. What was the etiquette in a situation like this? Probably I should ask Ted something about his life, but what kind of question would be appropriate?

Another waiter arrived with our bottle of wine, which Ted poured.

"How long have you been a dog groomer?" I asked rather tentatively.

"A couple of years. Of course I never intended to be a professional dog groomer. It was just something I did to make money. What I really wanted to be, just like about a million and a half other people, was an actor. Then I took a job out here for the summer, and like I said, I just stayed. I actually love the work. I love animals. When I was growing up my mom kept saying I should have been a veterinarian. She still says that to me sometimes, tells me it's not too late. I don't know. Frankly, I don't think I have what it takes to be a vet, and anyway, I don't want to be one. It's important work, but let's face it, I'm not for it and it's not for me. So I'm content to be a dog groomer." He picked up his wineglass and shook it, so that the wine lapped the rim in little waves.

"I know what you mean," I said, and I did. For years Susan had been complaining that I should have been an architect, insisting that I would have been happier, when the truth was she was just the tiniest bit ashamed of being married to a real estate broker. In her fantasies, "My husband is an architect" sounded so much better.

"My mother always wanted me to be an architect," I said now. "But it was just so she could tell her friends. For some reason people think real estate is a slightly shameful profession, like prostitution or something. They just assume on some level you make your living ripping people off. There's no way around it. An occupational hazard, I guess."

"Like dog bites," said Ted. He poured more wine.

"Oh, about that—" But Bobby was back to take our orders. He was pulling a green pad from the pocket on the back of his apron when another waiter came up to him from behind and whispered something in his ear. Suddenly they were both giggling wildly.

"You going to fill us in?" Ted asked, after the second waiter had left.

"I'm really sorry about this," Bobby said, still giggling. "It's just—" He bent down close to us, and in a confiding voice said, "Jill over at the bar brought in some like really good Vanna, just before work, and like, everything seems really hysterical to me? You know, like it's five years ago and I'm this boy from Emporia, Kansas?" He cast his eyes to the ceiling. "God, I'm like a complete retard tonight. Anyway, what did you say you wanted?"

Ted ordered grilled paillard of chicken with shiitake mushrooms in a papaya vinaigrette; I ordered a cheeseburger.

"Who's Jill?" I asked after Bobby had left.

"Everyone's Jill," Ted said. "They're all Jill."

"And Vanna?"

"Vanna White. It's what they call cocaine here." He leaned closer. "I'll bet you're thinking this place is really ridiculous, and you're right. The truth is, I kind of hate it. Only can you name me someplace else where two men can go on a date? I like the fact that you can act datish here, if you know what I mean." He smiled. Under the table our hands interlocked. We were acting very datish indeed.

It was all very unreal. I thought of Susan, in Queens, with her mother. She'd probably called the house two or three times already, was worrying where I was. It occurred to me, dimly and distantly, like something in another life, that Ted knew nothing about Susan. I wondered if I should tell him.

But I did not tell him. We finished dinner, and went to Ted's apartment. He lived in the attic of a rambling old house near the center of town.

We never drank more than a sip or two each of the cups of tea he made for us.

It was funny—when we began making love that first time, Ted and I, what I was thinking was that, like most sex between men, this was really a matter of exorcism, the expulsion of bedeviling lusts. Or exercise, if you will. Or horniness—a word that always makes me think of demons. So why was it, when we finished, there were tears in my eyes, and I was turning, putting my mouth against his hair, preparing to whisper something—who knows what?

Ted looked upset. "What's wrong?" he asked. "Did I hurt you?"

"No," I said. "No. You didn't hurt me."

"Then what is it?"

"I guess I'm just not used to— I didn't expect— I never expected—" Again I was crying.

"It's okay," he said. "I feel it too."

"I have a wife," I said.

At first he didn't answer.

I've always loved houses. Most people I know in real estate don't love houses; they love making money, or making deals, or making sales pitches. But Susan and I, from when we first knew each other, from when we were very young, we loved houses better than anything else. Perhaps this was because we'd both been raised by divorced parents in stuffy apartments in Queens—I can't be sure. All I know is that as early as senior year in high school we shared a desire to get as far out of that city we'd grown up in as we could; we wanted a green lawn, and a mailbox, and a garage. And that passion, as it turned out, was so strong in us that it determined everything. I needn't say more about myself, and as for Susan—well, name me one other first-in-her-class in law school who's chosen—*chosen*—basically to do house closings for a living.

Susan wishes I was an architect. It is her not-so-secret dream to be married to an architect. Truthfully, she wanted me to have a profession she wouldn't have to think was below her own. But the fact is, I never could have been a decent architect because I have no patience for the engineering, the inner workings, the slow layering of concrete slab and wood and Sheetrock. Real estate is a business of surfaces, of first impressions; you have to brush past the water stain in the bathroom, put a Kleenex box over the gouge in the Formica, stretch the life expectancy of the heater from three to six years. Tear off the tile and the paint, the crumbly wallboard and the crackly blanket of insulation, and you'll see what flimsy scarecrows our houses really are, stripped down to their bare beams. I hate the sight of houses in the midst of renovation, naked and exposed like that. But give me a finished house, a polished floor, a sunny day; then I will show you what I'm made of.

The house I loved best, however, the house where, in those mad months, I imagined I might actually live with Ted, was the sort that most brokers shrink from—pretty enough, but drab, undistinguished. No dishwasher, no cathedral ceilings. It would sell, if it sold at all, to a young couple short on cash, or a retiring widow. So don't ask me why I loved this house. My passion for it was inexplicable, yet intense. Somehow I was utterly convinced that this, much more than the sleek suburban one-story Susan and I shared, with its Garland stove and Sub-Zero fridge—this was the house of love.

The day I told Susan I was leaving her, she threw the Cuisinart at me. It bounced against the wall with a thud, and that vicious little blade, dislodged, rolled along the floor like a revolving saw, until it gouged the wall. I stared at it, held fast and suspended above the ground. "How can you just come home from work and tell me this?" Susan screamed. "No preparation, no warning—"

"I thought you'd be relieved," I said.

"Relieved!"

She threw the blender next. It hit me in the chest, then fell on my foot. Instantly I dove to the floor, buried my head in my knees and was weeping as hoarsely and furiously as a child.

"Stop throwing things!" I shouted weakly.

"I can't believe you," Susan said. "You tell me you're leaving me for a man and then you want me to mother you, take care of you? Is that all I've ever been to you? Fuck that! You're not a baby!"

I heard footsteps next, a car starting, Charlotte barking. I opened my eyes. Broken glass, destroyed machinery all over the tiles.

I got in my car and followed her. All the way to the beach. "Leave me alone!" she shouted, pulling off her shoes and running out onto the sand. "Leave me the fuck alone!" Charlotte romped after her, barking.

"Susan!" I screamed. "Susan!" I chased her. She picked up a big piece of driftwood and hit me with it. I stopped, dropped once again to my knees. Susan kept running. Eventually she stopped. I saw her a few hundred feet up the beach, staring at the waves.

Charlotte kept running between us, licking our faces, in a panic of barks and wails.

Susan started walking back toward me. I saw her getting larger and larger as she strode down the beach. She strode right past me.

"Charlotte!" Susan called from the parking lot. "Charlotte!" But Charlotte stayed.

Susan got back in her car and drove away.

At first I stayed at Ted's house. But Susan—we were seeing each other again, taking walks on the beach, negotiating—said that was too much, so I moved into the Dutch Boy Motel. Still, every day, I went to see the house, either to eat my lunch or just stand in the yard, feeling the sun come down through the branches of the trees there. I was learning a lot about the house. It had been built in 1934 by Josiah Applegate, a local contractor, as a wedding present for his daughter, Julia, and her husband, Spencer Bledsoe. The Bledsoes occupied the house for six years before the birth of their fourth child forced them to move, at which point it was sold to another couple, Mr. and Mrs. Hubert White. They, in turn, sold the house to Mr. and Mrs. Salvatore Rinaldi, who sold it to Mrs. Barbara Adams, a widow, who died. The estate of Mrs. Adams then sold the house to Arthur and Penelope Hilliard, who lived in it until their deaths just last year at the ages of eighty-six and eighty-two. Mrs. Hilliard was the first to go, in her sleep; according to her niece, Mr. Hilliard then wasted away, eventually having to be transferred to Shady Manor Nursing Home, where a few months later a heart attack took him. They had no children. Mr. Hilliard was a retired postman. Mrs. Hilliard did not work, but was an active member of the Ladies' Village Improvement Society. She was famous for her apple cakes, which she sold every year at bake sales. Apparently she went through periods when she would write letters to the local paper every week, long diatribes about the insensitivity of the new houses and new people. I never met her. She had a reputation for being crotchety, but maternal. Her husband was regarded as docile and wicked at poker.

The house had three bedrooms—one pitifully small—and two and a half baths. The kitchen cabinets were made of knotty, dark wood which had grown sticky from fifty years of grease, and the ancient yellow Formica countertops were scarred with burns and knife scratches. The wallpaper was red roses in the kitchen, leafy green leaves in the living room, and was yellowing and peeling at the edges. The yard contained a dogwood, a cherry tree and a clump of gladiolas. Overgrown privet hedges fenced the front door, which was white with a beaten brass knocker. In the living room was a dusty pair of sofas, and dark wood shelves lined with Reader's Digest Condensed Books, and a big television from the early seventies. The shag carpeting—coffee brown—appeared to be a recent addition.

The quilts on the beds, the Hilliards' niece told me, were handmade, and might be for sale. They were old-fashioned patchwork quilts, no doubt stitched together over several winters in front of the television. "Of course," the niece said, "if the price was right, we might throw the quilts in—you know, as an extra."

I was a man with the keys to fifty houses in my pockets. Just that morning I had toured the ten bathrooms of the $10.5-million oceanfront. And I was smiling. I was smiling like someone in love.

I took Ted to see the house about a week after I left Susan. It was a strange time for both of us. I was promising him my undying love, but I was also waking up in the middle of every night crying for Susan and Charlotte. We walked from room to room, just as I'd imagined, and just as I'd planned, in the doorway to the master bedroom, I turned him around to face me, bent his head down (he was considerably taller than me) and kissed him. It was meant to be a moment of sealing, of confirmation, a moment that would make radiantly, abundantly clear the extent to which this house was meant for us, and we for it. But instead the kiss felt rehearsed, dispassionate. And Ted looked nervous. "It's a cute house, Paul," he said. "But God knows I don't have any money. And you already own a house. How can we just *buy* it?"

"As soon as the divorce is settled, I'll get my equity."

"You haven't even filed for divorce yet. And once you do, it could take years."

"Probably not *years.*"

"So when *are* you filing for divorce?"

He had his hands in his pockets. He was leaning against a window draped with white flounces of cotton and powderpuffs.

"I need to take things slow," I said. "This is all new for me."

"It seems to me," Ted said, "that you need to take things slow and take things fast at the same time."

"Oh, Ted!" I said. "Why do you have to complicate everything? I just love this house, that's all. I feel like this is where I—where we—where we're meant to live. Our dream house, Ted. Our love nest. Our cottage."

Ted was looking at his feet. "Do you really think you'll be able to leave Susan? For good?"

"Well, of course, I— Of course."

"I don't believe you. Soon enough she's going to make an ultimatum. Come back, give up Ted, or that's it. And you know what you're going to do? You're going to go back to her."

"I'm not," I said. "I wouldn't."

"Mark my words," Ted said.

I lunged toward him, trying to pull him down on the sofa, but he pushed me away.

"I love you," I said.

"And Susan?"

I faltered. "Of course, I love Susan too."

"You can't love two people, Paul. It doesn't work that way."

"Susan said the same thing, last week."

"She's right."

"Why?"

"Because it isn't fair."

I considered this. I considered Ted, considered Susan. I had known Susan since Mrs. Polanski's homeroom in fourth grade. We played *Star Trek* on the playground together, and roamed the back streets of Bayside. We were children in love, and we sought out every movie or book we could find about children in love.

Ted I'd known only a few months, but we'd made love with a passion I'd never imagined possible, and the sight of him unbuttoning his shirt made my heart race.

It was at that moment that I realized that while it is possible to love two people at the same time, in different ways, in the heart, it is not possible to do so in the world.

I had to choose, so of course, I chose Susan.

That day—the day of Ed and Grace-Anne, the day that threatened to end with the loss of my beloved house—Susan did not call me at work. The morning progressed slowly. I was waiting for Ed and Grace-Anne to reappear at the window and walk in the office doors, and sure enough, around eleven-thirty, they did. The receptionist led them to my desk.

"I'm Ed Cavallaro," Ed said across my desk, as I stood to shake his hand. "This is my wife."

"How do you do?" Grace-Anne said. She smelled of some sort of fruity perfume or lipstick, the kind teenaged girls wear. We sat down.

"Well, I'll tell you, Mr. Hoover," Ed said, "we've been summering around here for years, and I've just retired—I worked over at Grumman, upisland?"

"Congratulations," I said.

"Ed was there thirty-seven years," Grace-Anne said. "They gave him a party like you wouldn't believe."

"So, you enjoying retired life?"

"Just between you and me, I'm climbing the walls."

"We're active people," Grace-Anne said.

"Anyway, we've always dreamed about having a house near the beach."

"Ed, let *me* tell about the dream."

"I didn't mean *that* dream."

"I had a dream," Grace-Anne said. "I saw the house we were meant to retire in, clear as day. And then, just this morning, walking down the street, we look in your window, and what do we see? The very same house! The house from my dream!"

"How amazing," I said. "Which house was it?"

"That cute little one for one sixty-five," Grace-Anne said. "You know, with the cedar shingles?"

"I'm not sure."

"Oh, I'll show you."

We stood up and walked outside, to the window. "Oh, that house!" I said. "Sure, sure. Been on the market almost a year now. Not much interest in it, I'm afraid."

"Now why is that?" Ed asked, and I shrugged.

"It's a pleasant enough house. But it does have some problems. It'll require a lot of TLC."

"TLC we've got plenty of," Grace-Anne said.

"Grace-Anne, I told you," Ed said, "the last thing I want to do is waste my retirement fixing up."

"But it's my dream house!" Grace-Anne fingered the buttons of her blouse. "Anyway, what harm can it do to look at it?"

"I have a number of other houses in roughly the same price range which you might want to look at—"

"Fine, fine, but first, couldn't we look at that house? I'd be so grateful if you could arrange it."

I shrugged my shoulders. "It's not occupied. Why not?"

And Grace-Anne smiled.

Even though the house was only a few hundred feet away, we drove. One of the rules of real estate is: Drive the clients everywhere. This means your car has to be both commodious and spotlessly clean. I spent a lot—too much—of my life cleaning my car—especially difficult, considering Charlotte.

And so we piled in—Grace-Anne and I in front, Ed in back—and drove the block or so to Maple Street. I hadn't been by the house for a few weeks, and I was happy to see that the spring seemed to have treated it well. The rich greens of the grass and the big maple trees framed it, I thought, rather lushly.

I unlocked the door, and we headed into that musty interior odor which, I think, may well be the very essence of stagnation, cryogenics and bliss.

"Just like I dreamed," Grace-Anne said, and I could understand why. Probably the Hilliards had been very much like the Cavallaros.

"The kitchen's in bad shape," Ed said. "How's the boiler?"

"Old, but functional." We headed down into the spidery basement. Ed kicked things.

Grace-Anne was rapturously fingering the quilts. "Ed, I love this house," she said. "I love it."

Ed sighed laboriously.

"Now, there are several other nice homes you might want to see—"

"None of them was in my dream."

But Ed sounded hopeful. "Grace-Anne, it can't hurt to look. You said it yourself."

"But what if someone else snatches it from under us?" Grace-Anne asked, suddenly horrified.

"I tend to doubt that's going to happen," I said in as comforting a tone as I could muster. "As I mentioned earlier, the house has been on the market for over a year."

"All right," Grace-Anne said reluctantly, "I suppose we could look—*look*—at a few others."

"I'm sure you won't regret it."

"Yes, well."

I turned from them, breathing evenly.

Of course she had no idea I would sooner make sure the house burned down than see a contract for its purchase signed with her husband's name.

I fingered some matches in my pocket. I felt terrified. Terrified and powerful.

When I got home from work that afternoon, Susan's car was in the driveway and Charlotte, from her usual position of territorial inspection on the front stoop, was smiling up at me in her doggy way. I patted her head and went inside, but when I got there, there was a palpable silence which was far from ordinary, and soon enough I saw that its source was Susan, leaning over the kitchen counter in her sleek lawyer's suit, one leg tucked under, like a flamingo.

"Hi," I said.

I tried to kiss her, and she turned away.

"This isn't going to work, Paul," she said.

I was quiet a moment. "Why?" I asked.

"You sound relieved, grateful. You do. I knew you would."

"I'm neither of those things. Just tell me why you've changed your mind since last night."

"You tell me you're in love with a man, you up and leave for three months, then out of the blue you come back. I just don't know what you expect—do you want me to jump for joy and welcome you back like nothing's happened?"

"Susan, yesterday you said—"

"Yesterday," Susan said, "I hadn't thought about it enough. Yesterday I was confused, and grateful, and— God, I was so relieved. But now—now I just don't know. I mean, what the hell has this been for you, anyway?"

"Susan, honey," I said, "I love you. I've loved you my whole life. Remember what your mother used to say, when we were kids, and we'd come back from playing on Saturdays? 'You two are joined at the hip,' she'd say. And we still are."

"Have you ever loved me sexually?" Susan asked, suddenly turning to face me.

"Susan," I said.

"Have you?"

"Of course."

"I don't believe you. I think it's all been cuddling and hugging. Kid stuff. I think the sex only mattered to me. How do I know you weren't thinking about men all those times?"

"Susan, of course not—"

"What a mistake," Susan said. "If only I'd known back then, when I was a kid—"

"Doesn't it matter to you that I'm back?"

"It's not like you never left, for Christ's sake!" She put her hands on my cheeks. "You *left,*" she said quietly. "For three months you *left.* And I don't know, maybe love *can* be killed."

She let go. I didn't say anything.

"I think you should leave for a while," Susan said. "I think I need some time alone—some time alone knowing you're alone too."

I looked at the floor. "Okay," I said. And I suppose I said it too eagerly, because Susan said, "If you go back to Ted, that's it. We're finished for good."

"I won't go back to Ted," I said.

We were both quiet for a few seconds.

"Should I go now?"

Susan nodded.

"Well, then, good-bye," I said. And I went.

This brings me to where I am now, which is, precisely, nowhere. I waited three hours in front of Ted's house that night, but when, at twelve-thirty, his car finally pulled into the driveway, someone else got out with him. It has been two weeks since that night. Each day I sit at my desk, and wait for one of them, or a lawyer, to call. I suppose I am homeless, although I think it is probably inaccurate to say that a man with fifty keys in his pocket is ever homeless. Say, then, that I am a man with no home, but many houses.

Of course I am careful. I never spend the night in the same house twice. I bring my own sheets, and in the morning I always remake the bed I've slept in as impeccably as I can. The fact that I'm an early riser helps as well—that way, if another broker arrives, or a cleaning woman, I can say I'm just checking the place out. And if the owners are coming back, I'm always the first one to be notified.

The other night I slept at the $10.5-million oceanfront. I used all the bathrooms; I swam in both the pools.

As for the Hilliards' house—well, so far I've allowed myself to stay there only once a week. Not because it's inconvenient—God knows, no one ever shows the place—but because to sleep there more frequently would bring me closer to a dream of unbearable pleasure than I feel I can safely go.

The Cavallaros, by the way, ended up buying a contemporary in the woods for a hundred and seventy-five, the superb kitchen of which turned out to be more persuasive than Grace-Anne's dream. The Hilliards' house remains empty, unsold. Their niece just lowered the price to one fifty—quilts included.

Funny: Even with all my other luxurious possibilities, I look forward to those nights I spend at the Hilliards' with greater anticipation than anything else in my life. When the key clicks, and the door opens onto that living room with its rows of Reader's Digest Condensed Books, a rare sense of relief runs through me. I feel as if I've come home.

One thing about the Hilliards' house is that the lighting is terrible. It seems there isn't a bulb in the house over twenty-five watts. And perhaps this isn't surprising—they were old people, after all, by no means readers. They spent their lives in front of the television. So when I arrive at night, I have to go around the house, turning on light after light, like ancient oil lamps. Not much to read by, but dim light, I've noticed, has a kind of warmth which bright light lacks. It casts a glow against the woodwork which is exactly, just exactly, like the reflection of raging fire.

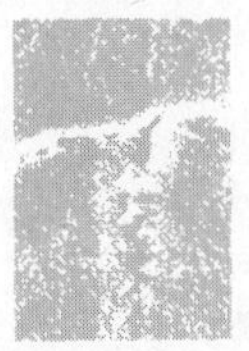

WHEN YOU GROW TO ADULTERY

ANDREW was in love with Jack Selden, so all Jack's little habits, his particular ways of doing things, seemed marvelous to him: the way Jack put his face under the shower, after shampooing his hair, and shook his head like a big dog escaped from a bath; the way he slept on his back, his arms crossed in the shape of a butterfly over his face, fists on his eyes; his fondness for muffins and Danish and sweet rolls—what he called, at first just out of habit and then *because* it made Andrew laugh, "baked goods." Jack made love with efficient fervor, his face serious, almost businesslike. Not that he was without affection, but everything about him had an edge; his very touch had an edge, there was the possibility of pain lurking behind every caress. It seemed to Andrew that Jack's touches, more than any he'd known before, were full of meaning—they sought to express, not just to please or explore—and this gesturing made him want to gesture back, to enter into a kind of tactile dialogue. They'd known each other only a month, but already it felt to Andrew as if their fingers had told each other novels.

Andrew had gone through most of his life not being touched by anyone, never being touched at all. These days, his body under the almost constant scrutiny of two distinct pairs of hands, seemed to him perverse punishment, as if he had had a wish granted and was now suffering the consequences of having stated the wish too vaguely. He actually envisioned, sometimes, the fairy godmother shrugging her shoulders and saying, "You get what you ask for." Whereas most of his life he had been alone, unloved, now he had two lovers—Jack for just over a month, and Allen for close to three years. There was no cause and effect, he insisted, but had to admit things with Allen had been getting ragged around the edges for some time. Jack and Allen knew about each other and had agreed to endure, for the sake of the undecided Andrew, a tenuous and open-ended period of transition, during which Andrew himself spent so much of his time on the subway, riding between the two apartments of his two lovers, that it began to seem to him as if rapid transit was the true and final home of the desired. Sometimes he wanted nothing more than to crawl into the narrow bed of his childhood and revel in the glorious, sad solitude of no one—not even his mother—needing or loving him. Hadn't the hope of future great loves been enough to curl up against? It seemed so now. His skin felt soft, toneless, like the skin of a plum poked by too many housewifely hands, feeling for the proper ripeness; he was covered with fingerprints.

This morning he had woken up with Jack—a relief. One of the many small tensions of the situation was that each morning, when he woke up, there was a split second of panic as he sought to reorient himself and figure out where he was, who he was with. It was better with Jack, because Jack was new love and demanded little of him; with Allen, lately, there'd been thrashing, heavy breathing, a voice whispering in his ear, "Tell me one thing. Did you promise Jack we wouldn't have sex? I have to know."

"No, I didn't."

"Thank God, thank God. Maybe now I can go back to sleep."

There was a smell of coffee. Already showered and dressed for work (he was an architect at a spiffy firm), Jack walked over to the bed, smiling, and kissed Andrew, who felt rumpled and sour and unhappy. Jack's mouth carried the sweet taste of coffee, his face was smooth and newly shaven and still slightly wet. "Good morning," he said.

"Good morning."

"I love you," Jack Selden said.

Immediately Allen appeared, in a posture of crucifixion against the bedroom wall. "My God," he said, "you're killing me, you know that? You're killing me."

It was Rosh Hashanah, and Allen had taken the train out the night before to his parents' house in New Jersey. Andrew was supposed to join him that afternoon. He looked up now at Jack, smiled, then closed his eyes. His brow broke into wrinkles. "Oh God," he said to Jack, putting his arms around his neck, pulling him closer, so that Jack almost spilled his coffee. "Now I have to face Allen's family."

Jack kissed Andrew on the forehead before pulling gingerly from his embrace. "I still can't believe Allen told them," he said, sipping more coffee from a mug that said WORLD'S GREATEST ARCHITECT. Jack had a mostly perfunctory relationship with his own family—hence the mug, a gift from his mother.

"Yes," Andrew said. "But Sophie's hard to keep secrets from. She sees him, and she knows something's wrong, and she doesn't give in until he's told her."

"Listen, I'm sure if he told you she's not going to say anything, she's not going to say anything. Anyway, it'll be fun, Andrew. You've told me a million times how much you enjoy big family gatherings."

"Easy for you to say. You get to go to your nice clean office and work all day and sleep late tomorrow and go out for brunch." Suddenly Andrew sat up in bed. "I don't think I can take this anymore, this running back and forth between you and him." He looked up at Jack shyly. "Can't I stay with you? In your pocket?"

Jack smiled. Whenever he and his last boyfriend, Ralph, had had something difficult to face—the licensing exam, or a doctor's appointment—they would say to each other, "Don't worry, I'll be there with you. I'll be in your pocket." Jack had told Andrew, who had in turn appropriated the metaphor, but Jack didn't seem to mind. He smiled down at Andrew—he was sitting on the edge of the bed now, smelling very clean, like hair tonic—and brushed his hand over Andrew's forehead. Then he reached down to the breast pocket of his own shirt, undid the little button there, pulled it open, made a plucking gesture over Andrew's face, as if he were pulling off a loose eyelash, and, bringing his hand back, rubbed his fingers together over the open pocket, dropping something in.

"You're there," he said. "You're in my pocket."

"All day?" Andrew asked.

"All day." Jack smiled again. And Andrew, looking up at him, said, "I love you," astonished even as he said the words at how dangerously he was teetering on the brink of villainy.

Unlike Jack, who had a job, Andrew was floating through a strange, shapeless period in his life. After several years at Berkeley, doing art history, he had transferred to Columbia, and was now confronting the last third of a dissertation on Tiepolo's ceilings. There was always for him a period before starting some enormous and absorbing project during which the avoidance of that project became his life's goal. He had a good grant and nowhere to go during the day except around the cluttered West Side apartment he shared with Allen, so he spent most of his time sweeping dust and paper scraps into little piles—anything to avoid the computer. Allen, whom he had met at Berkeley, had gotten an assistant professorship at Columbia the year before—hence Andrew's transfer, to be with him. He was taking this, his third semester, off to write a book. Andrew had stupidly imagined such a semester of shared writing would be a gift, a time they could enjoy together, but instead their quiet afternoons were turning out one after the other to be cramped and full of annoyance, and fights too ugly and trivial for either of them to believe they'd happened afterwards—shoes left on the floor, phone messages forgotten, introductions not tendered at parties: these were the usual crimes. Allen told Andrew he was typing too fast, it was keeping him from writing; Andrew stormed out. Somewhere in the course of that hazy afternoon when he was never going back he met Jack, who was spending the day having a reunion with his old college roommate, another art-history graduate student named

Tony Melendez. The three of them chatted on the steps of Butler, then went to Tom's Diner for coffee. A dirty booth, Andrew across from Jack, Tony next to Jack, doing most of the talking. Jack talking too, sometimes; he smiled a lot at Andrew.

When one person's body touches another person's body, chemicals under the skin break down and recombine, setting off an electric spark which leaps, neuron to neuron, to the brain. It was all a question of potassium and calcium when, that afternoon at Tom's, Jack's foot ended right up against Andrew's. Soon the accidental pressure became a matter of will, of choice. Chemistry, his mother had said, in a rare moment of advisory nostalgia. Oh, your father, that first date we didn't have a thing to talk about, but the chemistry!

At home that evening, puttering around while Allen agonized over his book, Andrew felt claustrophobic. He wanted to call Jack. Everything that had seemed wonderful about his relationship with Allen—shared knowledge, shared ideologies, shared loves—fell away to nothing, desiccated by the forceful reactions of the afternoon. How could he have imagined this relationship would work for all his life? he wondered. Somehow they had forgotten, or pushed aside, the possibilities (the likelihoods) of competitiveness, disagreement, embarrassment, disapproval, not to mention just plain boredom. He called Jack; he told Allen he was going to the library. The affair caught, and as it got going Andrew's temper flared, he had at his fingertips numberless wrongs Allen had perpetrated which made his fucking Jack all right. He snapped at Allen, walked out of rooms at the slightest provocation, made several indiscreet phone calls, until Allen finally asked what was going on. Then came the long weekend of hair-tearing and threats and pleas, followed by the period of indecision they were now enduring, a period during which they didn't fight at all, because whenever Andrew felt a fight coming on he threatened to leave, and whenever Allen felt a fight coming on he backed off, became soothing and loving, to make sure Andrew wouldn't leave. Andrew didn't want to leave Allen, he said, but he also didn't want to give up Jack. Such a period of transition suited him shamefully; finally, after all those years, he was drowning in it.

In skeptical or self-critical moments, Andrew perceived his life as a series of abandonments. This is what he was thinking about as he rode the train from Hoboken out toward Allen's parents' house that afternoon: how he had abandoned his family, fleeing California for the East Coast, willfully severing his ties to his parents; then, one after another, how he had had best friends, and either fought with them or became disgusted with them, or they with him, or else just drifted off without writing or calling until the gap was too big to dare crossing. There were many people he had said he could spend his life with, yet he hadn't spent his life with any of them, he saw now. Nathan and Celia, for instance, who it had seemed to him in college would be his best friends for all time—when was the last time he'd seen them? Five, six months now? Berkeley had severed Andrew from that ineradicable threesome of his youth, and now that he was in New York again it seemed too much had happened for them to fill each other in on, and in the course of it all happening their perceptions and opinions had changed, they were no longer in perfect synch, they weren't able to understand each other as gloriously as they once had because, of course, their lives had diverged, they did not have endless common experience to chew over, and on which to hone shared attitudes. After those first few disastrous dinners, in which arguments had punctuated the dull yawn of nothing to be said, he had given up calling them, except once he had seen Nathan at the museum, where they stood in front of a Tiepolo and Nathan challenged Andrew to explain why it was any good—a familiar, annoying, Nathan-ish challenge, a good try, but by then it was too late. All of this was guilt-inspiring enough, but what made Andrew feel even guiltier was that Nathan and Celia still saw each other, went to parties together, lived in the clutch of the same old dynamic, and presumably the same glorious synchronicity of opinion. They were going on ten years with each other even without him, and Andrew felt humbled, immature. Why couldn't he keep relationships up that long? As for leaving Allen for Jack—wouldn't it amount to the same thing? In three years, would he leave Jack as well?

Perhaps it was just his nature. After all, he had lived for the entire first twenty-two and most of the next six years of his life virtually alone, surviving by instinct, internal resources. This was not uncommon among gay men he knew; some reach out into the sexual world at the brink of puberty, like those babies who, tossed in a swimming pool, gracefully stay afloat; but others—himself among them—become so transfixed by the preposterousness of their own bodies, and particularly the idea of their coming together with other bodies, that they end up trapped in a contemplation of sex that, as it grows more tortured and analytic, rules out action altogether. Such men must be coaxed by others into action, like the rusty Tin Man in Oz, but as Andrew knew, willing and desirable coaxers were few and far between. For him sexual awakening had come too late, too long after adolescence, when the habits of the adult body were no longer new but had become settled and hard to break out of. Chronically alone, Andrew had cultivated, in those years, a degree of self-containment which kept him alive, but was nonetheless not self-reliance, for it was based on weakness, and had at its heart the need and longing for another to take him in. He remembered, at sixteen, lying in his room, his hands exploring his own body, settling on his hip, just above the pelvis, and thinking, No other hand has touched me here, not since infancy, not since my mother. Not one hand. And this memory had gone on for six more years. Had that been the ruin of him? he wondered now. Doomed by necessity to become self-contained, was he also doomed never to be able to love someone else, always to retreat from intimacy into the cozy, familiar playroom of his old, lonely self?

Outside the train window, the mysterious transformations of late afternoon were beginning. It was as if the sun were backing off in horror at what it had seen, or given light to. The train Andrew was on had bench seats that reversed direction at a push, and remembering how impressed by that he had been the first time Allen had taken him on this train, he grew nervous: suddenly he remembered Allen, remembered he was on his way to a man who considered his life to be in Andrew's hands. Already he recognized the litany of town names as the conductor announced them: one after another, and then they were there. By the crossing gate Allen sat in his father's BMW, waiting.

He smiled and waved as he stepped off the train. Allen didn't move. He waved again as he ran toward the car, waved through the window. "Hi," he said cheerily, getting in and kissing Allen lightly on the mouth. Allen pulled the car out of the parking lot and onto the road.

"What's wrong?" (A foolish question, yet somehow the moment demanded it.)

"This is the very worst for me," he said. "Your coming back. It's worse than your leaving."

"Why?"

"Because you always look so happy. Then you fall into a stupor, you fall asleep, or you want to go to the movies and sleep there. Jack gets all the best of you, I get you lying next to me snoring." He was on the verge, as he had been so many times in these last weeks, of saying inevitable things, and Andrew could sense him biting back, like someone fighting the impulse to vomit. Andrew cleared his throat. A familiar, dull ache somewhere in his bowels was starting up again, as if a well-trusted anesthesia were wearing off. It felt to him these days, being with Allen, as if a two-bladed knife lay gouged deep into both of them, welding them together, and reminded anew of its presence, Andrew turned futilely to the car window, the way you might turn from the obituary page to the comics upon recognizing an unexpected and familiar face among the portraits of the dead. Of course, soon enough, you have to turn back.

Andrew closed his eyes. Allen breathed. "Let's not have a fight," Andrew said quietly, surprised to be on the verge of tears. But Allen was stony, and said nothing more.

As they pulled into the driveway the garage doors slowly opened, like primeval jaws or welcoming arms; Sophie, Allen's mother, must have heard the car pulling up, and pushed the little button in the kitchen. A chilly dusk light was descending on the driveway, calling up in Andrew some primeval nostalgia for suburban twilight, and all the thousands of days which had come to an end here, children surprised by the swift descent of night, their mothers' voices calling them home, the prickly coolness of their arms as they dropped their balls and ran back into the warm lights of houses. It had been that sort of childhood Allen had lived here, after all, a childhood of street games, Kickball and Capture the Flag, though Allen was always the one the others laughed at, picked last, kicked. A dog barked distantly, and in the bright kitchen window above the garage Andrew saw Sophie rubbing her hands with a white dish towel. She was not smiling, and seemed to be struggling to compose herself into whatever kind of studied normalness the imminent arrival of friends and relatives demanded. Clearly she did not know anyone could see her, for in a moment she turned slightly toward the window, and seeing the car idle in the driveway, its lights still on, started, then smiled and waved.

A festive, potent smell of roasting meats came out the porch door. "Hello, Andrew," Sophie said as they walked into the kitchen, her voice somehow hearty yet tentative, and she kissed him jauntily on the cheek, bringing close for one unbearable second a smell of face powder, perfume and chicken stock he almost could not resist falling into. For Jack's sake he held his own. Of all the things he feared losing along with Allen, this family was the one he thought about most. How he longed to steep forever in this brisket smell, this warmth of carpeting and mahogany and voices chattering in the hall! But Allen, glumly, said, "Let's go upstairs," and gestured to the room they always shared, his room. Even that a miracle, Andrew reflected, as they trundled up the stairs: that first time Andrew had visited and was worrying where he'd sleep, Sophie had declared, "I never ask what goes on upstairs. Everyone sleeps where they want; as far as I'm concerned, it's a mystery." It seemed a different moral code applied where her homosexual son was concerned than the one that had been used routinely with

Allen's brothers and sister; in their cases, the sleeping arrangements for visiting boyfriends or girlfriends had to be carefully orchestrated, the girls doubling up with Allen's sister, the boys with Allen himself—a situation Allen had always found both sexy and intolerable, he had told Andrew, the beautiful college boys lying next to him in his double bed for the requisite hour or so, then sneaking off to have sex with his sister, Barrie. Well, all that was long past—Barrie was now married and had two children of her own—and what both Allen and Andrew felt grateful for here was family: it was a rare thing for a gay man to have it, much less to be able to share it with his lover. Their parents had not yet met each other, but a visit was planned for May, and remembering this, Andrew gasped slightly as the prospect arose before him—yet another lazily arranged inevitability to be dealt with, and with it the little residual parcel of guilt and nostalgia and dread, packed up like the giblets of a supermarket chicken. His half of the knife twisted a little, causing Allen's to respond in kind, and Allen looked at Andrew suspiciously. "What is it?" he asked. Andrew shook his head. "Nothing, really." He didn't want to talk about it. Allen shrugged regretfully; clearly he sensed that whatever was on Andrew's mind was bad enough not to be messed with.

"Well," Allen said, as they walked into his room, "here we are," and threw himself onto the bed. Andrew followed more cautiously. The room had changed hands and functions many times over the years—first it had been Allen's sister's room, then his brother's, then his, then a guest room, then a computer room, then a room for visiting grandchildren. It had a peculiar, muddled feel to it, the accretions of each half-vain effort at redecoration only partially covering over the leavings of the last occupant. There was archaeology, a sense of layers upon layers. On the walnut dresser, which had belonged to Allen's grandmother, a baseball trophy shared space with a Strawberry Shortcake doll whose hair had been cut off, a two-headed troll and a box of floppy disks. Odd-sized clothes suggesting the worst of several generations of children's fashions filled the drawers and the closets, and the walls were covered with portraits of distant aunts, framed awards Allen had won in high school and college, pictures of Barrie with her horse. The bed, retired here from the master bedroom downstairs, had been Sophie's and her husband Lou's for twenty years. The springs were shot; Allen lay in it more than on it, and after a few seconds of observation Andrew joined him. Immediately their hands found each other, they were embracing, kissing, Andrew was crying. "I love you," he said quietly.

"Then come back to me," Allen said.

"It's not that simple."

"Why?"

Andrew pulled away. "You know all the reasons."

"Tell me."

The door opened with a tentative squeak. Some old instinctual fear made both of them jump to opposite sides of the bed. Melissa, Allen's five-year-old niece, stood in the doorway, her hand in her mouth, her knees twisted one around the other. She was wearing a plaid party dress, white tights and black patent-leather Mary Janes.

"Hello," she said quietly.

"Melly! Hello, honey!" Allen said, bounding up from the bed and taking her in his arms. "What a pretty girl you are! Are you all dressed up for Rosh Hashanah?" He kissed her, and she nodded, opening her tiny mouth into a wide smile clearly not offered easily, a smile which seemed somehow precious, it was so carefully given. "Look at my earrings," she said. "They're hearts."

"They're beautiful," Allen said. "Remember who bought them for you?"

"Uncle Andrew," Melissa said, and looked at him, and Andrew remembered the earrings he had given her just six months before, for her birthday, as if she were his own niece.

"Look who's here, honey," he said, putting Melissa down. "Uncle Andrew's here now!"

"I know," Melissa said. "Grandma told me."

"Hi, Melissa," Andrew said, sitting up on the bed. "I'm so happy to see you! What a big girl you are! Come give me a hug!"

Immediately she landed on him, her arms circling as much of him as they could, her smiling mouth open over his face. This surprised Andrew; on previous visits Melissa had viewed him with a combination of disdain and the sort of amusement one feels at watching a trained animal perform; only the last time he'd been to the house, in August, for Sophie's birthday, had she shown him anything like affection. And it was true that she'd asked to speak to him on the phone every time she was visiting and Allen called. Still, nothing prepared Andrew for what he saw in her eyes just now, as she gazed down at him with a loyalty so pure it was impossible to misinterpret.

"I love you," she said, and instantly he knew it was true, and possibly true for the first time in her life.

"I love you too, honey," he said. "I love you very much."

She sighed, and her head sank into his chest, and she breathed softly, protected. What was love for a child, after all, if not protection? A quiet descended on the room as Andrew lay there, the little girl heavy in his arms, while Allen stood above them in the shrinking light, watching, it seemed, for any inkling of change in Andrew's face. Downstairs were dinner smells and dinner sounds, and Sophie's voice beckoning them to come, but somehow none of them could bring themselves to break the eggshell membrane that had formed over the moment. Then Melissa pulled herself up, and Andrew realized his leg was asleep, and Allen, shaken by whatever he had or hadn't seen, switched on the light. The new, artificial brightness was surprisingly unbearable to Andrew; he had to squint against it.

"We really ought to be going down now," Allen said, holding his hand out to Andrew, who took it gratefully, surprised only by the force with which Allen hoisted him from the bed.

Chairs and plastic glasses and Hugga Bunch plates had to be rearranged so Melissa could sit next to Andrew at dinner. This position, as it turned out, was not without its disadvantages; he was consistently occupied with cutting up carrots and meat. The conversation was familiar and soothing; someone had lost a lot of money in the stock market, someone else was building a garish house. Allen's sister sang the praises of a new health club, and Allen's father defended a cousin's decision to open a crematorium for pets. All through dinner Melissa stared up at Andrew, her face lit from within with love, and Allen stared across at Andrew, his face twisted and furrowed with love, and somewhere miles away, presumably, Jack sat at his drafting table, breaking into a smile for the sake of love. So much love! It had to be a joke, a fraud! Someone—his mother—must have been paying them! Wait a minute, he wanted to say to all three of them, this is me, Andrew, this is me who has never been loved, who has always been too nervous and panicked and eager for love for anyone to want actually to love him! You are making a mistake! You are mixing me up with someone else! And if they did love him—well, wouldn't they all wake up soon, and recognize that they were under an enchantment? Knowledge kills infatuation, he knew, the same way the sudden, perplexing recognition that you are dreaming can wake you from a dream. He almost wanted that to happen. But sadly—or happily, or perhaps just frustratingly—there appeared to be no enchantment here, no bribery. These three loves were real and entrenched. His disappearance from any one of them was liable to cause pain.

Even with Melissa! Just an hour later—screaming as her mother carried her to the bathtub, screaming as her mother put her in her bed—no one could ignore who she was calling for, though the various aunts and cousins were clearly surprised. Finally Barrie emerged from the room Melissa shared with her on visits, shaking her head and lighting a cigarette. "She says she won't go to sleep unless you tuck her in," Barrie told Andrew. "So would you mind? I'm sorry, but I've had a long day, I can't hack this crying shit anymore."

"You don't have to, Andrew," Sophie said. "She has to learn to go to sleep."

"But I don't mind," Andrew said. "Really, I don't."

"Well, thanks then."

Sophie led him into the darkened room where Melissa lay, rumpled-looking, in Cabbage Patch pajamas and sheets, her face puffy and her eyes red from crying, then backed out on tiptoe, closing the door three quarters. Immediately upon seeing him Melissa offered another of her rare and costly smiles.

"Hi," Andrew said.

"Hi."

"Are you all right?"

"Uh-huh."

"You want me to sing you a bedtime song?"

"Uh-huh."

"Okay." He brushed her hair away from her forehead, and began singing a version of a song his own father had sung to him:

Oh go to sleep my Melly-o
And you will grow and grow and grow
And grow and grow right up to be
A great big ugly man like me . . .

Melissa laughed. "But I'm a girl," she said.

"I told you, honey, this is a song my daddy sang to me."

"Go on."

And you will go to Timbuktu
And you'll see elephants in the zoo.
And you will go to outer space
And you will go to many a place.
Oh think of all the things you'll see
When you grow to adultery.

This last line, of course, caught him. It had always been a family joke, a mock pun. Had his father known something he hadn't?

"That's a funny song," said Melissa, who was, of course, too young to know what adultery meant anyway.

"I'm glad you liked it, but since I've sung it now, you have to go to sleep. Deal?"

She smiled again. Her hand, stretched out to her side, rested lightly now at that very point on his hip he had once imagined no one would ever touch. Now her tiny handprints joined the larger ones which seemed to him tonight to be permanently stamped there, like tattoos.

Though he'd left the light on, Allen was already tightly encased between the sheets by the time Andrew came to bed. He lay facing rigidly outward, and Andrew, climbing in next to him, observed the spray of nervous pimples fanning out over his shoulders. He brushed his fingers over the bumpy, reddened terrain, and Allen jumped spasmodically. Andrew took his hand away.

"Don't," Allen said.

"All right, I won't, I'm sorry."

"No, no. Don't *stop,* don't stop touching me. Please, I need you to touch me. You never touch me anymore."

Andrew put his hand back. "Don't," he said. "Stop. Don't. Stop. Don't stop, don't stop, don't stop."

"Thank you," Allen said. "Thank you."

"Switch off the light."

"You don't know," Allen said, "how much I've missed your hands."

"Allen, I've been touching you plenty," Andrew said.

"No, you haven't. You really haven't."

"This really is a stupid topic for an argument," Andrew said, not wanting to let on the sensation he was just now feeling, of a spear run through him, the whole length of his body. He reached over Allen's head and switched off the light. "Just relax," he said, and settled himself into a more comfortable position against the pillow. "I won't stop touching you."

"Thank you," Allen whispered.

In the dark things broke apart, becoming more bearable. His hand traveled the mysterious widths of Allen's back, and as it did so its movements slowly began to seem as if they were being controlled by some force outside Andrew's body, like the pointer on a ouija board. He had the curious sensation of his hand detaching from his arm, first the whole hand, at the wrist, and then the fingers, which, as they started to run up and down Allen's back in a scratch, sparked a small moan; this too seemed disembodied, as if it were being issued not from Allen's mouth but from some impossible corner or depth of the room's darkened atmosphere. Allen's back relaxed somewhat, his breathing slowed, and Andrew, with his index finger, scratched out the initials "J.S." My God, what was he doing? For a moment he lifted his hand, then thrust it back, ordering his fingers into a frenzy of randomness, like someone covering up an incriminating word with a mass of scribbling. But Allen didn't seem to notice, and breathed even more slowly. Andrew held his breath. What was possessing him he couldn't name, but cautiously he wrote "Jack" on Allen's back, elongating the letters for the sake of disguise, and Allen sighed and shifted. "Jack Selden," Andrew wrote next. "I love Jack Selden." His heart was racing. What if those messages, like invisible ink, suddenly erupted in full daylight for Allen to read? Well, of course that wouldn't happen, and closing his eyes, Andrew gave himself up to this wild and villainous writing, the messages becoming longer and more incriminating even as Allen moved closer to sleep, letting out, in his stupor, only occasional noises of pleasure and gratitude.

I SEE LONDON, I SEE FRANCE

I

HERE is Celia, not so many years later, sitting on a bench in a park in a village in Chianti, staring at her hands. Beyond the trio of little girls playing jacks, beyond the edge of the park and the crumbling cobbled houses, beyond the *fattorie* and the villas and the half-collapsed town wall, a glorious vista of hills rises, hills Celia can still not quite believe she is sitting in the midst of, hills which belong in the backgrounds of fifteenth-century paintings—dry yet supple, their greenness occasionally broken by rock, just beginning to burn under the late-spring sun. Christ might be kneeling for baptism in those hills, his waist wrapped in a sodden cloth; or the Virgin, in an open stone house, might be poised over her spinning wheel, awaiting the angel's visitation.

Celia is looking at her hands. They are city hands, more used to typing or sealing envelopes than they are to pulling tiny clams from their shells, or picking sprigs of wild thyme from fields at the sides of roads, or raking the uneven landscape of Seth's chest—Seth, the man who has brought her here, the man who, she is tempted to say (though she resists saying it), has saved her from all that. What intrigues her is that her hands *look* the same, the fingers a little puffy, the meat of the palms pale and blotched with red. Only when her hands change, she believes, will she have changed, only then will this new life become something she can believe is going to last. But so far the signs are minimal. Her nails are no longer chewed to the quick; the hairs on her wrists are bleaching from the sun. And her lifeline—so mysterious, Seth had said the first night they spent together, as he opened her palm and traced it—it's broken in the middle. Two distinct halves, and in the center a void, a gap. "They'll have grown together before I'm through with you," he concluded, wrapping her hand back up into a fist, and she'd flinched at the notion that he'd *ever* be through with her, even though she knew it was just a figure of speech. Now she looks carefully and wonders if the two halves really have grown a fraction of an inch closer to one another, or if she's just imagining it.

Across the street from the park sits the rented Fiat Panda that has brought them here; next to it, Seth waits for a farmer in a wobbling *Ape* to pass by on the road. Seth's arms are full of sandwiches and pastries he's bought at a little bar across the street, but before he crosses, he stops to chat with the driver of the *Ape*, a three-wheeled vehicle which is halfway between a truck and a motorcycle. Seth is a translator and interpreter, and since they're on their way to an important literary conference—his first Italian interpreting job in two years—he's talking to everyone he can, determined to oil the rusty wheels of what is, unbelievably, his fifth language.

Celia watches him nod as the farmer, with great, sweeping gesticulations, tells a story. She is thinking that even though it has been only three weeks since they arrived in Italy, the job she quit in New York, the apartment she sublet, seem as mysterious to her now as winter coats happened upon when cleaning a closet in August. And just as for years after graduating from college she dreamed that she'd missed an exam and had to go back to retake it, each night this week the plane that carried her to Rome has pulled up outside of whatever *pensione* they were sleeping in, and the stewardess has come through the door to tell her it's time to go back—back to her black Formica desk on 55th Street, her bumpy-floored apartment on 107th Street, the overstuffed trio of rooms on Kissena Boulevard in Queens where she was raised and where her mother still lives. Sometimes the New York dreams get mixed up with the college dreams—she sits down at the desk on 55th Street and instead of being handed a manuscript by her boss, Ruth Feldschmidt, she's handed a list of exam questions by her Italian Renaissance art professor, Lucy Cumberland, and then the paintings start flashing on the screen, and she has to identify them: artist, title, date, museum. It's a relief to wake up, after that, and see Seth's freckled back, and remember that yesterday she saw those paintings not flashed on a screen, but hanging in the museums the names of which Lucy Cumberland had made her memorize in the first place.

For Celia, Italy has always been a place recognized in the background of paintings. Behind the head of La Gioconda, or Isabella Sforza, or her husband, the Duca di Montefeltro, was a landscape of hills somersaulting down to dry, clay-colored valleys; overviews of cities burnished by the sun; and always, those strange, wonderful Italian trees: mysterious, noble cypresses lined along empty avenues like sentries; umbrella pines, with their green clouds of leaf; olives aligned in perfect orchard geometry. On her first trip to Florence, a college girl trying to make her way on almost no money, she stood in the big stone halls of the Uffizi, staring at those portraits, and hearing even there the din of the hot, crowded piazzas below. How she longed to carry herself through the frame, to enter, like the children in *The Voyage of the "Dawn Treader,"* the world of the picture, the better world behind the glass. But of course she could not.

She looks. Below the park where she sits a slope of yellowing grass rolls toward a tiny village where a waterwheel is turning. And of course, there are those mysterious trees, those very un-American trees. A flash, suddenly, of her childhood—the straight, heat-baked blocks of Kissena Boulevard in Queens, oak and elm and ash. Not a pleasant flash—she pushes it aside. And straining to absorb every detail of the view, swears she can see, when she looks toward Florence, the gargantuan, braided back of a Tuscan lady's head as she poses for her portrait, glorying in the countryside of her domain.

"Celia?" Seth says, and she turns. He has finished his conversation with the man in the *Ape* and is sitting down next to her. "Are you all right?"

"Yes," she says. "Fine."

"Good. I had a funny conversation with that man. He was telling me a story about a knight who fought a battle here in the fourteenth century. And he was speaking real Tuscan dialect, the old kind that no one speaks anymore. It was fascinating." He unwraps sandwiches. "*Bel Paese, prosciutto, salsiccia, tonno*—take your pick." She does so silently, reverently. It is eleven o'clock in the morning, and they are on their way to lunch at the villa of some friends of Seth's from when he lived in Rome, ten years earlier.

"But you can't drive on an empty stomach," Seth says. "And anyway, what's the point of Italy if you don't eat in every town you stop in? Who knows what you might miss?"

It's been only a few months since Celia found Seth, since he swept her off her feet and out of her life. Now, when people ask how they met, they say it was at a party—a lie mutually agreed upon, since both are too embarrassed to admit the truth: that they were introduced into each other's lives through one of those phone lines that randomly connect women and men, men and men—in this case, a number, 970-RMNC, geared especially toward those seeking "romance." Celia is convinced that her description of herself over the phone that evening—not false, exactly, but elusive, embellished—implanted in Seth's mind an image of an object of desire which somehow, miraculously, the truth of her has failed to obliterate. When he looks at her, the urgency in his eyes can only mean that he still sees the fantasy she presented to him on the telephone, not who she really is. She wonders how long this can last.

A mutual love of travel—in Italy especially—was something they started talking about even during that first conversation. Seth had lived in Rome for five years; Celia had gone three times, once for a month in college, twice for two weeks each during her working years—vacations long planned, long saved for, and terribly lonely, spent mostly in museums, or sitting in cafés, always waiting for love to spring out from behind a painting or across a piazza and claim her. It never did. She and Seth had their first date in an Italian restaurant on Bleecker Street—an extraordinary, expensive restaurant, Seth's choice, where they ate imported tiny salad leaves with olive oil and lemon, roasted artichokes, whole garlic cloves baked to the point of sweetness. A week later Celia quit her job; they bought tickets.

Now, only two months since they first happened upon each other over the telephone, they are driving together along a back road near Siena, on their way to the reconstructed *fattoria* of Alexander and Sylvie Foster, and Seth is filling Celia in. "They've had an amazing life," he is saying, as he opens the window to let out his cigarette ash. "Both of them have very famous fathers—Alexander's was Julian Foster, the painter, and Sylvie's was Louis Roth, the conductor. And they've been married since they were sixteen. Sixteen! Can you imagine? They met on the southern coast of France, in Sanary, where their parents both had summer houses. A boy and a girl, just kids, with an enormous amount of wealth between them. They'd grown up in unreal places—Sylvie in East Hampton, Alex on the French coast. And they didn't want to live in the world. So they bought this farm. They bought it twenty years ago, when they were maybe eighteen. And they've lived there ever since, raised their daughters there. When they need money, Alex sells one of his father's paintings and that keeps them going maybe five, six years. And their house! You'll be astonished. It's the closest thing I've seen to paradise."

"How amazing," Celia says. But what she means is, How amazing that other people can have had such extraordinary lives, when my life has been so—what is the word? So *un*extraordinary. And suddenly she envisions these people she has never met, sixteen years old, strolling along a French beach, in love. Whereas she, at sixteen . . . There are tears in her eyes, she is bottomed out with grief, scooped hollow, suddenly so light, so tightly filled with air, that like a balloon, she might lift from the seat of the car, float out the window and over the hills. Travel, she knows, heightens the emotions; tears and laughter and rage come upon her as easily as a blush.

"It's an odd part of Italy around here," Seth says. "People call it 'Chiantishire,' because it's so filled with English and Australians. And they're all very tight with each other, they gossip all the time. For some reason there's particularly a lot of gossip about Sylvie, maybe because her father's so famous. For instance, once I met a Spanish woman who said, 'Oh, Sylvie Foster, Louis Roth's daughter. I heard she had a glass shower built in the middle of her living room and likes to shower in front of her guests.' Such a strange idea, that one! But people imagine all sorts of outrageous things about each other which really say much more about themselves, don't they? And Sylvie *is* brash. She'll probably be checking you out, seeing if you fit her standards, if you're good enough for me. But don't be intimidated."

"I'll try," Celia says, even though Seth's description has made her pale. These are not the sort of people she's used to. (Well, for that matter, most of her life she's been around people she wasn't used to. Her mother used to call her "my scholarship girl" when she was in college, and even though it's been ten years, and most of her student loans have finally been paid off, she still thinks of herself as a scholarship girl—fraudulent, somehow, not quite belonging, brought into the houses of these rich, sophisticated people more as a gesture of charity than a reflection of the value of her company. She has stayed in huge Southampton mansions, eaten dinner at the apartments of famous film stars, and still, each time, she quakes with fear, convinced that this once they'll see through to who she really is.)

Soon they're pulling up to the Fosters' farmhouse. Three cars are parked in front. "The house is called 'Il Mestolo,' " Seth says, getting out and stretching his legs. "That means 'the ladle.' Because of the way the hills slope down to this sort of plateau, and the house and barn and outbuildings are leveled on the plateau, like bits of vegetable and pasta in a soup being ladled into the bowl." He smiles with appreciation. "It's an old name. It predates the Fosters."

"*Carino!*" calls a rugged-looking woman with streaked gray hair, dressed in overalls, who is striding out of the farmhouse. She is clutching one breast rather oddly, and continues clutching it as she and Seth embrace, kiss each other on both cheeks, exchange a torrent of fast Italian which seems to Celia unnecessary, given that they're both Americans. Awkwardly Celia stands, looks at the sky, waits for them to include her, prays Seth will save her before she has to introduce *herself* to the reedy, windblown-looking man, also in overalls, who is now coming out of the kitchen, reaching out a hand.

"I'm Alex Foster," he says.

"Hello," Celia says. "I'm Celia." She doesn't think to mention her last name. And like a man awakened from a trance, Seth jolts, mid-sentence, back into English, and slides out of Sylvie's embrace.

"I'm sorry," he says. "I was so happy to see Sylvie I forgot to introduce Celia." He clears his throat. "So: Alex, Sylvie, this is Celia Hoberman, my fiancée."

It almost makes Celia not want to get married, she likes the sound of "fiancée" so much.

"A pleasure, Celia, a pleasure," says Sylvie, in a clipped British accent with just the slightest Tuscan undertone. "Come in, come in. Ginevra and Fabio and Ginevra's mother have just arrived."

She leads them into a large farmhouse kitchen where wooden rocking chairs circle an enormous stone fireplace. Each of the chairs has a ladle painted on the back. A huge pot of water is boiling on an ornate antique stove with polished brass fixtures, above which hang maybe a dozen bronze and stainless-steel ladles. Two women and a man are sitting in the rocking chairs. The older woman has feathery blond hair and is waving a fan over her face. Although she is scrupulously powdered, her forehead shines in the heat. She is wearing a cream-colored silk blouse and skirt, stockings and pointy-toed alligator shoes. Next to her, the younger woman and the man argue in muted, deep voices. The younger woman is boxy, with short-cropped brown hair, the man handsome and Nordic; both are wearing cotton turtlenecks and blue jeans.

Sylvie, Celia notices, is still clutching her breast in that odd way. She notices Celia staring, laughs, says in a mock-Cockney accent, "I'm such a peasant I've got a chick on me tit!"

"What do you mean, a chick, on your tit?" Seth says.

"Just what I said." And reaching into her blouse, she presents to them a small, yellow-feathered chick, which wobbles on her palm. The old woman by the fireplace fans her face even more furiously.

"The mother abandoned it, left it to die. So I'm keeping it warm. Such a farm woman I've become, after all these years!"

"Let me introduce you," Alex says to Celia. "Ginevra, Fabio, this is Celia."

The younger man and woman, abandoning their argument, stand up. Ginevra says "Ciao," and shakes Celia's hand briskly. Fabio's handshake is like a glove being pulled off. "Scylla?" he says. "Like the monster?"

"No, Celia. Ce-li-a."

"Ah, Celia! *Certo.*" He pronounces it "Chaylia."

"And this is Signora Dorati, Ginevra's mother," Alex says.

The older lady stands and reaches out a hand gloved in lace and jewels.

"Ciao," Celia says.

Signora Dorati looks alarmed at this overly familiar greeting, and withdraws her hand. "*Piacere,*" she murmurs, her voice faint, and returns to her chair.

"And where are the girls?" Seth asks, breaking the silence of Celia's mortification. "I must say hello to them!"

"Out at the pool, swimming," Sylvie calls, her head buried in a high cabinet from which she is pulling boxes of pasta. "You know Francesca leaves for school in England in a month. Can you believe it? She's almost sixteen."

"Where's she going?"

"Cheltenham, of course," says Alex.

"Francesca! Sixteen! It's hard to imagine!"

"And Adriana's almost thirteen, and looks twenty," Sylvie says. "Boys come around all the time asking for her."

"It's hard for her," says Alex. "Francesca can't wait to grow up, but Adriana clings to childhood. The last thing she wants to be is the woman her body makes her resemble. She'd like to stay a child forever." He looks wistful, as if he sympathizes with that desire.

"I must see them," Seth says now. "Come on, Celia." And grabbing her hand, he leads her out the back kitchen door, past an arbor covered with grapevines, a table set for lunch, the barn where Alex makes his sculptures, a chicken coop, an herb garden. Around a hedgerowed bend, the swimming pool sits on a ledge, littered with floating toys, the ladleful of soup itself.

A girl is swimming in the pool, her red hair floating out around her head. Another girl, slightly older and also red-haired, stands over her on a diving board, positioning herself for the dive.

"Adriana! Francesca!" Seth calls.

"Seth? Seth, is that you?" the older girl says. And abandoning her dive, she runs across the grass, catching Seth in an embrace from which he lifts her, effortlessly, into the air.

"My God, you've grown up!" he says.

"You look the same," Francesca says, laughing.

"Seth!" calls Adriana, hoisting herself from the pool and running up to join her sister. She pulls on Seth's hand, dances around him in a frenzy of appreciation. Sylvie was right: she does look twenty. She is tall, with olive-colored skin, a flat waist, large pretty breasts. The sort of body Celia's always envied. A woman's body. Yet there is an old doll lying on the grass, and the bathing suit Adriana wears—much too small and patterned with bears—is clearly that of a child.

"Adriana, Francesca, this is Celia," Seth says. "My fiancée."

"Hello," they say, and shake her hand, but it's only out of politeness. Celia is invisible to them. She listens, fascinated, as they barrage Seth with information about their lives—the dress Francesca wants to buy to take to England, but her mother won't let her, the

Nintendo video game their uncle Martin sent Adriana for her birthday from the States, the Bon Jovi concert next week in Florence. "You must play Nintendo with me!" Adriana cries. "You will, won't you? Promise?"

"Promise."

"And you'll convince Mummy to let me go to the concert?" asks Francesca.

"Of course."

What odd accents they have! Part British, part Italian. But unlike Sylvie's accent, not acquired, not chosen—no, this is the voice of being raised at once in two worlds, the voice of placelessness.

"You must swim with us, Seth!" Francesca says.

"Yes, you must!"

"But I don't have my bathing suit!"

"Then swim in your underwear!"

"Well—" He looks pleadingly at Celia.

"Go ahead," she says. "I'll play lifeguard."

"All right, then. Why not?"

Instantly the girls are tearing at his clothes, one pulling a shoe off, the other unbuttoning his shirt, until he's down to his underpants, at which point, of course, lunging and grasping, they drag him into the water with them. Celia steps back from the splash, watches, still as a statue, a thin smile frozen on her mouth, filled with—what can she call it? Well, it's obvious. Grief.

What is here—what the people here have—is beauty. Whereas what she has—what she's always had, what is irrefutably hers in the world—is nothing anyone would ever call beautiful. Books: *Nancy Drew and the Mystery of the Ivory Charm.* Good Humor ice cream bars. Dry sidewalks, the gridded streets and avenues, playing jacks when it was cool enough at sunset.

Suddenly she feels a cold, wet tentacle grasp her ankle. She jumps back, nearly screams. But it's only Seth, reaching his arm from the swimming pool.

"Let me guess what you're thinking," Seth says.

"All right."

"You're thinking that this is the most beautiful place in the world. So beautiful it makes you sad, it breaks your heart, because you can never have it. But you can have it. I'll give it to you, Celia."

She turns away from him, toward the view of the walled city. "Only . . . It's not that I want to live here *now,* it's that I want to *have* lived here. To have grown up here. Or rather, to be the sort of person who grew up in this sort of place with that sort of parents, and feel the things that sort of person could feel which a different sort of person—the sort of person I am, for instance—could never feel. And not feel the sort of things the sort of person I am has to feel—does this make sense?"

"You don't have to be trapped anymore," Seth says. "I've saved you from feeling trapped. I've taken you away from your dreary apartment and your dreary job. Look where we are now and be happy. You don't have to go back."

It seems important to Seth that Celia understand that he has saved her, and for a moment she wonders how much this "saving" really was for her benefit, and how much for his, and if it really matters.

"Well, of course," she says finally, laughing, and mostly to please him. "It's just that I can't quite believe it."

"Believe it," Seth says. And letting go of her leg he returns, splashing, to pool games.

II

Celia grew up in a few rooms on the fourth floor of a brick apartment building fringed with fire escapes. One of hundreds, thousands of identical buildings all over Queens, yet she never got lost, never mistook one for another, never had any trouble distinguishing where her friends lived. You noticed the differences when you actually *lived* among so much sameness: Her building, for instance, had the drugstore across the street. And another building, where her friend Janet Cohen lived, was covered with climbing vines. And Great-aunt Leonie's building had the lady who filled her balcony each year with expensive lawn furniture, and could be seen sunning herself in harlequin-shaped sunglasses and a white one-piece bathing suit as late as November and as early as March.

Across the street, on the stoop next to the drugstore, Hasidic boys traded "Torah Personalities" the way most boys trade baseball cards. "I'll give you a Rev Mordechai Hager for a Yehuda Zev Segal!" "You've really got Menachem Mendel Taub?" There was at dusk the thwack of the jump rope against the sidewalk, the elaborate reverberating chants of double-dutch.

> *"I see London, I see France,*
> *I see Celia's underpants!"*

Street games: Capture the Flag, Spud.

> *"Eeny meeny miny mo,*
> *Catch a tiger by the toe,*
> *If he hollers let him go,*
> *My mother says that you are not It."*

The Good Humor man, twice a day, ringing his bell. Chip Candy. Red, White and Blue. Nutty Buddy.

Upstairs lived Celia's mother, Rose, and her grandmother, Lena. There was no father; he had died before Celia ever had a chance to meet him, in a bus accident. Celia had rich uncles and aunts: in Westchester, in Great Neck, one in California. On holidays she'd visit them, watch her cousins as they played effortlessly in great pools, sleep in pull-out trundle beds in rooms that were impossibly big, impossibly good-smelling and filled with toys. Then she and Rose and Lena would head back to Queens, to the stuffy apartment house in the old neighborhood where the three of them had been left behind, presumably because her father, who was expected to get rich, died instead.

What they did, Celia's mother and grandmother, was watch television. Especially when Celia was a teenager and in college, when her mother had gotten so fat it was hard for her to move outside the apartment, and her grandmother was more or less bedridden. In that overheated, shag-carpeted room with its plastic-covered flowery sofas, and shelves full of tchotchkes, and old dinner dishes piled on breakfast trays, they'd eat Pepperidge Farm cookies and fight over the remote control. Rose got up from her armchair now and then to do a little dusting or clean a plate. Lena stayed mostly in bed. All over the room were elephants: glass elephants, china elephants, stuffed elephants. They were what Rose collected, what everyone gave her. Every birthday, every Mother's Day, another elephant. The TV, in Celia's memory, never goes off. It is on at dawn when she gets out of bed and goes into the kitchen for milk (later coffee): morning talk shows, exercise shows her mother observes with detached bemusement while eating crullers. It is on at midday when she comes home for lunch: soap operas. It is on all night: the evening news, and then situation comedies and cop shows, and more news. Celia usually fell asleep to the sound of *Honeymooners* reruns, old episodes of *The Twilight Zone* she knew by heart.

The soap operas, however, were most important, in particular *The Light of Day,* which was Lena's favorite. It seemed to make her genuinely suffer, this show; if on Friday the heroine was left dangling from a small plane while a villain crushed her fingers with his shoes, there would be no living with Lena that weekend. What had drawn them to the show in the first place was a story line that occurred in the mid-seventies, concerning a sweet girl nun who found herself torn between her faith and the pleas of a handsome, severely smitten Jewish boy determined to woo her away from the convent. Anxiety bled with a little bit of love was the formula of this soap opera. If love for the nun started Rose and Lena watching, anxiety for her fate compelled them to keep watching—especially after the nun went off to a war-torn Central American country to do good works, and wound up being kidnapped by guerrillas. The cycle was eternal, and designed to addict: an adored heroine had to be in trouble if you were going to care about her at all. Soon Lena and Rose became experts, they predicted things long before they happened: too much happiness meant something terrible, a psychopath, a car accident. Vague tiredness boded terminal illness or unwanted pregnancy.

For years, day after day, *The Light of Day* evolved. Hairdos changed, as did clothes. Occasionally new actors would replace old ones, the transformation explained by a quick car accident and facial reconstruction. The show seemed never to have begun (though Celia knew it had, once, before her birth). Apparently it would never end. And there was no assurance that the characters' suffering would end, either. Whereas in a movie you could pretty much assume a hostage taken at the beginning was a hostage saved at the end, here torture, detainment, misunderstanding might drag on for months.

The year Celia was applying to colleges, Lena became preoccupied with the fate of a couple on the show, a girl named Brandy and a boy named Brad. They were in love, but a series of miscommunications mostly engineered by an evil older woman named Mallory had led each to believe the other was cheating. Finally Brandy called Brad and left a message on his answering machine: "If I hear from you tonight, I'll know you love me; otherwise, I'll assume you don't." Then Mallory stole the tape. Brandy assumed Brad didn't love her, but of course, Brad had never heard the message. Mallory continued to stir up trouble until finally Brad, despairing, sure that Brandy didn't love him, allowed himself to be seduced by and then to become engaged to Mallory. Brandy, in the meantime, kept almost finding the incriminating tape, which Mallory had saved and hidden inside a jade statue in the museum where Brandy worked. This jade statue seemed to have mysterious powers. Then Mallory started putting drugs in Brandy's coffee, slowly addicting her, making it look like she was going mad.

All through this Lena roiled in bed, shuffling and moaning: "Oy, oy!" She said it was killing her; she said it was giving her an ulcer. "If I have to die soon," Lena said, "let me at least die knowing that Brandy and Brad got back together." So Rose wrote a letter to the show, and showed it to Celia first, to make sure the grammar was perfect.

Dear Sirs and Mesdames [it read]:

For many years my mother, Mrs. Lena Lieberman, aged eighty-nine, and myself have been loyal viewers of your show, *The Light of Day.* We have seen the characters through thick and thin, good and bad. Lately, however, my mother has been very disturbed by the extended troubles being suffered by Brandy and Brad. Surely seven and a half months is long enough for such a sweet and loving pair of young people to have to endure the evil doings of Mallory, not to mention painful and unnecessary separation! Life is short, as we all know. I myself lost my husband in 1959, and watching the travails suffered by Brandy and Brad, I can only think what a shame it is that they are wasting their youthful years apart when very likely anything can and will happen to them in the near future. Youth is golden, and should be enjoyed. If you don't mind my quoting the name of a rival (and in my opinion much inferior) program, each of us has only one life to live.

Sirs and mesdames, let me come to my point. My mother is an old woman not long for this world. She is sick, and her anxiety for Brandy and Brad is making her sicker. I doubt I am exaggerating when I say it could be the straw that breaks the camel's back. A life is at stake here, and that is why I am writing to ask you, with all speed, to bring Brad and Brandy back together, marry them to each other, punish the wicked Mallory. Only knowing they are reunited in matrimony will my elderly mother breathe easy, and die peacefully.

Yours sincerely,
Rose (Mrs. Leonard) Hoberman

Celia didn't think much about the letter except to wonder whether her mother really was as far gone as she sounded, or whether this was some joke going on between Rose and herself. She was busy with her college applications, and filling out scholarship forms, and entering competitions (the Optimists' Club Speech Competition, theme: Together we will . . . ; the Ladies' Auxiliary of B'nai B'rith; Young Women of Merit Awards), doing everything she could to scrounge up all the money she'd need for school. When she got the letter informing her of her acceptance, she couldn't wait for the elevator; instead she raced up the stairs, shouting, "Ma! Ma!" But her mother didn't hear her. She had a letter of her own. "Celia!" she said breathlessly as Celia ran into the living room. "Listen, listen! It's from the show!"

"Ma, I've got great news!"

"Listen to this letter, you won't believe it!"

Dear Mrs. Hoberman:

I received your letter, and was sure to share it with our writers and cast, all of whom join me in wishing your mother a speedy recovery. While it is our policy never to reveal what's going to happen on *The Light of Day* in advance—even the actors only see the scripts a few days before shooting—I believe I can assure you that all is going to work out for Brandy and Brad, and that Mallory will receive her comeuppance.

In conclusion, let me say that viewers such as you and your mother mean everything to us here at *The Light of Day*; we hope you'll accept the enclosed autographed photo of Mark Metzger (Brad Hollister) and Alexandra Fisher (Brandy Teague) as a token of that appreciation.

Very sincerely yours,
Donna Ann Finkle
Public Relations Associate

"It's amazing," Rose cried. "They listened to us! They answered!" And Celia, all at once, fell silent in her rapture, for she understood, as if for the first time, how rarely her mother had been listened to, and how even more rarely answered.

"Now, I'm sorry, honey, sit down and tell me your news." But Celia was quiet.

"Celia. I'm waiting."

Celia sat next to her mother on the sofa, indifferent to the crunch of plastic underneath her. For a year now she'd anticipated the moment she'd receive this letter, she'd imagined herself tearing open the envelope, reading the words "We are happy to inform you," then throwing her arms up to the sky, because they signaled the end of one life—a life of stuffy entrapment, washed-out colors, dirty air—and the beginning of another, a glamorous life, a glorious life, a life of books and green grass and ivy-covered walkways. But now, sitting with her mother while Rose clutched her own letter, Celia saw that it wouldn't matter; she saw that though she might walk through those halls, she'd do so as a ghost, a guest, a stranger, the same way she walked the commodious halls of her Westchester and Long Island relatives. How could college make a difference when her mother was still here, trapped in where and who she was? No matter what, Celia knew, she too would always end up back in this apartment, on this sofa. Never listened to. Never answered.

"I got in," she said hopelessly. Her mother turned. "You did what?"

"I got in."

Then Rose screamed in a way that reminded Celia of the noises Great-aunt Leonie's parrot made. "You got in! She got in!" And jumping to her feet, Rose called toward the bedroom: "She got in! Mama, Celia got in!" She opened the window, leaned out, screamed so all the neighbors could hear, and the Hasidic boys across the street: "My Celia, Celia Hoberman, is a scholarship girl! She got in!"

Three months later, in August, Brandy married Brad. Mallory, exposed and humiliated, left town, swearing she'd be back to get even. Rose took Celia up to New Haven. Everything according to clockwork, except for Lena, who didn't die until two years later, and by then Brad was an alcoholic failure, and Brandy a famous TV talk-show host, played by a different actress and carrying the child of a mysterious stranger named Señor Reyes.

Celia came down from New Haven when her grandmother died, even though it was the middle of exam week. Her Westchester aunts and uncles were sitting in the living room, looking uncomfortable and crowded. Rose was serving them cups of tea. Without even saying hello, Rose instructed Celia to bring a plate of cookies in from the kitchen. Celia took off her coat and got the cookies. "You remember these cookies, Belle?" Rose was saying to her sister. "Seidman's Bake Shop? It's still around. The neighborhood hasn't changed that much, in the end."

"They're delish, honey," Belle said.

"You know, Celia's in the middle of exams at Yale. Tell Aunt Sadie your major, honey."

"Art history."

"Not too many career options there!" Uncle Louis said.

"My Marc's majoring in economics *and* political science at Brown," Aunt Belle said. "He's planning on law school."

"Now that's a sensible major."

"Bring some more tea, Celia. The funeral's in half an hour."

Celia went back into the kitchen. Her mother followed her, closed the door and dropped herself onto a chair, looking defeated and collapsed.

"I feel so ashamed," she said. "I feel like such a failure."

"Don't feel that way, Mama," said Celia.

"I do. They pity me."

Suddenly Rose fell to the floor, weeping. "Mama," she cried, clutching Celia's knees. "Mama."

"Mama, no," Celia said. "I'm Celia."

"Mama, come back," Rose called into Celia's scabby knees. "Come back, Mama. Mama."

III

Lunch is still ten minutes off when Celia and Seth get back from the pool, so Alex takes them on a tour of Il Mestolo. "It was a wreck when we bought it," he explains as he leads them down stony corridors to the room where Sylvie has set up her spinning wheel. "Then slowly, over the years, we worked on it, picking up furniture here and there at estate sales. It wasn't until Francesca was born that we put in electricity and got a phone."

There is a huge bathroom, the size of a bedroom, with a toilet built into a marble bench, and a tub on claws, big enough to hold a family. Much of the furniture Alex made himself, in his shop in the barn—fanciful sofas and beds with elaborate animal carvings in the moldings, down-stuffed cushions wrapped in brightly colored cotton fabric. But it is the girls' rooms that take Celia's breath away. In each is a handcarved sleigh bed of dark cherry, above which Alex has painted a mural. The background of the mural in Adriana's room is sky blue, the letters of her name, spread out against it, festooned with birds—every imaginable bird, each species distinct and colorful and exact. "Francesca," by contrast, floats in an undersea green, surrounded by fish. "Like the Grotto of the Animals," Alex says, as Celia stares admiringly. "Outside Florence, in a place called Castello. A little leftover of the Mannerist period. You go into this grotto, and what you see is a stone-carved catalogue of the birds of the air, the beasts of the land, the fish of the sea. This is my slightly less ambitious version."

There are differences between the rooms. Whereas Adriana's is neat and filled with toys—as many handmade by Alex, Celia notices, as bought at town shops—Francesca's is a mess, the covers thrown off the bed, underwear tangled on the floor, Bon Jovi and Guns 'n Roses posters thumbtacked into the great sea wall. The posters make Celia flinch with pain—a defacement—but Alex is blasé. "The worst thing in the world," he says, "is to tell children how to lead their lives. Their rooms belong to them. The murals are my gift, to make of what they wish. I've always thought it a mistake to expect appreciation from your children. You'll never get it that way."

From the kitchen, Sylvie calls out, "Al-ex! Lunch!" so they head outside to the table under the grape arbor. Seth has told Celia that at formal Italian meals, the eldest guest is always seated at the host's right, so she is surprised when Sylvie—who clearly knows better—seats Signora Dorati at Alex's left. The old woman once again flutters her fan frantically, her face tight with distress. Celia is seated between Ginevra and Fabio. Ginevra, she knows from Seth, is a famous poet, although not a very productive one: two slim white volumes over twenty years, published by the best literary house.

While Alex fills glasses with wine, Adriana and Francesca, freshly dressed, their hair still wet from the pool, emerge from the kitchen, bearing huge, steaming bowls of pasta. Ah, pasta! Celia has always loved it, and now, as she spoons *penne* into a bowl handpainted by Alex with purple garlic bulbs, she sees that Sylvie is an expert. The tubed *maccheroni* are luminous with bits of sausage, basil, tomato, glints of yellow garlic. What a far cry from the spaghetti and meatballs of her childhood, the overcooked, mushy noodles swimming in a bright red bath of watery, sweet tomato sauce, the whole plate periodically dented by boulders of ground beef and bread crumbs! Her mother used to sing a song as she cooked it, to the tune of "On Top of Old Smoky," her voice loud in the cramped, steamy kitchen:

> *On top of spaghetti, all covered with cheese,*
> *I lost my poor meatball, when somebody sneezed.*
> *It rolled off the table, and onto the floor*
> *And then my poor meatball rolled out of the door . . .*

Celia puts down her fork. Oh, her poor foolish, sad mother! She is overwhelmed, suddenly, by the poverty of her childhood, by all she didn't know, all she didn't even know to ask. Here, of all places, in Chiantishire, sitting at this perfect table with these beautiful people under a grape arbor on a gloriously sunny spring day, she is haunted.

"The weather will be bad tomorrow," Ginevra says. "I can feel it."

"How?" asks Seth. "Today is beautiful."

"Today beautiful, tomorrow hot, humid, uncomfortable. My mood always tells me. I'm getting depressed."

"Ginevra can recognize the bad weather coming," Fabio says. "And she's right much more than the newspaper."

"Well, I'm not going to haul in the garden furniture yet!" Sylvie says, still stroking the small bulge in her breast. "Anyway, Ginevra, why should we listen to you? You've been in a bad mood since you lost your manuscript. I don't trust your senses so much."

This last remark is greeted by a tense silence. Ginevra puts down her fork and rubs her forehead.

"Really, Sylvie," Alex says.

"Well, it's not like a death," says Sylvie, her back tensing defensively. "I'm tired of avoiding the subject."

"I just don't think one should refer to tragedies . . . quite so casually—"

"No, Alex, never mind," Ginevra says. "It's all right. I don't know if Seth told you, but I'm sometimes a poet. Sometimes, because I don't write very often—I have great blocks. And last year I was working on a poem, a long poem, which I loved like a person. I loved it so much I carried it with me everywhere. And I lost it. So for a year I've been in grief, and everyone is silent about my poem as if it were my lover who is gone."

Again, a tense silence stretches out. "That must have been terrible," Celia says at last.

"Terrible, yes," Ginevra says. "I suppose. Yes."

"Ginevra is a wonderful cook," Seth says now, brightly, to change the subject. "You know, Ginevra, Celia's very interested in Italian food. Maybe you could give her lessons."

Ginevra looks at Celia and smiles. "Are you ready to be an

obedient pupil?" she says. "Because the Italian kitchen, it is only about obedience. Obedience to the old ways."

"Ginevra is a perfectionist," Fabio says. "Last week in Rome, she made a duck. And she drove miles and miles to a little village in Lazio to buy the duck, because it had to be just so. And then she spent an hour picking through the vegetables at Campo dei Fiori because they had to be just so. And then she spent three hundred fifty thousand lire for caviar and *tartufi* even though she cannot pay her house. And then—"

"*Basta,* Fabio, *basta*—" Ginevra covers her mouth, laughing.

"No," Sylvie says. "Not *basta.* Go on."

"And then she made the duck, and we ate, and it was the most delicious duck we ever taste, and we tell her, 'Ginevra, it is marvelous,' but she takes one taste and says, 'No, no, it's awful, throw it away, throw it away,' and starts taking our plates from us. She is mad!"

Ginevra is still laughing. "I told you, the fourth taste wasn't right!"

"The fourth taste?" Seth asks.

"There were supposed to be five tastes, and the fourth—"

"*Che cosa?*" asks Signora Dorati, bewildered, and Alex offers her a quick summation in Italian, at the end of which she laughs halfheartedly. She has not touched her pasta. He pours more wine for himself and her.

A barrage of heavy-metal music stuns the atmosphere; apparently Francesca has put on one of her Bon Jovi records.

Sylvie puts down her glass, closes her eyes and rubs her temples. Francesca, nonchalant and challenging, comes out of the kitchen, picks up some empty bowls, goes back in.

"Alex," Sylvie says, "can't you do something?"

"Do what? You do something for once."

"You're useless," Sylvie says. Then she turns and shouts, "Will you please shut that dreadful noise down?"

"All right, all right!"

The music is turned off, not down, the needle pulled from the record with a violent scratch meant to be heard.

There is a quiet which feels dangerous, like the moment after the screams of someone dying have finally stopped.

"So, Celia," Sylvie says, with a smile that seems to cost, "tell us about yourself. Where did you grow up?"

"New York."

"Really! Me too. Though mostly in East Hampton. Did you ever go to East Hampton?"

"Not until I was grown up."

"And where did you go to school?"

"Bronx Science."

"I was at Spence. I dated a boy from Bronx Science once. Gerald Ashenauer. Did you know him?"

"No, I didn't."

"Well, of course not, you're probably just decades younger than me, aren't you?"

"Not *decades.*"

"And what kind of work do you do?"

"For God's sake, Sylvie, don't interrogate the poor girl," Alex says, pouring more wine. "After all, she's only come to lunch."

"I don't mind answering," Celia says. "Only it's not very glamorous. I was a proofreader and copy editor."

"Any kind of work sounds glamorous to me," Alex says, "never having done any myself."

"Why do you say 'was'?" Sylvie asks.

"Celia's quit her job," Seth says. "We're not going back. We're going to stay here in Italy."

"Oh, jolly good for you!" Alex says, lifting his wineglass. "Wonderful. A new wave of expatriation, that's what we need over here. A shot in the arm, since all the British around here are so bloody boring."

Francesca and Adriana come out from the kitchen again.

"We've washed the bowls, Mummy," Adriana says.

"Thank you, sweetie."

"Mummy," Francesca says, "can't I please go to the Bon Jovi concert next week?"

Sylvie's hand once again cradles her breast. "We'll talk about it another time, Francesca."

"But Seth says it's all right, he says nothing will happen and he likes Bon Jovi, don't you, Seth?"

"Uh—yes," Seth says. "Absolutely."

No one laughs.

"Please, Mummy."

"Just say yes," Alex says.

"I said we'd talk about it later," Sylvie says.

"Oh, I'm so sick of you!" Then Francesca picks up an empty bowl from the table and smashes it against the bricks, where it shatters loudly: her father's beautiful, hand-painted bowl.

Signora Dorati gives the only audible gasp.

Sylvie is standing in an instant. "Get in the house," she says, but though Adriana runs indoors, Francesca doesn't move. "You're fakes, you and Daddy," she says, "you haven't worked a day in your lives, you just sit out here on your asses. I'd rather be dead than grow up like you." Then her eyes bulge, and she brings her hand tentatively to her teeth, as if to stuff the words back in.

"Mummy, I—"

"Get in the house," Sylvie says again, with dental precision, her voice dangerous. Francesca turns, and is gone.

"Excuse us just a moment," Sylvie says. "Just your run-of-the-mill family catastrophe."

She follows her daughter into the house. Signora Dorati, fluttering her fan, whispers something furiously to Ginevra, who whispers something back. Signora Dorati wipes her brow with a handkerchief.

"I think," Alex says, "that a toast is in order, don't you, Seth?"

"Ah, sure," says Seth. "What shall we toast? Mothers and daughters?"

"I was thinking, not working a day in one's life. Sitting on one's bum." He is pouring himself yet another glass of wine.

"Here's to bum-sitting, then," Seth says.

"Cin-cin," Ginevra says. The glasses clang.

The chick on Sylvie's tit, in spite of her best efforts, has died. With a sort of sentimentalist's imitation of peasant hardness—her face stoic, her lower lip not quivering one bit—she buries the small, feathered corpse in the garden. Francesca and Adriana, their eyes red but dry, watch her, don't say a word. Then the three of them disappear into the kitchen together, the girls clinging to their mother's arms, tied to her by some blood bond not even broken pottery can threaten, and from which Celia is naturally, painfully excluded.

On the patio, Seth practices his Italian on a bored-looking Signora Dorati. "*Che meraviglia,*" she responds tiredly to everything he says. "*Che bravo. Che stupendo.*" Ginevra and Fabio play a foolish game of Ping-Pong at a green table. Once the ball goes rolling under Signora Dorati's chair, but she has apparently been so defeated by the events of the afternoon that she hardly notices when her daughter reaches under her legs to get it.

Then Alex—drunk, but pleasantly so—invites Celia for a tour of his studio, and together the two of them head off down the hill toward the old barn. "Now you'll get to see my 'work,' " he says, making little quotation marks around the word with his fingers.

"I can't wait," Celia says, as he pulls open the wide, scarred doors. Inside the barn the air is dark and moist, and all around them are animals—willowy, spindly, brass tigers and antelopes, gazelles, stone cats, their eyes painted black.

"So you see," he says, "I have my own grotto of the animals."

Looking at all these animals, the first thing Celia thinks of is her mother's shelves and shelves of elephants.

"They're fantastic," she says.

"My daughter's right," Alex says. "There's no reason for Francesca to take me and Sylvie seriously, to listen to us. We're anachronisms. Useless, really. Look at what I do all day! A toy man!" He laughs. "When they were young, that was fabulous, there was nothing better a father could be than a toyman. But now—well, you only have to look at what happened. I don't understand these young people. They're so—practical. They have no romance in them. Francesca, especially. She says her ambition is either to be a rock star or go to work on the stock exchange and make her first million pounds by the time she's thirty. Sixteen years old, and talking like that. Whereas when I was sixteen—well, a lot has changed."

Celia cautiously strokes the neck of a ceramic giraffe painted with blue spots.

"Do you sell them?" she asks.

"Now and then, through friends. I don't have much of a mind for business. Once Sylvie and I went to New York to talk to some gallery people, people who'd known my father—very intimidating, those people were, not encouraging and not very kind. We fled back here as fast as we could. We really aren't made for the world, you see. Francesca is. She'll go to England, get a job, be a Sloane Ranger in London, just like she says. And maybe on the way she'll join a punk band, she'll live in a tenement in Brixton. The world. Adriana's more like us. I'm not so sure about Adriana."

He has led Celia over to the working space of his studio. Here the animals are smaller—the size of hands and fingers. She notices a brass elephant, like many of the other animals, so spindly she's afraid it will break in half when she picks it up. But it doesn't.

"My mother collects elephants," she says.

"Then why don't you give her this one?"

"What?" Celia puts the elephant down. "No, no, I didn't mean that, really. Oh, you probably think I mentioned my mother just because I hoped you'd offer, when really—"

"Just give it to her," Alex says, pressing the elephant into her palm. "After all, there's nothing else for me to do with them. If you don't take it, it'll just sit here getting dusty."

Celia is flustered from too much speech. "Well, then, all right. Thank you." She looks again at the tiny elephant.

"We were beastly this afternoon," Alex is saying. "I hope you'll forgive us. My family has a tendency to behave rather animalistically, to just express ourselves all over the place, and sometimes that can be a bit of a strain for visitors. Signora Dorati, for instance. Somehow I don't suspect we're going to be receiving an invitation to lunch at *her* villa anytime soon." He laughs halfheartedly. "Supposed to be quite a splendid villa, too. I would've liked to have seen it."

"Well, *I* didn't mind," Celia says. "It made me feel like one of the family."

"You're kind," Alex says.

The tiny elephant in Celia's palm looks up at her, its face inscrutable but knowing, as if it has a secret to tell but no mouth.

"You can't imagine how much my mother will appreciate this," Celia says. "Why, she'll probably clear a whole shelf for it, a special shelf, and when her friends come in, Mrs. Segal or Mrs. Greenhut or the ladies from the block association, she'll gather them round and say, 'Now look at this, Elaine, this elephant was made by a real artist in Italy. My daughter Celia got it for me. Isn't it gorgeous?' 'Oh, gorgeous!' 'Now don't touch, it's fragile!' "

Alex laughs mildly. "I wish everyone I gave a sculpture to was so enthusiastic," he says. "Most often they just sort of shrug. If I'm visiting the person, and I'm lucky, it'll turn up in the bathroom, and I'll look under the sink and see the bowl of flowers it's been brought out to replace for the afternoon."

"Oh, I doubt that," Celia says.

But Alex once again doesn't seem to have heard her. And once again, this strange afternoon, it seems to Celia as if a piece of fragile thread, spun like spider's web, has been cast out across the ocean, from this ancient Tuscan barn to her mother's apartment in Queens, pulling these two disparate places into a nearness so intimate she feels as if she could reach across the darkness and brush Rose's arm. She has known for some time now that Seth cannot save her, at least the way he says he wants to, that he can never "take her away from all that"; no one can ever take anyone else away from all that. There are always those threads, billions of them, crisscrossing and crossing again, wrapping the world in their soft, suffocating gauze.

The futility, the falseness of her romance with Seth—each of them playacting for the other the role of something long sought, long needed—she sees clearly now, but at a remove: the sort of truth you can gaze at for years; ponder; affirm; ignore.

Yes, she sees it all now; sees that she will stay in Italy, no matter how ardently her better judgment tells her not to; sees that, to the extent that it's possible, she'll become a different person from the person she used to be. And then one day she'll be walking down the cobbled street of her own Tuscan village, thinking about something properly Italian—olive trees, maybe, or art—when suddenly that mysterious thread will start to tighten, and Queens and Tuscany will be pulled to somewhere in the middle of the ocean, and briefly, magically merged. She'll turn and see, sitting on a bench in her own piazza near where the old men smoke cigars and play dominos, two Hasidic boys trading rabbi cards. And two little girls playing jump rope. And hearing the thwack of the jump rope against the pavement, she'll feel her feet start to dance, and want to jump herself, jump until the rope slipping under her is no longer anything real, is just a blur of speed. "I see London, I see France . . ." (But of course they didn't see any of those places, didn't even imagine they'd ever see any of those places.) Who, after all, is speaking? And in what language? And how can those boys be here, and her mother's voice calling to her down this ancient cobbled street? "Celia, come home, dinner's ready! It's spaghetti and meatballs! Your favorite!"

CHIPS IS HERE

HERE is why I decided to kill my neighbor:

On a rainy morning in midsummer, after several failed efforts, my cat finally managed to scale the fence that separated my yard from Willoughby Wayne's. The cat landed on all four feet in the narrow space behind a privet hedge. At first he sat there for a moment, licking his paws and acquainting himself with his new situation. Then, quite cautiously, he began making his way through the brushy underside of the hedge toward Willoughby's lawn. Unfortunately for him, the five Kerry blue terriers with whom Willoughby lives were aware of the cat's presence well before he actually stepped out onto the grass, and like a posse, they were there to greet him. The cat reared, hissed and batted a paw in the face of the largest of the Kerry blues, who in turn swiftly and noisily descended with the efficient engine of his teeth. "Johnny! Johnny!" I heard Willoughby call. "Bad dog, Johnny! Bad dog!" There was some barking, then things got quiet again.

A few hours later, after I'd searched the house and checked most of the cat's outdoor hiding places, I called Willoughby. "Oh, a young cat?" he said. "Orange and white? Yes, he was here. Needless to say I did my best to introduce him to my pack, but inexperience has resulted in their maintaining a very puppylike attitude toward cats; the introductions—shall we say—did not go well. I interceded delicately, breaking up the mêlée, then, for his own good, lifted the feline fellow over the fence and deposited him in the field adjacent to my property. I believe he was quite frightened by Johnny, and suspect he's probably hiding in the field even as we speak."

I thanked Willoughby, hung up and headed out into the field that adjoins both our yards. It was a fairly wild field, unkempt, thick with waist-high weeds and snarls of roots in which my dog, accompanying me, kept getting trapped. I'd be thrashing along, breaking the weeds down with a stick and calling, "Kitty! Here, kitty!" when suddenly the dog would start barking, and turning around I'd see her tangled in an outrageous position, immobilized by the vines in much the same way she often became immobilized by her own leash. Each time I'd free her, and we'd continue combing the field, but the cat apparently chose not to answer my repeated calls. I went back three times that afternoon, and twice that night. In the morning I canvassed the neighbors, without success, before returning to comb the field a sixth time. "Still looking for your young feline?" Willoughby called to me over the fence. He was clipping his privet hedge. "I'm really terribly sorry. If I'd had any idea he was *your* cat I most certainly would have hand-delivered him to you on the spot."

"Yes, well," I said.

"For whatever it's worth, it was right here, right here where I'm standing, that I lifted him over."

"Well, I've been meaning to ask you. He *was* all right when you handed him over, wasn't he? He wasn't hurt."

"Oh, he was perfectly fine," Willoughby said. "Why, I would never put an injured cat over a fence, never."

"No, I'm sure he's just hiding somewhere. I'll let you know when I find him."

"Do," Willoughby said, and returned to his clipping. The thwack of the clippers as they came down on the hedge followed me through the field and out of the field.

* * *

I'm not sure what it was, but the next day something compelled me to search Willoughby's yard. I waited until he wasn't home, then, like my cat before me, crept stealthily through a side gate. From their outdoor pen the Kerry blues growled at me. I circled the lawn, until I was standing at the place where Willoughby was standing when he claimed to have put the cat over the fence. On the other side of the fence a thorny bush blocked my view of the field, and just to the left of it lay my cat, quite dead. I didn't make a sound. I went around the other way, into the field, and dug behind the bush, in the process cutting myself quite severely on the brambles. There was a gash running from the cat's chest to near his tail.

I picked up the carcass of my cat. His orange-and-white markings were still the same, but he was now just that—a carcass. I went to the house and got a garbage bag and shovel, and then I buried my cat in the overgrown field.

On the way home, climbing over my own fence, I decided to kill my neighbor.

At home I took a shower. The soap eased me. I considered methods. I felt no urge to confront Willoughby, to argue with him, to back him up against a wall and force him to confess his lie. I did not want to watch him writhe, or try to wriggle away from the forceful truth inhabiting my gaze. I simply wanted to kill him—cleanly, painlessly, with a minimum of fuss and absolutely no discussion. It was not a question of vengeance; it was a question of extermination.

Of course a shotgun would have been best. Then I could simply ring his doorbell, aim and, when he answered, pull the trigger.

Unfortunately, I did not own a shotgun, and had no idea where to get one. Knives seemed messy. With strangulation and plastic bags, there was almost invariably a struggle.

Then, drying myself after the shower, I noticed the andirons. They were Willoughby's andirons; nineteenth-century, in the shape of pug dogs. He had loaned them to me one night in the winter. I'd lived next door to him for three years by then, but for the first two years I was living with someone else, and he hadn't seemed very interested in us. We'd exchanged the merest pleasantries over the fence. All I knew of Willoughby at that point was that he was exceedingly red-cheeked, apparently wealthy, and a breeder of Kerry blue terriers. It was only when the person I was living with decided to live somewhere else, in fact, that suddenly—at the sight of moving vans, it seemed—Willoughby showed up at the fence. "Neigh-bor," he called in a singsong. "Oh, neigh-bor." I walked up to the fence and he told me that one of his dogs had escaped and asked if I'd seen it, and when I said no he asked me over for a drink. I didn't take him up on the offer. One day my dog managed to dig under the fence to play with his Kerry blues, and when she returned there was a small red Christmas-tree ornament in the shape of a heart fastened to her collar. It hadn't been there before.

A few nights later a smoldering log rolled out of my fireplace, setting off the smoke alarm but bringing no one but Willoughby to the rescue. He was wearing a red sweatsuit and a Vietnam jacket with his name printed over his heart. I thought, Rambo the Elf.

"I must loan you a pair of andirons," he said happily as he looked down at the charred spot on my rug. "Firedogs, you know. I'll be right back."

"Ah—no need. I'll buy a pair."

"No, no, you must accept my gesture. It's only neighborly."

"Thanks very much, then. I'll come by and pick them up in the morning."

Willoughby beamed. "Oh, too eager, I am always too eager when smitten. Well, yes, then. Fine." But in the morning, when I woke up, the andirons were waiting on my doorstep, along with a piece of notepaper illustrated with a picture of a Kerry blue terrier. On it, in red pen, was drawn a question mark.

From the fireplace, now, I picked one of the andirons up. It was cold and slightly sooty, yet it felt heavy enough to kill. "Blunt instrument," I said aloud to myself, savoring the words.

My dog was sitting in the backseat of the car. Since the cat's disappearance, this had become her favorite resting place, as if she feared above all else being left behind, and was determined to make sure I didn't set foot out of the house without her being aware of it. Now, however, I was traveling on foot, and figuring that anywhere I could walk was close enough not to pose a threat to her, she remained ensconced. It was a bright, sunny day, not the sort of day on which you would think you would think of killing someone. As I passed each house and turned the bend toward Willoughby's, I wondered when my resolve was going to lessen, when, with a rocket crash, I'd suddenly come to my senses. The thing was, it was the decision to kill Willoughby that felt like coming to my senses to me.

Halfway to his house, a Jeep Wagoneer pulled up to the side of the road ahead of me. On the bumper was a sticker that read, THE BETTER I GET TO KNOW PEOPLE, THE MORE I LOVE MY DOGS, and leaning out the driver's window was Tina Milkowski, the proprietress of a small, makeshift and highly successful canine-sitting service. She was a huge woman, three hundred pounds at least.

"How you doing, Jeffrey?" she called.

"Not bad," I said. "How are you, Tina?"

"Can't complain." She seemed, for a moment, to sniff the air. "Where's the Princess today?"

"Home. She's spending the afternoon in my car."

"Hope you left the windows open. Say, what you got there? Firedogs?"

"They're Willoughby's."

Tina shook her head and reached for something in her glove compartment. "He's a strange one, Willoughby. Never been very friendly. The dogs are nice, though. He give those firedogs to you?"

She pulled a stick of gum out of a pack and began chewing it ruthlessly. I nodded.

"I didn't know you two were friends," Tina said in what seemed to me a suggestive manner.

"We're not friends. In fact, I'm on my way to kill him."

Tina stopped chewing. Then she laughed—a surprisingly high, girlish laugh, given her hoarse, bellowslike voice.

"Now why do you want to kill Willoughby?"

"One of his dogs murdered my cat. Then he threw the corpse over the fence into the field. But he told me the cat was alive, that he'd thrown the cat alive into the field because he didn't know it was my cat, and for three days now I've been searching that field for my cat when the whole time he was dead. At least I hope he was dead. It's possible he threw the cat over injured and let him bleed to death, though I can't believe, I honestly can't believe . . ."

I believed Tina had seen her fair share of the crimes human beings commit against one another; for this reason, perhaps, it was the crimes human beings commit against animals toward which she brought her harshest judgment.

She narrowed her eyes. "Listen, honey, don't do anything you'll regret. Think of it this way. His dog kills the cat, he throws it over, he isn't even thinking, probably. He figures it was a wild cat, pretends it'll just disappear. Then you ask him, he never knew it was your cat, and he just makes something up. On the spur of the moment. Probably he's over in that church right now saying a hundred Hail Marys and praying to Jesus to forgive him."

"It was worse than that." I cleared my throat. "Look, there's no point in going into details."

"The doggy probably didn't know what he was doing. Sometimes they just act instinctually."

"I don't blame the dog. I blame Willoughby."

Tina chewed her gum even more ferociously. For a few moments we were silent, her Wagoneer idling, until I realized what it was she was waiting for me to say.

It was easy enough. I laughed. "Don't worry," I said, "I'm not *really* going to kill him. I'm just going to bring back his andirons and have it out with him."

"You sure you're all right? You want to come by for a cup of coffee and talk it over?"

"Really, it's okay. Anyway, Tina, do I look like a murderer?"

She smiled, and I saw how tiny her mouth was, lost in her huge face. "You don't look to me," she said, "like you could kill a deer tick if it was biting you on the face."

I was learning something about murder. Before—that is, before the cat—I had always assumed that when the thought of killing someone enters the mind, a sudden knowledge of its consequences rears up almost automatically in response, saving the would-be killer from himself by reminding him, in glorious Technicolor, of all the cherished things he stands to lose. Today, however, no vision of jail cells or courtrooms or electric chairs entered my head. Nothing compelled me to replace the gun gratefully in its holster, the knife happily in its drawer, the firedog cheerily in its fireplace. The urge to kill had fogged every other feeling; walking down the street in its grip, I could see nothing but the immediate goal, and that goal was so clear, so obvious, it seemed so justly demanded, that the rest of the world, the world after the murder, the world of repercussions and punishments, receded and became dimly unreal. Indeed, as I approached Willoughby's house and rang his doorbell, I felt as if I were no longer a person; I felt as if I were merely a function waiting to be performed.

"Good afternoon," Willoughby said automatically as he pulled open the door; then, faced by mine, his face sank.

He looked down quickly. "I see you're returning my andirons."

"Yes," I said.

"Please come in." Willoughby led me into his living room. He was wearing a bright purple polo shirt and green shorts. I had one andiron in each hand, and what I hadn't counted on was having to put one down in order to kill him with the other one.

"I'll just take those from you," he said.

I allowed him to remove the andirons from my hands and replace them in his fireplace, along with several other sets.

"Have you found your little cat?"

"Yes. He was dead. Just where you threw him over."

Willoughby seemed to do some quick thinking, then said, "Oh dear, how terrible. I suspect one of those roaming dogs must have gotten to him. You know, with no leash law, this town is full of roaming, wild dogs. Most irresponsible of their owners, but I've always felt the folk here were a cretinous brood." He shook his head, turned from me, sat down on the edge of a settee.

"The corpse was at the exact spot where you told me you set him over the fence—alive."

"It is possible the dog—the wild dog—brought the corpse back after killing him, or—or did it right then—right after I—put him over." Willoughby coughed. "I am truly most terribly sorry about your cat. You know, Johnny really is very frightened of cats. He killed another—killed a cat once, another cat, that is. It was wandering in that field, and it attacked him. The cat attacked him. Viciously. He reacted in self-defense. With that cat, of course, the other cat, not with yours. In your case I interceded in the nick of time and removed the cat unharmed." He looked up at me. "Are you sure I can't induce you to take *some* libation?" he said.

"I'm going to kill you," I said.

Willoughby stood. "I'll call the police," he said. "I'll scream. My neighbor can be here in thirty seconds. My dogs are trained to kill. Believe me, I've dealt with thugs like you before and I know what to do. Many people have tried to take advantage of me, and not one has ever succeeded. There's a gun in that drawer. There's a knife in the kitchen. I was in Vietnam. I'm trained to kill. I know karate. I'm warning you. Stand back! Johnny! Johnny!"

His eyes were bulging. He stood pressed against a sliding glass door, as if pinned back, as if he were waiting for knives to land in a pattern around his body. Then he pulled the door open and ran out into the backyard. The dogs came leaping to him. He ran past them, toward the side gate which opened into the field, and then he ran out the gate, not bothering to close it. The dogs huddled around the open gate, but hesitated to follow their master through it.

I turned around and left Willoughby's living room. I closed his door behind me. I did not kill him, and I went home.

I did not know my cat well when he died. I had had him just over a month. But I liked him, and I was beginning to look forward to our life together. Not much distinguished him from other young cats. He was orange and white, and looking at him always made me hungry for those orange popsicles with vanilla ice cream inside. He liked to romp around the house, to play with balls of string, to climb trees and to hide. For hours he and Johnny sat across the fence from each other, staring, not making a move. He climbed tablecloths, and the smell of tuna fish made him yowl with an urgent desire which I could not seem to talk him out of. At first he had been wary of my dog, but then they grew loving toward each other. He used to nip at her legs for hours, trying to get her to play with him, while she sat there, unreacting, an enduring, world-weary matron. Sometimes he'd bat her face with his paw, and his claws would stick in her wiry fur.

When I got home from Willoughby's that afternoon my dog was still in the car. The paint on the driver's door, I noticed, was scratched from her nails. I got in and pulled out of the driveway. From where she was lying behind the backseat she lifted her head like the stuffed dog with the bobbing head my aunt kept in the back of her car in my childhood. She jumped onto the seat. I opened the back window a little, and she nudged her nose through the crack, sniffing the wind. We passed the empty field next to Willoughby's house, and I saw Willoughby on the side of the road, barefoot, red-faced and panting. I honked, and his mouth opened, and he ran across the street. In my rearview mirror I watched him grow smaller and smaller until I turned a corner and he disappeared. Soon we were in open country—long fields where corn had been planted in narrow even rows.

Once, on a snow-blind winter night, I had heard Willoughby whistling. I stood up and went to the back door. There he was, just on the other side of the fence. "Jeffrey," he said, "are you really my friend?"

"Excuse me?" I said.

"I'm asking if you're really my friend," he said. "I must know, you see, because the Lord has seen fit to lock me out of my house, and I must rely upon the kindness of strangers."

"Wait a minute. You're locked out?"

"Afraid so."

"Have you lost your key?"

"No, I haven't lost my key."

"Is the lock broken, or frozen?"

"There's nothing wrong with the lock."

"Well, I don't understand then—"

"The *Lord* has seen fit to lock me out of my house. It is a test. I must throw myself upon the mercy of strangers, the kindness of strangers. I must be humble."

"Call a locksmith," I said, and went back inside.

A few hours later the phone rang. I let the answering machine pick it up. "Jeffrey, among the many things you may not ever forgive me for is calling you at this indecent hour," Willoughby said. "It's ten—or rather, two o'clock." For a long while he was silent. Then he said, "Whenever you're ready, I'll be waiting. And my house is all alit by the Christmas tree."

When I got back from my drive that afternoon, the phone was ringing. "Excuse me," said a voice I didn't recognize. "Is this Mr. Jeffrey Bloom?"

"It is."

"Oh, hello. You don't know me, I'm your neighbor, Mrs. Bob Todd?"

"Hello," I said. I knew the house: a standard poodle, a children's pool and a sign in front which read, THE BOB TODDS.

"I'm sorry to bother you in the evening, Mr. Bloom, but Tina

Milkowski told me what happened to your little kitty and I wanted to extend my sympathies. It's just monstrous what that Willoughby Wayne did."

"Thank you, Mrs. Todd."

"Willoughby has been a nuisance ever since he moved into the Crampton place. Piles of money from his grandfather, and nothing to do with it. Now that was a man. Norton Wayne, he had character. But you know what they say, every family spawns one bad seed, and Willoughby Wayne is it. Always yammering on about his family tree. One poor couple, they were new at the club? They thought they had to be polite. I was at the next table, and I heard. Willoughby told them his family tree from 1612. Forty-five minutes, and he didn't even pause to take a breath. And those dogs. They bark like crazy, annoying the whole neighborhood. Then one day a few years ago he was leaving the club, and he hit a woman. He was drunk."

"My goodness," I said.

"And he's never married. I don't have to tell you *why.*" Mrs. Bob Todd hiccupped. "Everyone says it's the Jews that are wrecking the neighborhood, but if you ask me, it's the old good-for-nothings like Willoughby. Nothing but trouble. Now I'm not rich, but I've lived in this town my whole life, and I can tell you honestly, I think you Jewish people are just fine."

"Thank you," I said.

"Anyway, dear, the reason I'm calling is Tina and I have decided to take some action. This has just gone far enough, with Willoughby and those dogs, and we're going to do something about it. I've already complained to the dog warden, and now I'm going to start a petition to have Willoughby thrown off the board of the Animal Protection Society. He has no business being on that board, given what he did, no business whatsoever."

"Mrs. Todd," I said, "really, this isn't necessary—"

"Oh, don't you worry. You won't have to lift a little finger. Your kitty's murder will be avenged!"

I was quiet. "Thank you," I said again.

"You're very welcome," she said. "Good-bye." She hung up.

I looked outside the window. My dog was flat on her back, being licked by an elderly Labrador named Max, neither of them deterred from this flirtation by the fact that one was spayed and the other neutered. And suddenly I remembered that I had an appointment for my own cat's neutering just the next week. I'd have to cancel it in order to avoid being charged.

I put the phone down. I was sorry I'd mentioned the whole thing to Tina Milkowski, and thus inadvertently begun the machine of vengeance rolling. Revenge anticipated is usually better than revenge experienced. (Then again, when I had wanted to kill Willoughby, it hadn't felt like revenge, what I'd wanted—or had it?)

I decided to clip a leash onto my dog and take her for a walk. It was the dog-walking hour. The Winnebago of our local mobile dog groomer was parked in Libby LaMotta's driveway, Libby pacing nervously alongside while within that mobile chamber her cocker spaniel puppy, Duffy, was given a bath. We waved. Across the street Susan Carlson had Nutmeg, her Manx cat, on a leash. We waved. Further down the street Mrs. Friedrich was watering her plants. She often spoke wistfully about the "big, velvety balls" of which *her* cat, Fred, had finally to be deprived, once he'd sprayed too many sofas. We waved. Then I passed Mrs. Carnofsky, quite literally dragging her resistant Dandie Dinmont terrier behind her, unmoved by the scraping sounds the dog's paws were making against the pavement, the wheezing and choking as he gasped against the tug of his collar, determined to pull her back to a pile of shit a few feet down the sidewalk. "He won't budge," she said. Her blue-gray hair was exactly the same tint as her dog's. We did not wave.

As for Willoughby—just past midnight that night there was whistling at the fence. There he stood, in his elf suit, having somehow climbed through or over the privet hedge.

"Jeffrey," he said.

"What is it, Willoughby?"

"Why do you hate me so?"

"I don't hate you," I said honestly.

"If you don't hate me, then why are you persecuting me?"

I crossed my arms, and turned away from him. "Look, I'm sorry I said I wanted to kill you. I was just angry. I'm not going to kill you. I apologize."

"Nadine Todd called me this evening and she said the most horrid things. She called me a monster and a drunk and worse. She's going to have me thrown off the board of the Animal Protection Society."

"I really didn't have anything to do with that, Willoughby—"

"The Animal Protection Society is one of my great loves. Disregarding the humiliation for the moment, you'll be taking away one of the few ways in the world in which I'm able to feel truly useful."

"I'm sorry," I said. "Really, I have nothing to do with it. Mrs. Todd is acting on her own."

He looked away. "I am lost and forlorn. I have nowhere to turn. I throw myself upon your mercy."

"Good night, Willoughby," I said, and went inside.

A few minutes later there was a knock on the door.

"Do with me what you will," Willoughby said, and threw his arms out at his sides, like Christ.

"Willoughby, it's past midnight."

"The Lord has directed me to you, Jeffrey. He has told me to throw myself upon your mercy. I must learn to be humble, to act humbly."

"Is it humble to barge uninvited into someone's house in the middle of the night? Is that humble?"

"I am a pathetic and desperate man," Willoughby said. He hung his head in shame.

"All right," I said. "Come in."

He smiled, then, came through the door gratefully, and sat down on the sofa. My dog ran up to him from where she was sleeping, barked, sniffed at his haunches. He reached down and stroked her neck. There was something incalculably gentle and expert about the way he stroked her neck, and I wondered, for a moment, if he suffered from a kind of autism; if, in lieu of his clumsy and imperfect relations with humans, he had developed an intricate knowledge of the languages and intimacies of dogs. There were people who, for all the affection they felt, hadn't the foggiest idea how to stroke a dog. They pushed the fur the wrong way, their hands came down rough and ungentle. I suspected Willoughby was like this with people, and always had been.

I brought him a cup of tea, which he thanked me for. The dog had crawled into his lap and gone to sleep. "This is not, of course, the first time that I've been the object of persecution and derision," Willoughby was saying. "Even when I was a little boy it happened. My parents for some reason insisted I attend public school. Another child circulated a petition which read, 'We, the undersigned, hate Willoughby Wayne.' I didn't understand why. I had tried to ingratiate myself with those children, in spite of the enormous gulf which separated us." Tears welled in his eyes. "The ancient Hebrews were cursed with the vice of avarice, and often I have felt the modern Hebrews have inherited that vice, yet in spite of this I feel deeply for the persecution they suffered at the hands of the Nazis, for I too have suffered such persecution." And like a litany, he incanted: "I am a pathetic and desperate man."

I sat down next to him. "You don't have to be that way," I said.

"I am very set in my ways." His hand, I noticed, was on my thigh, following, even at this dark moment, its sly and particular agenda. I moved it away. The dog lifted her head, sniffed, and jumped barking onto the floor.

"I'll call Mrs. Todd," I said. "I'll try to persuade her not to throw you off the board. But I can't guarantee anything. Now I have to go to bed."

Willoughby stood up. I handed him a Kleenex and he blew his nose. "I assure you," he said at the door, "that when I threw your cat over the fence, he was unharmed," and I realized that whether or not this was true, he believed it.

"Good night, Willoughby," I said.

"Good night, Jeffrey." And I watched him go out the door and head down the street. I was remembering how when I was digging the grave that afternoon, I'd kept repeating to myself over and over, "It's just a cat, just an animal, with a small brain, a tail, fur." Then I started thinking about the night my dog—spooked by thunder—bolted out the front door and ran. For three hours I'd driven through the neighborhood, calling her name, knocking on doors. Various sightings were reported in a direct line from Mrs. Friedrich's house, to the Italian deli by the train station, to the laundromat; then the trail disappeared. Finally I went to bed, making sure her dog door was open for her, while outside the storm railed on, and my dog, lost somewhere in it, struggled to make her way home. And what a miracle it was when at four in the morning she jumped up onto my bed—filthy, shivering, covered with leaves and brambles. Like the dogs of legends, she had found her way back.

I thought I'd *had* my brush with death then. I thought from then on I might be spared.

It must have been at that moment—when I was digging the grave, remembering how nearly I'd lost my dog—that the thought of murder came to me, growing more vivid with each thwack of the shovel against the stony earth. Really, I was no better than Willoughby; I just hadn't been alone so long.

"I am a pathetic and desperate man," I said to myself—trying the words on for fit—and standing in the doorway, watched Willoughby stumble home, bereft in the starlight. All along the street, houses were dark, and inside each of those houses were people with cats and dogs, and stories to tell: the time Flossie fell four stories and broke a tooth; the time Rex disappeared for weeks, then showed up one afternoon on the back porch, licking his paw; the time Bubbles was mangled under the wheels of a car. They would tell you, if you asked them, how they had to put Darling to sleep; how Fifi went blind, then deaf, then one day just didn't wake up; how Bosco could jump through a hoop; how Kelly swam under water; how Jimbo begged, how Millie spoke, how Sophie ate nothing but tuna fish. The night was brisk, and somewhere distantly a dog barked. My dog growled, then barked in response. The distant dog barked back. Their conversation, like mine and Willoughby's, might, I knew, go on all night.

Here is my story: When I was young, my family lived in Cleveland, and we had a dog named Troubles. Next door was a dog named Chips, and sometimes in the afternoon, when Chips wandered into our yard, my sister would yell, "Troubles, Chips is here! Chips is here!" and Troubles would leap up from wherever she was sleeping and bound into the yard to see her friend. Then we moved away to California, and Troubles got old and cranky and seemed no longer to like other dogs. Chips was still in Cleveland, or dead; we didn't know.

One day my sister had a friend over. They were going through the old photo albums from Cleveland, and my sister was telling stories. "All we had to do," I heard her saying to her friend, "was yell, 'Troubles, Chips is here! Chips is here!' and then—" And before she could even finish the story Troubles had leapt into the room once more, barking and jumping and sniffing the air. Something had lasted, in spite of all the time that had passed and the changes she had weathered, the trip cross-country, and the kennel, and the cats. My sister put her hand to her mouth, and tears sprang in her eyes, and like the young enchantress desperate to reverse the powerful incantation she has just naively uttered, she cried out, "Troubles, stop! Stop! Stop!" but it did no good. Nothing would calm Troubles, and nothing would dissuade her, as she barked and jumped and whined and nosed for that miraculous dog who had crossed the years and miles to find her.

ROADS TO ROME

FULVIA'S house: old, swollen bricks, a buckling terra-cotta floor. A child could stand inside the fireplace. In the middle of the kitchen is an oval oak table, big enough to seat twenty, which Fulvia bought at an auction of retired theater-set furniture. For many years she'd noticed it on the stage of the Rome Opera, where perhaps the grandeur of the gestures put its massiveness in perspective; more than one of the guests has joked today that Fulvia's house may not be such a far cry from all of that. "Anyway, I feel like a minor character in Puccini," Giuliana told Marco, laughing, out on the patio. Below them lush hills spread out, and in the distance, in the plain, they could see the spa—Terme di Saturnia—where until recently Fulvia spent most of her days, lazing in the hot sulfurous waters.

It is a lukewarm, drizzly afternoon, late in spring. Outside Fulvia's house rain beats at the metal roofs and hoods of the twenty or so cars parked in the moss-covered courtyard. "My family," Fulvia jokes to the American from where she's lying, half covered in a blanket, on the worn velvet sofa by the fireplace. "Look around you, try to figure it all out." The American turns. Giuliana, Fulvia's daughter, has just come in from the patio with Marco. He was her best friend when they were teenagers, and then when he was sixteen he and Fulvia became lovers and she swept him off to Paris. For possibly unrelated reasons Giuliana ran away to India, became a junkie, then settled in Singapore, where she is now married, the mother of three children Fulvia has never seen. Across the room is Rosa, Fulvia's closest friend and Marco's mother, and his sister, Alba. Grazia, Marco's wife, sits at the huge oval table with Alberto, the man she lives with. The man Marco lives with is the American. His name is Nicholas. Laura has just emerged from the bathroom; she is the mother of a little boy, Daniele, whom Marco has raised as his own, even though, biologically, technically, he is not his son. Daniele is outside, playing with Alba's little girl, whose name is also Rosa.

"I think I've got it clear who everyone is," Nicholas says.

"Not for long," jokes Fulvia, and coughs violently. "More are coming. More come every day. Everyone wants to say good-bye because I am the queen and I'm dying. The queen! It's funny. It's amazing, really. Look at all these people, they are rich, well-educated, they are the best Italy has to offer. And they are ruined, every single one of them. You can't guess. If you knew the drugs they've put into their veins, the things they've seen and done—corrupt, utterly." She smiles, as if this pleases her.

"What are you saying about me now, *cara?*" Marco asks, in English. "You think you can tell Nicky anything, no one will understand, but you forget that some of us have been living in New York a long time now."

"Nothing you haven't already heard from me," Fulvia says, laughing, then breaks into a rasping, huge, dangerous smoker's cough.

Fulvia seems determined to die the way she has lived all these years: with drama and pronouncements. Just this morning a famous movie star whose villa is down the road came to pay a visit. Much was made over the movie star, pasta with truffles was prepared for her, as well as a rabbit and a salad of wild greens. Afterwards, from her place on the couch, Fulvia told the movie star she ought really to take more care choosing her films.

"And wasn't that just like Fulvia," Rosa says, after the movie star has left. She is drying dishes and speaking—ostensibly—to her daughter Alba, though Fulvia is within full hearing range. "Does it matter that poor Marina couldn't get a part in a decent film if her life depended on it? Does it matter that she is about to be divorced and must take pills to sleep?" She shakes her head. "The creature deserves our pity, not Fulvia's meanness."

"You're too sentimental, Rosa!" Fulvia calls from the living room. "The woman is richer than the Pope. As for those American films she's been in lately, she'd be wiser to make nothing than that kind of *trippa.*"

"Fulvia, you haven't even seen Marina's latest films," Rosa says. "Not that that ever stopped you from passing judgment." (Fulvia, for most of her life, has been a kind of all-purpose cultural critic for a famous Communist newspaper.)

"*I* saw one of Marina's films," says Giuliana. "She was a mafiosa whose daughter decided to leave the family. It was dubbed in Chinese, so it was hard for me to understand."

"Probably better than the original. And you're telling me to waste my money on garbage like that?" Fulvia laughs hoarsely. "Bring me a cigarette, *carissimo,*" she calls to Nicholas, who waits for someone to object, then, when no one does, fetches the ever-present box of Rothmans from the table.

"You're jealous, that's all," Rosa is saying. "You would have liked to be a movie star too."

"Oh, Rosa, shut up! You're the one who's jealous. You always have been, since we were girls."

"And why's that?"

"Because I'm prettier," Fulvia says.

"Ah, I see."

"Because people care about me so, and want to visit me, and no one likes you."

"Yes, it's true," Rosa says. "I'm an ugly duckling. What is her name, Cinderella? Every summer Fulvia invites half of Rome to this house, and who washes all the dishes? Who cooks the pasta?"

"You've always been the housewifely type," Fulvia says. "Unlike you, I'm glamorous. Like that American soldier from the waterfall called me, during the war. La Glamorosa."

"Marina told me something about that English lord down the road," Giuliana says, coming into the room. "She says he likes to make love to women while wearing rubber boots inside of which he's put live canaries. He bounces on the balls of his feet and feels the crunch—"

"Giuliana, that is the most ridiculous thing I've ever heard," Rosa says.

"No, it's true," Giuliana says. "Marina went there for lunch last week, and there'd been a party the night before. When she walked in, there were ten pairs of boots lined up and the floor was covered with feathers."

"Bah!" Rosa says. "*Ridicolo.*"

"I don't know why you can't believe it," says Grazia. "Stranger things have happened, and within the walls of this house."

"The only people more twisted than the rich Italians around here," Fulvia says, "are the rich English."

"Marina is a sick woman," Rosa says.

"I wonder if that's where Dario got it from," says Laura.

"What?" Grazia asks.

" 'La Glamorosa.' "

Fulvia waves her cigarette in annoyance. "It was my mistake to tell Dario too many stories when he was young."

Laura, looking distressed, says, "I'm sorry, Fulvia, I didn't mean to mention all that."

"You think just because I'm dying I've become sentimental? I'm not sentimental." She blows out smoke dramatically. "No, 'bored' is a better word to describe my feelings about Dario these days. Bored with his *myth.* He was a naughty boy, and I loved him, but I am as bored with him as I am with Marina's movies."

"I saw Dario do Marina once," Alba pipes in. "It was marvelous, he looked just like her."

"Fulvia," says Rosa, "you are not really so callous."

Fulvia extinguishes her cigarette in an empty bottle of cough syrup. "I at least have no delusions. I say the truth. If people don't like it, they can leave my house."

"Excuse me," Marco says, and walks out of the room, onto the balcony. Everyone watches him.

"Well, well, well," Grazia says, after a few seconds.

"Who is Dario?" Nicholas asks.

Rosa, who is drying her hands on a dish towel, stops suddenly.

"I have to use the toilet," Fulvia announces, rather grandly.

"Speaking of Dario?" Laura asks. Grazia suppresses a laugh.

"Very funny," Fulvia says. "Rosa, can you get over here and help me? There's not much time."

"Yes, yes," Rosa says wearily. "Giuliana?"

"I'm coming."

Even though she can barely walk, Fulvia refuses a wheelchair. She says she prefers being carried around, "like a queen." "Careful! Careful!" she scolds Giuliana as the two women pick Fulvia up from the sofa. "Don't be a clumsy girl."

"A mother of three, and she still calls me a clumsy girl."

"When you start supporting yourself, then I'll call you a clumsy woman," Fulvia says as Rosa closes the bathroom door behind them.

"La Glamorosa," Alba is saying. "That must have been part of his act too. Like when he did Marina Albieri."

"La Glamorosa!" says Alberto, Grazia's boyfriend, who up until this point has been busily engaged in cleaning his pipe. He grabs a tablecloth from a pile on the cabinet, drapes it over his shoulder and starts singing.

"That's a Patty Pravo song," Laura says. "Did Dario do it? My Brazilian husband was so in love with her in 1968."

"You have a Brazilian husband?" Nicholas asks.

"Perhaps, *caro.* Unless he's dead. I haven't heard a word from him since 1972, nor do I care to."

Though Nicholas has been living with Marco in New York for just under a year now—Marco is employed by a large international drug company; Nicholas works at a bookstore—this is the first time they've traveled to Italy together. Of course, Nicholas was nervous about meeting Marco's large, strangely shaped and strange-sounding family—fearful that they wouldn't like him, that they'd find him boring, bourgeois or parochial. Fulvia especially. Everything Marco told Nicholas about Fulvia scared him. Marco had grown up with Fulvia and her children, and when he was sixteen and she was fifty, she'd taken him as her lover. It didn't matter that Marco was the son of her best friend, Rosa, or that she'd changed his diapers; what she wanted, he said, Fulvia took. They lived together in Fulvia's apartment in Paris for just over a year—the only year in their lives that Fulvia and Rosa didn't speak, and don't speak about still. (That was considered the major calamity, the split between Fulvia and Rosa.) In those days Fulvia liked Marco to make love to her while holding her wrists together behind her back, and once he did this so tightly her wrists turned blue and started to bleed. Being a boy, he began, almost immediately, to weep, but Fulvia managed to calm him, wrap her wrists in gauze, and get by herself to the hospital, where she had to do quite a bit of talking to convince the doctor that what he was treating was not, as it appeared, a suicide attempt. Of course, the truth sounded so improbable that finally the doctor believed her.

It was Fulvia who told Marco he was gay. Announced it to him, in fact, quite casually, at a restaurant.

"And how do you know that?" a flustered Marco had asked her. (He was just sixteen, and easily unnerved.)

"A woman knows these things about a man," Fulvia said. "Anyway, am I right?"

"I'm not sure."

"I'm right," Fulvia said. And she was. "But don't worry over it, *amore.* It's your nature. It's good. Just start sleeping with other boys and don't feel guilty."

Marco was nothing if not obedient. He went off to find a boy, and found many. Eventually, for reasons mysterious to everyone except the two of them, he married Grazia, who was not thirty but twenty years older than he was. They lived together for a few years. Then Marco moved to New York with Laura, whose son he'd adopted, and Grazia moved to Milan with Alberto. Fulvia took as a new lover the doctor who'd treated her wounds and was eager to try out that sexual position her fondness for which had brought her to his hospital in the first place. His name was Caino, and he spent his summers in Capri, with his wife.

Almost instantly after Marco went off to find boys, Rosa and Fulvia became friends again, which was lucky, since summer was coming, and everyone was in an uproar about what would happen with the house if Rosa and Fulvia were fighting. Later, Grazia insisted Fulvia had timed it that way. An affair was an affair, but the summer house—that was a different matter.

Technically, it's Fulvia's house. She inherited it from her parents, who died in the war—they were both Resistance fighters—and since their youth, she and Rosa and all their husbands and children have shared it. When Fulvia dies, it will become Rosa's property—"the least I deserve," Rosa joked, after the pronouncement was made. "After all, Fulvia, have you once planted a seed or painted a wall or boiled a pot of water? I was the *casalinga,* summer after summer. It should have been mine years ago."

"Don't forget who found the furniture."

"Don't forget who dusted it."

"*Puttana.*"

"Don't call me a *puttana,*" Rosa said. "*I've* only had *two* husbands." And Fulvia laughed. "Come here," she called to Nicholas. She cleared a space on the sofa in the living room, the sofa from which she conducted the business of the house, then slapped the space like a baby's bottom, shouting, "Sit! Sit!" Nicholas sat. "Now tell me, are you having a good time here? Are you enjoying your new Italian relatives?"

"I'm loving it," Nicholas said. "I can't tell you how much I wish I'd grown up in a household like this. I think about Marco's childhood and I get envious—mine was so boring by comparison."

"Don't say that!" Fulvia clucked her tongue. "I know what it looks like to you. You think it was all warmth and singing, *la mamma* and *il papà* and pots of pasta and wine pouring out of the bottle onto the floor. But there was more to it than that, *caro.* Corruption. Cruelty. Not to mention the drugs. You know all our children used heroin—even Marco."

"I know."

She beckoned him closer. "I'll tell you a secret. Every one of these people in this house, every single one, I'd just as soon they would leave today and never come back. Except for Rosa. Without Rosa I'd be dead. Rosa walks out that door, I die."

"Ridiculous," Rosa muttered from the other sofa, where she was reading the newspaper.

"Rosa is the only person I love," Fulvia went on. "If God had had any sense at all, he would have made us lesbians. But, unfortunately, we're both too fond of *cazzo* for that. A pity. We would have treated each other better than any of our husbands. No, don't think the men had anything to do with it. *We* built this family, Rosa and me. We raised all the children together, didn't we, Rosa?"

Absorbed in her paper, Rosa only murmured a concurrence.

"Ah, I'm getting boring," Fulvia said. "Now, *caro,* tell me about you. Your dull family."

"Well," Nicholas said, "my mother's a schoolteacher, and my father's—"

"A schoolteacher! I was supposed to be a schoolteacher when I was a girl! Can you imagine? Me? I can't. Anyway, I lost the chance for that glamorous career when I married Carlo. I had to settle for being a famous journalist and cultural arbiter. Sad, when I could have been a schoolteacher."

"*Cagna,*" Rosa said, under her breath.

"*Porca,*" Fulvia muttered. They both giggled.

On the balcony, Marco stands, his back to the house, the household, Fulvia. In the distance, at the bottom of the hills, are the famous hot springs: a spa with pools, and down the road from it, a waterfall where you can swim without paying. At Nicholas's insistence, they went at midnight the night they arrived, even though Marco was jet-lagged and would have preferred to wait until the morning. But Nicholas was emphatic. He'd been hearing about the waterfall for too long. Now he saw: Naked men with big muscles and bulging stomachs stood under the dark heavings of water, their eyes cast up to a sky thick with stars. Women and babies. Grandmothers, their breasts distended. There was a strong, ugly smell of rotten eggs. "The sulfur," Marco explained, pulling his shirt off. "Smells like farts, doesn't it? But you'll grow to love it soon."

And Nicholas has. Since their arrival a week ago he's gone every afternoon to the spa, lying limp in the hot pool, or allowing the pounding weight of an artificial waterfall to beat his back. In the evenings he goes back to the natural waterfall, sometimes for hours. There are a big pool and a small pool at the spa. Near the big pool is a little fountain, a perpetual trickle, with plastic cups and a sign extolling the water's health-giving properties. At first the thought of drinking the stuff repelled Nicholas, but by the second day he was ready, and lined up behind a family of fat Germans for his first taste of the acrid, sulfurous water. He could barely get it down, but once he had, felt purified.

"There's not a wrinkle on my body," Fulvia boasted, the one afternoon she felt well enough to go down to the spa. "And I'm ninety-seven years old."

"Fulvia, don't be absurd," Rosa said. "Everyone here knows you're just ninety-six."

Even so, when Fulvia pulled off her bathrobe, people gasped or turned away. She laughed. "You think I've been making it up, the dying part?" she asked, pulling loose the gathered leg-holes of her bathing suit. "Skinny, yes. But even at the hospital the doctors couldn't keep their hands off me. Such *skin.* And you know why? This water. Help me, will you?" And Marco and Nicholas eased her in. Instantly she fell silent, and dropped her head back into the water, so that her hair floated out like strands of seaweed, her mouth open.

"Stay with me," she said. "I'm so skinny I might go down the drain."

On the porch, the rain has stopped. Small puddles reflect the peeling stucco that covers the old house. From where Marco stands, there is a good view of the spa, the brightly suited bathers standing out like colored beads against the green water. Nicholas touches Marco's shoulder, and Marco flinches before turning.

"Oh, hi."

"Are you all right?"

Marco stretches. "Yes, all right."

"Why did you leave the room?"

"I just didn't feel like listening to Fulvia and my mother chatter." He puts his hands on Nicholas's shoulders. "So how are you enjoying my—shall we say—family?"

"I'm a bit perplexed," Nicholas admits. "Everyone seems to be married to someone who's dead, or in South America, or living with someone else, and they don't care."

"Marriage Italian style," Marco says, laughing. "Haven't you read about it in books? But there's an explanation. In a country where divorce has only been legal for fifteen years, people just get used to finding—shall we say—alternatives. For centuries we couldn't divorce, and now that we can, nobody sees the point in taking the trouble when probably if you get remarried you'll just end up divorcing again anyway. Why, look at Fulvia. I can't even remember who she's married to. The men she married, the men she lived with, they all blend together."

"It's just different than what I'm used to," Nicholas says. "I mean, my sister's divorced. A lot of my friends too. But in America, even if you get a divorce, at least it's a big deal. You don't just leave a marriage behind like a shirt that doesn't fit you anymore."

"Why?"

"Because it has emotional ramifications."

"A marriage is a legal document. A legal document does not have, as you say, emotional ramifications unless you give them to it."

Both of them lean over the railing, staring down at the plain.

"Who's Dario?" Nicholas asks.

"Ah, the Dario question," Marco says. "Dario was Fulvia's son."

"But why isn't—"

"He's dead. He killed himself seven years ago."

Nicholas catches his breath. "I didn't know," he says.

"Of course not. I didn't tell you."

"Why?"

"Because," Marco says. "Why don't you ask Fulvia? Fulvia will be more than glad to give you the whole story. All the gory details, including the shit."

"Shit?"

"Ask her." Then Marco turns and goes back into the house. Nicholas follows. From the front door he watches as Marco gets into Grazia's little Fiat and drives off.

"Coprophagy," Alberto is saying to Alba. "That's the technical term for it."

"I've never heard that word before."

"So you've learned something new for the day, haven't you? And what a thing to learn."

"Sit down," Fulvia says, making room for Nicholas on the sofa. "Sit down and Fulvia will tell you the whole story."

Nicholas sits down. Fulvia is flanked on one side by Rosa, who is knitting, and on the other by Grazia, who is running her fingers through her pale blond hair. Giuliana and Laura mill about, pretending not to listen.

"My son," Fulvia begins, "was a strange young man. He liked to wear dresses and eat shit."

Nicholas blinks.

"A coprophagist," Grazia says. "He had a whole philosophy about it."

"Why, look at him!" Rosa says. "The poor boy is shocked. Oh dear, Fulvia, it's like you're the worldly *principessa* in some Henry

James novel, corrupting the innocent American. But there it is. He asked."

"Well, if he's shocked, he shouldn't be," Fulvia says. "Worse things go on in New York. And every day."

"I've just never heard of someone eating—"

"It's not an ordinary practice," Fulvia says. "Then again, Dario was not an ordinary young man. He had theories."

"For him, it was the ultimate transgression," Grazia says. "The ultimate sin, the ultimate, unspeakable, unforgivable sin. And once you'd done it, well—you pierced through—what was it he called it?—the membrane of ordinary morality. You entered a kind of ecstasy, a freedom. You committed the final transgression, and it felt wonderful."

"My son was full of shit—if you'll excuse the expression. He just wanted to shock."

"He'd read a lot of the Marquis de Sade. There was a scene where the nobleman who is the hero, after doing every imaginable thing, every vile thing, announces that he is going to take the village idiot into a room and once there do something with him so unspeakably obscene the other people in the book won't ever in their dreams be able to imagine what it is. Then he leads the village idiot into the room and closes the door. The others wait. After about ten minutes, he comes out and announces he's done it. He's done the unspeakable thing with the village idiot. Then they all sit down and he gives them a thirty-page lecture on hedonism."

"Really, Grazia, you were rather too taken in by Dario—"

"Dario was fascinated by de Sade. He wanted to know what it was the nobleman and the village idiot had done. He wanted to do it. You see, he was determined to show all of us what a joke our bourgeois lives were. He wasn't ashamed of being homosexual. He was a beautiful boy, Dario, and he looked beautiful in dresses. Sometimes he sang."

"La Glamorosa," Rosa says.

"Dario," Fulvia says, "liked attention, and never felt he got enough from me. That was all there was to it. He wanted to impress me. But I never attended one of his evenings."

"He said the taste of shit was ambrosial," Grazia continues, rather dreamily. "He wanted me to try it, but I thought I'd throw up. I never did, that I knew of. But once he gave a party and baked a big *torta di cioccolata.* And he put it in it—the shit. And everyone at that party kept saying, 'But *Madonna,* this is the best *torta* I've ever tasted! So delicious! Dario, what is your recipe?' "

"Really, Grazia," Rosa says, "must you remind us?"

"Well, anyway," Fulvia says, "to make a long story short, Marco became Dario's lover. Don't ask me why; Marco was very impressed by him. He even went on stage once and made love. That was when Dario was performing."

"Performing?"

"Yes, it was the early seventies, when even intelligent people were behaving like fools. Dario would get on a stage, recite some of his ludicrous texts, lift up his dress and squat—"

"But Fulvia, you're too hard on him!" Grazia says. "You were never there, you never saw. It's true, seen from today, it was a bit strange. But what he read was—brilliant. And when you watched him—what he did—it seemed beautiful."

"Grazia, you're a stupid *vacca.* You'll fall for anything, even today when most people have gotten their brains back in order. I never understood what Marco saw in you, except you allowed him to get away with his own stupidity, which I never did."

"Fulvia, please," Rosa says.

"Oh, shut up, Rosa, I'm dying. I'll say the truth, for once."

Grazia stands. "You really think you're the queen, Fulvia. And like a queen, you assume that just because you're cruel, you're right. But you're not always right."

She turns and marches out of the room.

"*Che sensibilità!*" Fulvia says. "Hand me a cigarette." Nicholas obliges. "So, to get on with the story: As time went on, the fashions changed. Fewer and fewer people came to Dario's performances.

He was—how would you say it in English—'a flash in the bedpan'?"

Nicholas doesn't laugh. He is looking at the door through which Grazia has just passed.

"Of course," Fulvia says, "there were drugs. And even though nobody was listening to him anymore except stupid Grazia, he was still having his delusions of grandeur. He thought he was the Savior, the Messiah. Naturally Marco became sick of this soon enough, and left him. Dario was alone. The drugs were getting bad. Finally he took an overdose. They found him in the morning. He wasn't trying to get attention, for once. He just wanted it over." She blows smoke.

"Fulvia acts cold," Rosa says. "But that's just her way of hiding her pain."

"Oh shut up, Rosa. Don't speak for me. I act cold because I *am* cold."

"Marco never told me any of this," Nicholas says.

"Marco made a big exit, going to New York. He said he never wanted to have anything to do with any of us ever again. It doesn't surprise me one bit that he never mentioned Dario to you."

"Dario was a disturbed boy, but he had something," Rosa says. "He had charm and a certain real genius. A kind of genius. It was just that everyone mistook it for another kind of genius. He acted like a messiah, and everyone was looking for a messiah, so that's what they turned him into."

"You're too kind to him, Rosa."

"You're too cruel."

"Perhaps. But I made him." Fulvia takes a drag from her cigarette. "Now, for God's sake, will someone empty this ashtray? And close the window! I feel a wind coming up."

Years before, during the war, when they were girls, Fulvia and Rosa lived alone in the house near Saturnia with an old crone and her cretinous son. They were being hidden, protected. Fulvia's parents, they thought, were still alive; Rosa's were fighting it out in Rome. One night the two girls sneaked out of the house to take a swim at the waterfall. It was winter and there wasn't any heat; the hot water warmed them up. A pair of soldiers surprised them, where they were splashing, and the dread they felt, those first few moments, looking into the soldiers' faces and wondering if they were Nazis, was worse than anything either of them had ever imagined they might have to feel. They covered their breasts with their hands and waited to see what would happen next. "You think they speak English?" one of the soldiers said. He was tall, blond, with fair skin. He seemed to be making a noble effort not to look at their bodies. The other soldier, who was shorter and more muscular, couldn't keep his eyes from Fulvia's breasts. "I'm not sure," he answered. Then he stepped forward, and clearing his throat, said, "We are Americans. *Americani.* We've come to liberate you. From the Nazis." The soldier spoke slowly and very loudly, as if he imagined an increase in volume might help to bridge the gap between languages. "*Liberazione,*" he tried. "The war is over."

"We understand English," Fulvia said. "But is it true? We cannot believe it. The war is over?"

"Maybe you could bring us our towels," Rosa said.

"Oh yes," said the shorter soldier, and taking the towels from the tree, threw them out to where the girls were standing, knee deep, in the water. Rosa and Fulvia covered themselves. They were both laughing, yelling, really, with joy and disbelief. Could it be true? The war over?

"Come in the water!" Fulvia said. "You must come in the water! The war is over!" She flung aside her towel and traipsed onto the shore toward the two soldiers, who stepped back. "Oh no," the taller soldier said. "We can't." But the shorter was already taking off his shirt. "Hell, Wayne, why not?" he asked. "Shit, the war's over." Soon he was naked, splashing in the hot water with Rosa and Fulvia, while Wayne stood staring on the shore.

"Come on, Wayne!" called the shorter soldier. "Get your clothes off!"

"Yes, come on, Wayne!" Rosa called. She jumped out of the water and started tearing at the soldier's uniform with wet hands.

"Well, why not?" Wayne said finally. From the village on the hill, a sound of screaming was starting up. The girls climbed onto the soldiers' shoulders and battled each other for a while, and then the four of them broke into pairs and moved together to opposing shadowy regions. In one corner of dry grass and moonlight, the shorter soldier, whose name was Nelson Perkins, Jr., called Fulvia "La Glamorosa" and after they made love gave her chewing gum. In another, Wayne Smith asked Rosa to come back to America and marry him.

Fulvia thought Rosa was crazy, and told her so. "You're nineteen, the war is over, you have everything ahead of you! How can you waste it all on a silly American? You'll go mad with boredom wherever it is he lives—what is the place called, Canvas?"

"I love him," Rosa said stoically.

"Love him! You hardly know him! Trust me, Rosa, very soon you'll find another man to love—an Italian, preferably with some power and intellect. If you'll pardon my saying so, your Wayne has eaten too much *granoturco*; they say it makes them feebleminded."

"Shut up, Fulvia. Why must you always know what's best for other people? You're envious of me, that's all."

"Envious!"

"Because my soldier loves me, and yours couldn't care less. Wayne told me, Nelson said he thought you were—what was his word—'uppity.' He said you were uppity."

"Rosa, you are a fool."

"Fine, if that's what you think. I'll go. Then we'll see." And she went. They got married in a Presbyterian church in Kansas City. Then, for almost a year, Rosa lived—irony of ironies—in Rome, Kansas, the wife of an auto mechanic, while Fulvia—fueled, some said, by rage over her parents' death—worked her way through a number of powerful men and eventually got a job interviewing people for a newspaper. She later wrote a column in which she expressed her resentment at the assumption that she'd only gotten where she was because of who she'd slept with; at the time she'd done it, she pointed out, sleeping with them was the only way for an intelligent woman to get powerful men to listen to her in the first place. Then she named the men. The article, like much of what Fulvia wrote, caused a stir, and had people arguing for a month. All this while Rosa—just nineteen—tried to make a go of it in Rome, Kansas, got pregnant, had a miscarriage. Her arrival had been greeted by an article in the local newspaper, a clipped copy of which she still keeps stowed in a kitchen drawer in Saturnia:

WARTIME ROMANCE
Rome Boy Marries Rome Girl

> Private Wayne Arthur Smith, 20, son of Mr. and Mrs. Ludlow J. Smith of Ellsworth Street, Rome, Kansas, was married yesterday to Rosa Signorelli, 19, of Rome, Italy. The bride and bridegroom met in Italy, where Private Smith was stationed.
>
> Private Smith, who is employed at Sam's Service Station on Mott Avenue, is a graduate of Rome Regional High School. He and his bride plan to make their home in the new development on Warren Drive.
>
> The bride's parents, Mr. and Mrs. Luigi Signorelli of the Appian Way, Rome, Italy, did not attend the nuptials.

So Rosa ended up living in a blue asbestos-shingled house near a wheat field. Every day Wayne got up near dawn and drove his pickup truck to the garage. Rosa played bridge with his mother and sisters, made elaborate *torte* for the church bake sales, which, because they were not frosted pink, no one wanted, and searched futilely for foods that would at least approximate the tastes she'd grown up with—good, green olive oil, fresh pecorino cheese, ripe tomatoes. But the oil was like soap scum, the tomatoes pale orange and mealy, the cheese the consistency of pencil erasers. Rome, Kansas, the late 1940s: It might seem a strange place for a sophisticated Roman girl, the child of intellectual leftists, to end up. And yet, how many more couples like them did the war produce? Differences become detectable much more slowly when there's a language barrier; also, in the flummox of the aftermath, the joyous, wrecked catharsis that marked the end of the war, such differences might have seemed romantic, exciting, there might have appeared something deeply challenging about the prospect of crossing such barriers and thereby—in a small, private way—healing the broken world. They went off to America, in love, got married, in love; it took Rosa nearly a year to realize what a mistake she'd made.

Fortunately, she was not the kind of girl who digs her grave and lies in it. The first time Wayne blackened her eye she was gone. It wasn't hard; she didn't feel settled; the whole marriage had seemed like a dream, a sojourn, some sort of penance for the war. She was young, she healed easily; as soon as she got back to Rome—the real Rome—she would just start afresh, it would all seem distant and quick and nothing to be regretted. These days, she remembers with visceral clarity that windy afternoon she stood at the bus depot in Rome, Kansas, makeup covering her blackened eye. Wayne was at the garage; he didn't even know she was leaving. She had just enough money to get her to New York; once there, she planned to wire Fulvia, who'd just married a rich industrialist from Milan and would certainly provide fare for the boat. There is an illusory calm about this memory; a sensation of peace and clarity, of having finally come to her senses, which cannot be accurate, since, looking back forty years on the incident, Rosa realizes she must have been panicked and terrified that somehow he'd find her and drag her home. The bus glides down the long, straight road, its headlights seeming to warble and shimmer in the gasoline fumes. It pulls up to the depot, enveloping her in dust and the smell of diesel fuel. She lifts her little suitcase to the driver, steps up. Light, free, young. On the bus there is only one other passenger, an old woman with a back stiffened by church chairs. The woman is wearing a high, elaborate hat covered with flowers in candy tones of yellow and red. Rosa looks at the hat and she finds she can't help but laugh. She laughs and laughs. The woman looks at her, surprised, then enraged. Rosa can't stop laughing.

By six o'clock, they're in another state; she can see Wayne stepping into the house in Rome, Kansas, calling for her. Of course she's left no note.

Three weeks later she was back in Italy.

Fulvia had a party for her, with champagne. At the party were a number of men Rosa decided she would like to go to bed with. She forgot about Wayne Smith, forgot about him completely, until the letter came to her parents' house, inquiring as to her whereabouts. She tore it up. There were no communications, then, for a long time, and Rosa, who was in love again, decided to pretend the marriage hadn't really happened—after all, it was an American marriage, it had never been officially registered in Italy, therefore it didn't really count. She married her second husband, Paolo, without even mentioning the first to him, without a thought as to the consequences, and they stayed married for almost twenty years without hearing a word from Wayne Smith. Then one day in the early seventies—they were living in Rome, Marco was fifteen and Alba ten—Rosa received an official communication from a lawyer in Salina, Kansas. She remembers standing by her mailbox, staring at the unfamiliar, foreign-looking envelope, pulled back, suddenly, over decades, as if a bill she'd once neglected to pay, and assumed she had evaded, had just found her, hugely multiplied by interest into an astronomical fee. She opened the letter. After considerable effort—several years', it seemed—Wayne Smith had finally tracked her down. And suddenly in her mind she was dragged back to Rome, Kansas, strung up while Wayne's mother and sisters laughed and applauded, whipped by the woman in the high flowered hat, before being taken back to Wayne's blue-shingled house. What was the dream and what the reality? Perhaps all of this—her marriage to Paolo, her children—was the dream. Perhaps she was about to wake up and find herself back there, in Rome, Kansas, scrubbing potatoes, while Wayne, in the living room, drank beer and polished his fist.

But in fact, all Wayne wanted was a legal divorce. He was now the president of a company that manufactured spare parts for tractors, the lawyer wrote, lived in Dallas and was eager to remarry. Naturally this put Rosa in a rather sticky situation: Which husband, she wondered, would take priority?

Fortunately, Fulvia knew people in the right offices who owed her favors. A number of bribes were paid; certain documents were rewritten so that the marriage between Rosa and Paolo had never happened, and thus the marriage between Rosa and Wayne could be discreetly dissolved. Rosa assumed that she and Paolo would then remarry, but it turned out Paolo had a girlfriend he'd been planning to move in with for a while now and just hadn't known how to tell Rosa about. So that was that. Rosa, vowing she'd never marry again, started spending more and more time at Fulvia's house near Saturnia, less and less in Rome. She visited the waterfall sometimes, and thought about Wayne Smith, and felt guilty for having just abandoned him like that. Finally she wrote to him in care of the lawyer in Salina, Kansas; it was a long letter, one she spent days on. In it she tried to explain to him why she'd left him; they were both so young, after all, and so traumatized by the war, she said, and then it had just seemed like a dream—hadn't it seemed like a dream to him? Anyway, she wrote, she was sorry she hadn't bothered to formalize the divorce. She hoped it hadn't caused him too much inconvenience. She hoped he and his new wife were very happy. She told him about her life in Italy, included snapshots of her children and Fulvia's children. She told him how famous Fulvia was, how they went to the waterfall frequently, these days, and reminisced. Did he have any news of Nelson Perkins, who'd called Fulvia "La Glamorosa" and given her chewing gum?

But Wayne Smith never wrote back.

Fulvia, who had just divorced her third husband, felt little sympathy. "You were stupid to marry him," she said. "I told you then."

"I wish," Rosa said, "you had more gentleness, Fulvia. Yes, it was a mistake, yes, I shouldn't have done it. But even so, when I think back now to the girl I was then, the thrill I felt, getting on that boat with Wayne, or the thrill I felt coming back to Rome, for that matter—I don't know if I'll ever feel anything like that again. It was my adventure, my madness of youth, and I'm glad I had it."

"If you want to call spending a dreary year in the middle of nowhere your madness of youth, that's your choice," Fulvia said. "To me it was madness plain and simple." Then she went out to meet a politician for an illicit rendezvous. Rosa, as often happened in those days, was left to take care of the children.

Later that afternoon, after she got back from the market, Rosa found Dario in her bedroom. He was wearing a pink chenille evening gown which she herself hadn't been able to fit into for years, and was admiring himself in the mirror. He was just sixteen. He looked good. "La Glamorosa," he said, and smiled.

She stayed in the doorway, didn't let him know she'd seen him. She thought, So Fulvia isn't as all-knowing as she thinks she is, then tiptoed away, storing the discovery for rumination and future use.

What she didn't know was that the "politician" Fulvia had gone off to have an illicit rendezvous with was Marco.

This afternoon, Grazia takes Nicholas on a walk along a decaying cobblestone path which begins at the crumbling village wall in Saturnia, on top of the hill, and passes by Fulvia's house. It's an ancient Roman road, dating from the time of Nero. The bumpy, herniated path narrows and widens and occasionally disappears altogether under the weeds and grasses which are choking it, but Grazia seems to know it well, and they never lose the trail. "But does it really go all the way to Rome?" Nicholas asks, and Grazia nods. "If you kept walking and walking through these hills, eventually you'd end up at Fulvia's apartment." She laughs, shielding her eyes with her hand. The sun is huge now, the same red-orange as the yolks of the eggs Rosa picks up every morning from a chicken farm outside the village. It gives the dry grasses which cover the hills the golden cast of wheat ready to be threshed.

"It's beautiful here, no?" Grazia says. "Fulvia and Rosa talk about Saturnia like it's their place, but they're Romans, they don't really know. I grew up near Grossetto, on a farm. We had olive groves. My father used to drive me when he took the olive oil to Rome. I know everything of this countryside."

"Yes?"

"Maremma, it's called. The swamp. It used to be a swamp, in the fourteenth century. Now it is a wild land, full of *cinghiali.* Our dogs, the *Maremmani*, are the fiercest in Italy, and white as snow."

They continue their downward trek. Nicholas has to make a conscious effort to slow himself down in order to avoid getting too far ahead of Grazia, who takes tiny steps, and studies the misshapen cobblestones cautiously, as if in fear of tripping over pebbles.

"I wanted to talk to you more about Dario," she says after a few minutes. "Fulvia paints such an ugly picture. And I thought you should know more."

"She must suffer a lot, otherwise she wouldn't have to act so callous."

"But you make a mistake. You assume Fulvia has a heart. Fulvia has no heart. In the old days, she always acted hard, but underneath she was soft. Now she's hard even underneath. Marco will tell you it's jealousy, that she went mad because he chose Dario instead of her. But the truth is, Fulvia didn't care about Marco after he married me. No, the only reason Fulvia is jealous is because Dario's genius was something she couldn't take credit for. Imagine! Fulvia Bellini, the great cultural critic, the maker and breaker of reputations, has a son who is suddenly famous all over Italy, and she's had nothing to do with it! In fact, she's discouraged him! She couldn't stand that. Even now, she wants to punish Dario's memory." They stop for a moment, and Grazia turns to face Nicholas. "I'll tell you a secret. Dario's writings, the things he read during the performances? I've saved them all. I keep them in a safety-deposit box in Milano. They are works of brilliance, as the world will someday know. Well, just after Dario died—he'd entrusted his papers to me—I tried to get them published. I approached every publisher in Italy, and one by one, they refused me. And you know why? Because of her. Because they were afraid of her. Believe Fulvia when she tells you how much power she has. It's all true. She kept those writings from being published because she couldn't stand the idea that someday her son would be more famous than she was. But he will. In a few years' time, no one in the world will remember who Fulvia Bellini was. But Dario—he will be one of the great ones." Grazia smiles. "Have you seen a picture of him?"

"No."

She opens her purse and pulls from it a snapshot of a young man with dark-blond hair, freckles, bright green eyes. "Such eyes!" she says. "He used to recite in the performance a poem Fulvia said to him when he was small, something she made up:

Verdi come le acque di Saturnia, gli occhi del mio bambino.
Caldo come le acque di Saturnia, il cuore del mio bambino.
Fragrante come le acque di Saturnia, la cacca del mio bambino.

"What that means is: 'As green as the waters of Saturnia, my little son's eyes. As hot'—hot? No, 'As warm as the waters of Saturnia, my little son's heart. As fragrant as the waters of Saturnia, my little son's shit.' "

Grazia is, for a moment, triumphantly silent.

"He couldn't resist that. He found that so funny. If she had any idea of the future, singing that little poem, can you imagine? But now you see the truth. Fulvia loved him best of all. It's true, she couldn't say anything loving to him without making it a joke in the end, even when he was just a *bimbo.* But she loved him anyway. And Dario was the only man who broke with her instead of the other way around. I'll tell you something else." Again Grazia stops, leans close. "The night Dario killed himself, Marco was with him. Marco had been trying to leave him for months. And Dario said to him, 'If you leave me tonight, Marco, I'll kill myself.' And Marco walked right out the door."

Nicholas looks down into Grazia's face as she tells him this. Her face is pale and fat and looks like the face of one of those very innocent Madonnas, as chubby and unknowing as the babies they hold in their arms.

"I'm telling you this for your own good," she says. "I'm telling you this so you'll understand. Marco was my husband. I know him better than Fulvia, better than Dario."

"Thank you," Nicholas says uneasily.

There is, in the distance, the sound of engines. The ancient road has met up with the new road, the road for cars.

"It's why Marco left, you see. He couldn't stand the guilt."

A car rounds the bend, slows. It is Alberto, with one arm around Alba. Grazia seems hardly to notice.

"Did someone call a taxi?" Alberto calls to them in English, across the little field. And Alba laughs.

In the late afternoon, Fulvia naps. The house shuts up, quiets down, in deference to her. Most everyone is down at the spa, lounging in the waters, or having mud baths, or themselves napping. Only in the kitchen is there activity, where Rosa, assisted by a girl from the village, has started preparations for the evening supper. The wine bottles are yet to be uncorked, the tablecloth is yet to be spread, a heady odor of garlic and olive oil wafts from the stove, where Rosa is making a *soffrito.*

"Understand, Nicholas," she is saying, "we're all fools. But none of us so much as Grazia."

Then it's time for the dinner, which, like every meal in this household, is a messy, complicated affair, starting at ten and lasting until one, with a crowd of people whose names Nicholas can't keep straight gathered around the huge operatic table, and big bowls of pasta and risotto making the rounds, and prosciutto and cheeses and *bollito misto,* and of course, gallons of wine—expensive bottles from Montalcino and Montepulciano as well as casks of the locally produced, pale yellow *vino dei contadini.* By the end of the evening the table is strewn with walnut shells, and the peels of clementines, and wineglasses in which cigarette butts have been snuffed out.

"*Dio,*" Rosa mutters, surveying the huge pile of dishes to be done. "*Mai più.* Never again."

"But Mamma, Simonetta's coming in the morning," Alba reminds her. "She'll take care of it. Go to bed, Mamma."

Rosa shakes her head. "You know that Simonetta's been threatening to quit. She says there's just too much work to be done here, when she could get the same money washing a plate and a glass for Signora Favetta down the road. No, I must start now. I must get some of this cleared away."

In the end, only Nicholas volunteers to help her—Nicholas, the American, raised to believe you can never do too much for people who are putting you up for free.

They are just starting the ritual business of plunging plates into steaming water when Fulvia calls from the sofa, "I want to go to the waterfall!"

"Absolutely not," Rosa says. "You're a sick woman, Fulvia, you can't just go out swimming at one in the morning."

"Don't treat me like an old lady," Fulvia says. "I do what I want. Marco! Take me to the waterfall!"

"But you've got to think of your health!"

"I've got to think of my sanity! Really, Rosa, every night this week, I've sat through dinner, then watched as everyone went off to the *cascata* except for you and me, the two *vecchie.* Enough of that!"

"Do what you want then," says Rosa, turning from the sink to face her. "Kill yourself. I have dishes to wash."

"You always have dishes to wash! Leave the dishes! I forbid you to do the dishes!"

"Simonetta—"

"Forget Simonetta, you're as much a fool as she! Now get my swimming suit."

Rosa turns again from the sink, marches into the living room, stands over her friend. It seems, for a moment, as if she's going to say something terrible, unforgivable; indeed, even Fulvia looks as if she wonders if this time she's gone too far. But whatever it is

Rosa is about to say she apparently chooses to keep to herself. Her shoulders sink. "Marco, help Fulvia into her bedroom," she says. Then she leaves the room.

"I think we'll go down now and you can join us later," Alberto says. "Alba and I. Anyone else want to come?"

"Go ahead," says Grazia. She doesn't look at them.

"Fine. Ciao, then," Alberto says, and before anyone else has a chance to ask for a ride, he and Alba are out the door. Laura goes to put the children to bed, and then only Nicholas and Grazia are left at the table. He watches while with small and vicious fingers she tears the peel of a clementine into tiny pieces.

At the falls, lowering Fulvia into the water proves to be an even more complicated business than it was at the pool. "Careful, you *caproni!*" she chastises, as they ease her in. "Slowly! Ah, yes, that feels wonderful." Immersed, she leans her head back, her body wraithlike in the dark water. "Stay with me, Nicholas," she says.

"Of course."

"Fulvia, it's too cold," Rosa says. She herself is still dressed, and standing at the edge of the water. "You shouldn't be here."

"Oh get lost, Rosa. You and Marco. Let me talk to the *ragazzo.*"

"Don't tell me what to do," Rosa says, and Nicholas notices a surprising, new inflection of hurt in her voice.

"Come on, Mamma," Marco says. And he leads his mother around to the other side of the little pond under the waterfall, where Alberto and Alba are cavorting.

"You know, I only feel good when I'm in the water these days," Fulvia says. "Too bad I'm so weak, otherwise I'd be here all day. I've been swimming in these springs for sixty years, since I was a very little child. Even before the hotel existed, Rosa and I used to come and swim here. And once, at the end of the war, we met an American soldier. He looked a bit like you: same freckles."

"And he called you 'La Glamorosa,' " Nicholas says.

"Yes," Fulvia says, wrapping her arms around her chest. "His Italian was bad, but creative. He was at least trying to speak the language, which is more than I can say for most of those soldiers. And what a lover he was. My God!" She laughs, then stops laughing. "Dario was shameless about using my life in his so-called performances. For that I forgive him."

"But not for much else, I gather."

"Oh, I don't blame Dario. Dario was merely disturbed. No, I'll tell you who I blame. Them." And she points across the water, at her swimming friends. "They'll deny it now—all except stupid Grazia—but every one of them was there, at Dario's performances. They all sat in the audience, in those cafés and clubs, their hands on their laps, watching my son make an idiot of himself. Now they speak skeptically, like it was some craziness of other people. But you can mark my words, when Dario ate his shit on stage, the people in the audience cheering him on were these people: serious intellectuals, bourgeois, from good families. The way Grazia talks about him—that was how they all spoke of him, in those days. That's what makes me so angry: If they hadn't been so taken in, they could have stopped him. They could have saved him."

For a moment, she almost looks sad.

"But if you wanted to stop him, why didn't you talk to him?"

"Would he listen to me? I'm his mother." She laughs and shakes her head. "No, I couldn't do it. These people, my friends, they could have just stopped paying attention to him. That would have been all it took. Unfortunately, they liked watching him think he was a messiah too much. And soon enough he really believed what he started out pretending to believe. That's all it takes, you know. You convince one person, you've convinced yourself."

The contrast between the cool air and the hot water makes Nicholas's teeth start to chatter, but Fulvia doesn't seem to notice.

"People will drool at anything. They'll drool over a boy in a dress eating shit until something else comes along to grab their attention, which is exactly what I predicted, and exactly what happened. Soon Dario was threatening to kill himself ten times a day. Every time I came over, every time Marco came over, when we left, he'd threaten to kill himself. Of course, by that time, no one else was bothering to visit him. Dario was alone in the end. For that I can never forgive them."

"Even Rosa?"

"Even Rosa."

Little wavelets of water are splashing around Fulvia. She leans back, regal, silent. The wavelets get bigger. It's Rosa, who's put on her swimming suit and is walking in the shallows toward them.

"Have you had enough yet?" she says. "Because I, for one, am ready to go to bed."

"Rosa, why must you always spoil my fun? I never hired you to be my nursemaid. Now go away."

"Oh fine!" Rosa says. "In that case, why don't we settle the bill now for thirty years of cooking, cleaning, taking care of your children—"

"Rosa, I said go away!"

"—wiping their asses, wiping *your* ass, I don't even have to mention Dario's ass—"

"Shut up, Rosa!"

"What do you think the total ought to come to, Fulvia? Well, I'll have my lawyers call you to settle, because I've had enough of it, I'm sick and tired of being your dishrag and listening while you rave on as if anyone cares anymore, and treating me like a worthless piece of garbage. And now, saying I didn't try to help Dario. I might as well have been his mother, since you never lifted a finger for the boy."

Fulvia, still immersed in the water, puts her hands over her ears and screams—a single, sharp, hoarse tone, ascending in pitch and volume.

"What's going on here? Are you two at it again?" It's Marco, who's come over from the other side of the falls.

"And you!" Rosa says, turning on him. "Why should I listen to you? You, who let her take you into her bed when you were a boy? The shame I felt, the betrayal."

"I will not listen to this!" Fulvia shouts, hands over her ears.

"All jealousy, of course," Rosa says. "Jealousy because I at least had two normal, healthy children, while Fulvia was blessed with a junkie daughter and a son who, if there's anything worse than a child who's a junkie—well, he was determined to find out what it was and become just that."

Suddenly Fulvia thrusts out an arm, grabbing Rosa by the leg, pulling her down. Rosa screams and tumbles. Obscenities fly back and forth in the air, until finally the two women lie in a heap, wet and muddy, weeping. "Don't talk that way about my children!" Fulvia is saying. "Don't you dare say such things about my children!"

"Why not? You do."

"I loved Dario. I did everything for Dario."

"And now you speak of him like you wish he had never been born!"

"That's my right!"

"How?"

Fulvia sits up, rubs her eyes. "I'm a dying woman, Rosa, it's not fair to interrogate me like this." And Rosa falls silent.

"Are you two finished?" Marco asks, sounding annoyed, and they look up at him. Rosa starts to laugh.

"Imagine," Rosa says, "being chastised by your children."

"I suppose the day had to come," Fulvia says. "They couldn't be more foolish than we are, so I guess that means they have to be wiser." She coughs and presses her fingers against her temples. "I'm tired," she says. "Rub my shoulders, Rosa. Oh, Rosa, I'm tired of hurting."

"You see, she *does* need me," Rosa says. "And I'll take care of her. She knows I'll take care of her." And turning from where she's sitting, in the wet sand, Rosa begins to massage Fulvia's shoulders.

Fulvia closes her eyes, giving herself over to the strength of Rosa's hands. Across the pond, Alberto has Alba on his shoulders; he is singing, and strutting, and she is screaming for him to put her down. The waterfall pounds gracelessly around them.

When Rosa's massage is finished, she and Fulvia share a cigarette. "I tell you," Fulvia says, "he looks just like him."

"Fulvia, your memory's playing tricks on you."

"Looks just like who?" asks Nicholas.

"The American soldier. The one I met here at the end of the war."

"Fulvia's feeling romantic tonight," Rosa says, handing the cigarette to Fulvia.

"He had freckles, and he came from Ames, Iowa," Fulvia says. "His name was Nelson Perkins, and he gave me chewing gum."

"Fulvia looked him up once, when we were in New York. She called information in Ames, Iowa. She actually found him."

"I said I was the little Italian girl he met at the springs of Saturnia and made love with and gave chewing gum. And now, I said, I was a cultural critic, and I was in New York City to write about the ballet. I don't think he remembered me. He sold cars, he said. Oldsmobiles. He was married and had some children. He sounded nervous, like he was afraid I'd had a child and was going to ask him for money."

"Fulvia was sad, though she pretended she wasn't."

"No, I wasn't." And suddenly she turns and takes Nicholas's face in her hands.

"You look just like him," she says, smiling. "Really, you could be him."

"One American looks like another to Fulvia."

"And here, in this pond, we swam, and he told me I was a glamorous Italian girl and he had saved me from the Nazis. Maybe you can too, *caro.* Save me."

Her face is suddenly radiant, her hands warm against Nicholas's cold cheeks.

"But I don't know how," Nicholas says.

"Yes you do," says Fulvia. "It's simple. Just pick me up on your shoulders and carry me away."